Form L 31

~~WELWYN GARDEN CITY~~ ASCHAM

Hertfordsh

COUNT

70

This book should   **e**
latest

DATE OF RETURN	DATE OF ~~RETURN~~	~~RETURN~~

9/12

Hertfordshire
COUNTY COUNCIL

Community Information

Please renew/return this item by the last date shown.

So that your telephone call is charged at local rate,
please call the numbers as set out below:

	From Area codes 01923 or 0208:	From the rest of Herts:
Renewals:	01923 471373	01438 737373
Enquiries:	01923 471333	01438 737333
Minicom:	01923 471599	01438 737599

L32b

English Reprints

ROGER ASCHAM

The Scholemaster

Written between 1563-8.   Posthumously published

FIRST EDITION, 1570 ; COLLATED WITH
THE SECOND EDITION, 1572

EDITED BY

EDWARD ARBER

F.S.A. ETC. LATE EXAMINER IN ENGLISH
LANGUAGE AND LITERATURE
TO THE UNIVERSITY OF
LONDON

LONDON
CONSTABLE AND CO LTD
1935

CONTENTS

PRINTED IN GREAT BRITAIN

THE SCHOLEMASTER.

INTRODUCTION.

T is a part of the Divine Providence of the World, that the Strong shall influence the Weak: not only on the Battlefield and in Diplomacy; but also in Learning and Literature. Thus the Nations of Modern Europe have been influenced by the Writings of Greece and Rome: and they have influenced each other, in turn, with their own Power and Beauty in Thought and Expression. Thus, Modern English has been subject in succession to the influence of Classical Literature in the time of Ascham; to the literary fascination of Italy, in the age of Elizabeth; of France, at the Restoration; and of Germany, in more recent times: without at all ceasing in the natural progression of its innate capabilities, for all the fashions and forms which, for a time, it pleased to adopt. In like manner, English Literature has allured the German, the Frenchman, and the Italian: thereby restoring benefit for benefit in the commerce and free trade of the Mind.

2. The stream of Ancient Literature and Cultivation, which, after the fall of Constantinople, advanced from East to West; at length reached our shores in the reign of Henry the Eight. In the planting and engraftment of Classical learning in England at that time, St. John's College, Cambridge, —founded on 9th April 1511—had a most distinguished share. Its Master and Fellows—whether they adhered to the older or the newer 'faith'—strove alike most earnestly to promote the new 'learning.'

THOMAS NASHE, writing—twenty years after Ascham's death—somewhat severely ,on 'our triuiall translators,' in his address *To the Gentlemen Students*, prefixed to R. Greene's *Menaphon*, 1589: bears honourable testimony to the worthiness of this College. . . . "I will propound to your learned imitation, those men of import, that haue laboured with credit in this laudable kinde of Translation; In the forefront of whom, I cannot but place that aged Father *Erasmus*, that inuested most of our Greeke Writers, in the roabes of the auncient *Romaines*; in whose traces, *Philip Melancthon, Sadolet, Plantine*, and manie other reuerent Germaines insisting, haue reedified the ruines of our decayed Libraries, and merueilouslie inriched the Latine tongue with the expence of their toyle. Not long after, their emulation beeing transported into *England*, euerie priuate Scholler, *William Turner*, and who not, beganne to vaunt the smattering of Latine, in English Impressions. But amongst others in that age, Sir *Thomas Eliots* elegance did seuer it selfe from all equalls, although Sir *Thomas Moore* with his Comicall wit, at that instant was not altogether idle: yet was not Knowledge fullie confirmed in hir Monarchie amongst vs, till that most famous and fortunate Nurse of all learning, Saint *Iohns* in *Cambridge*, that at that time was as an Vniuersitie within it selfe; shining so farre aboue all other Houses, Halls, and Hospitalls whatsoeuer, that no Colledge in the Towne, was able to compare with the tythe of her Students; hauing (as I haue hearde graue men of credite report) more candles light in it, euerie Winter Morning before fowre of the clocke, than the fowre of clocke bell gaue stroakes; till Shee (I saie) as a pittying Mother, put too her helping hande, and sent from her fruitfull wombe, sufficient Schollers, both to support her owne weale, as also to supplie all other inferiour foundations defects, and namelie that royall erection of *Trinitie Colledge*, which the Vniuersitie Orator, in an Epistle to the Duke of *Somerset*, aptlie tearmed *Colonia diducta* from the Suburbes of *Saint Iohns*. In which extraordinarie conception, *vno partu in rempublicam prodiere*, the Exchequer of eloquence Sir *Ihon Cheeke*, a man of men, supernaturally traded in al tongues, Sir *John Mason*, Doctor *Watson, Redman, Aschame, Grindall, Leuer, Pilkington*: all which, haue either by their priuate readings, or publique workes, repurged the errors of Artes, expelde from their puritie, and set before our eyes, a more perfect Methode of Studie.

3. THOMAS BAKER in his *History of the College of St. John the Evangelist, Ed.* by J. E. B., Mayor, 1869; tells us that about 1520-30, "12d per week was allowed in commons to a fellow, and only 7d to a scholar. These were times when £120 was sufficient to found a fellowship [for the private foundations usually run thereabouts], and when £6 per an. was enough to maintain a fellow," *p.* 81, "as £3 per annum was enough to found a scholar," *p.* 99.

Baker also gives us a Statement of the finances of the College when Doctor Metcalfe became its third 'master, about Dec. 1518, which fully corroborates Ascham's account at *p.* 133: which Statement may be thus summarized :—

Total revenues from lands	.	.	.	234 14 4
Less value of private foundations				48 0 0
				186 14 4
Less the ordinary charges incident to these revenues				125 9 9
Remaining to the sustentation of all such as be to be found of the said lands, *i.e.*, for their only commons, stipend, and livery yearly	.	.	.	61 4 6
The charges of these viz. of the master, twenty-eight fellows, six scholars and of several servants, is yearly	.	.	.	162 8 0
	Excess of Outgoings over Receipts		£101	3 5

Yet Doctor Metcalfe in ways like those described by Ascham, as well as by obtaining the property of the suppressed Nunneries of Higham and Bromehall, raised the finances of the College to a flourishing condition, until it was spending £1000 a year (equal to £15,000 now) in the spread of knowledge.

4. But the College was not more fortunate in wealth than in learning when, in 1530, Roger Ascham, a Yorkshire lad of 15, entered it. John Cheke had been elected Fellow on the 30th of March in that year : and John Redman became a fellow on 3d of November following. Ascham thus distinctly attributes the race of Scholars that were bred up in St. John's College to the unwearying efforts of these two men. "At Cambridge also, in S. Johns Colledge, in my tyme, I do know, that, not so much the good statutes, as two Ientlemen, of worthie memorie, Syr *Iohn Cheke*, and Doctour *Readman*, by their onely example of excellency in learnyng, of godnes in liuyng, of diligence in studying, of councell in exhorting, of good order in all thyng, did breed vp so many learned men in that one College of S. Iohns, at one time, as I beleue, the whole Vniuersitie of *Louaine*, in many yeares was neuer able to affourd," *p.* 67.

As Redman became Master of King's College in 1542, and Cheke went to Court on 10 July 1544 to be Tutor to Prince Edward; the period of Study to which Ascham so gladly and so often reverts in this his last work, ' my swete tyme spent at Cambridge,' would not exceed fifteen years, at the longest ; so far at least as the time during which Cheke and Redman gave so mighty an impulse to classical Learning.

5. These Planters of the ancient Literature in England hoped well of their Mother Tongue. The more they learnt of the subtilty of Greek eloquence or the cunning elegance of Roman prose : the more they desired that English might be kept pure, the more they believed it to be capable of a worthy literature.

ROGER ASCHAM while a Fellow of St. John's, deliberately wrote his *Toxophilus*, published in 1545, in plain and pure English; thus, how strangely to us, *defends* himself. "If any man woulde blame me, eyther for takynge such a matter in hande, or els for writing it in the Englyshe tongue, this answere I may make hym, that whan the beste of the realme thinke it honest for them to vse, I one of the meanest sorte, ought not to suppose it vile for me to write: And though to haue written it in an other tonge, had bene bothe more profitable for my study, and also more honest for my name, yet I can thinke my labour wel bestowed, yf with a little hynderaunce of my profyt and name, maye come any fourtheraunce, to the pleasure or commoditie, of the gentlemen and yeomen of Englande, for whose sake I tooke this matter in hande. And as for ye Latin or greke tonge, euery thing is so excellently done in them, that none can do better: In the Englysh tonge contrary, euery thinge in a maner so meanly, bothe for the matter and handelynge, that no man can do worse. For therein the least learned for the moste parte, haue ben alwayes moost redye to wryte. And they whiche had leaste hope in latin, haue bene moste boulde in englyshe: when surelye euery man that is moste ready to taulke, is not moost able to wryte. He that wyll wryte well in any tongue, muste folowe thys councel of Aristotle, to speake as the common people do, to thinke as wise men do; and so shoulde euery man vnderstande hym, and the iudgement of wyse men alowe him. Many English writers haue not done so, but vsing straunge wordes as latin, french and Italian, do make all thinges darke and harde," *p.* 18. *Ed.* 1868.

THOMAS HOBY, afterwards knighted, having, after many delays, finished his translation of Baldassare Castiglione's work, spoken of so highly by Ascham at *p.* 66: in his *Epistle*, has the following. "As I therefore haue to my smal skil bestowed some labour about this piece of woorke, euen so coulde I wishe with al my hart, profounde learned men in the Greeke and Latin shoulde make the lyke proofe, and euerye manne store the tunge accordinge to hys knowledge and delite aboue other men, in some piece of learnynge, that we alone of the worlde may not bee styll counted barbarous in oure tunge, as in time out of minde we haue bene in our maners. And so shall we perchaunce in time become as famous in Englande, as the learned men of other nations haue ben and presently are."

While the work was yet in MS., Hoby sent it to Sir JOHN CHEKE to look over. Cheke wrote the following letter in reply; which is important as coming from one who, Sir T. Wilson says, had 'better skill in our English speache to iudge of the Phrases and properties of wordes and to diuide sentences: than any one else had that I haue knowne.' It is also interesting as showing that uniform spelling had nothing to do with clean English.

This letter was written while Sir John was fading out of life; for shame at his recantation of the Protestant faith at his pardon, for having acted—out of zeal for that faith—as Secretary of State to Lady Jane Grey. He died in the Sept. following of that year, 1557, at the house of his friend Peter Osborne, in Woodstreet. The letter is printed verbatim at the end of the first edition of *The Courtier*, 1561.

⁋ To his louing frind Mayster Thomas Hoby.

FOr your opinion of my gud will vnto you as you wrrit, you can not be deceiued: for submitting your doinges to mi iudgement, I thanke you: for taking this pain of your translation, you worthilie deseru great thankes of all sortes. I haue taken sum pain at your request cheflie in your preface, not in the reading of it for that was pleasaunt vnto me boath for the roundnes of your saienges and welspeakinges of the saam, but in changing certein wordes which might verie well be let aloan, but that I am verie curious in mi freendes matters, not to determijn, but to debaat what is best. Whearin, I seek not the bestnes haplie bi truth, but bi mijn own phansie, and shew of goodnes.

I am of this opinion that our own tung shold be written cleane and pure, vnmixt and vnmangeled with borowing of other tunges, wherein if we take not heed bi tijm, euer borowing and neuer payeng, she shall be fain to keep her house as bankrupt. For then doth our tung naturallie and praisablie vtter her meaning, when she borroweth no conterfeitness of other tunges to attire her self withall, but vseth plainlie her own with such shift, as nature craft, experiens, and folowing of other excellent doth lead her vnto, and if she want at ani tijm (as being vnperfight she must) yet let her borow with suche bashfulnes, that it mai appeer, that if either the mould of our own tung could serue us to fascion a woord of our own, or if the old denisoned wordes could content and ease this neede we wold not boldly venture of vnknowen wordes This I say not for reproof of you, who haue scarslie and necessarilie vsed whear occasion serueth a strange word so, as it seemeth to grow out of the matter and not to be sought for: but for mijn own defens, who might be counted ouerstraight a deemer of thinges, if I gaue not thys accompt to you, mi freend and wijs, of mi marring this your handiwork. But I am called awai, I praī you pardon mī shortnes, the rest of mī saienges should be but praise and exhortacion in this your doinges, which at moar leisor I shold do better.   From my house in Woodstreete the 16 of Iuly, 1557.

                                    Yours assured IOAN CHEKE.

These three instances may suffice to show the close connection between their study of the ancient Literature and their care over their native speech. Some of these Classical Students were the best Prose Writers of their time : just as the best Poets then, were those who drew their inspiration from Italy.   The two literary influences prepared a way, by creating a favourable literary atmosphere, for our Master Writers in Elizabeth's reign, Spenser and Shakespeare ; Bacon and Hooker.

6. Of these Classical Pioneers, Sir JOHN CHEKE was the chief. His influence on the *English* Literature of that and the next age has hardly been adequately recognized : partly because his principal work was Oral Teaching : and partly because only three or four of his thirty to forty known writings (many now lost) are in English. Sir Richard Sackville calls him ' the best Master . . . in our tyme,' at *p.* 21. Ascham quotes him ever and anon in this work as an authority from whom there was hardly any appeal, and in particular, relates at *pp.* 154-159, with a fresh memory, Cheke's criticism of Sallust, made to him about twenty-five years before.   Cheke was a Teacher of Teachers.   The influence of simply Oral Teachers rests chiefly in the hearts and minds of the Taught, and it shows itself most in their after Lives and Works. Cheke taught Edward VI. ; Sir W. Cecil ; W. Bill, 7th Master of St Johns ; R. Ascham ; Sir T. Wilson ; and many more celebrities of that time : and their characters and careers reflect his teaching.

T, afterwards Sir T. WILSON, in his *Epistle*, dated 10 June 1570, to Sir W. Cecil [It would be an interesting list, if English books were grouped according to their *dedicatees* : as showing the influence of the Nobility and Gentry on Literature], prefixed to his translation of the *Olynthiacs of Demosthenes* into English : thus ably conveys to us a conception of the surpassing abilities and character of Sir John Cheke.

" Great is the force of vertue (Right Honorable Counseller) to wynne loue and good will vniuersally, in whose minde soeuer it is perfitelye knowne, to haue once gotte a dwelling. I speake it for this ende, that being solitarie of late time from my other studies, and musinge on this world, in the middest of my bookes : I did then (as I haue oftentimes else done) deepelye thinke of Sir Iohn Cheeke Knyght, that rare learned man, and singular ornament of this lande. And as the remembrance of him was deare vnto me, for his manifolde great gifts and wonderfull vertues : so did I thinke of his most gentle nature and godly disposed minde, to helpe all those with his knowledge and vnderstanding, that any waye made meanes vnto him, and sought his fauour. And to say for my selfe amongest others, I founde him such a friende to me, for communicating the skill and giftes of hys minde, as I cannot but during my life speake reuerentlye of so worthie a man, and honor in my hart the heauenly remembrance of him.   And thinking of my being with him in Italie in that famous Vniuersitie of Padua : I did cal to minde his care that he had ouer all the Englishe men there, to go to their bokes : and how gladly he did reade to me and others, certaine Orations of Demosthenes in Greeke, the interpretation wherof, I and they had then from his mouth. And so remembring the rather this world by the very argument of those actions : I did then seeke out amongest my other writings for the translation of them, and happily finding some, although not all : I was caried streightwayes (I trust by Gods good motion) to make certaine of them to be acquainted so nigh as I coulde with our Englishe tongue, aswell for the aptnesse of the matter, and needefull knowiedge now at this time to be had : as also for the right notable, and most excellent handling of the same.   And here must I saye, confessing mine owne weakenesse and imperfection, that I neuer founde in my life any thing so harde for me to doe. . . .

Maister Cheeke (whome I dare match with any one before named for his knowledge in the Greeke tongue,) hauing traueyled in Demosthenes as much as any one of them all, and famous for his learning throughout Europe : yet was he neuer so passing in his translations that no exception coulde be made against him.   And then what shall I thinke of my selfe, after the naming of so manye excellent learned men, but onely submit my doings to the favour of others, and desire men to beare with my weakenesse. For this must I needes confesse, that I am altogither vnable to doe so in Englishe, as the excellencie of this Orator deserueth in Greeke. And yet the cunning is no lesse, and the prayse as great in my iudgement, to translate any thing excellently into Englishe, as into any other language. And I thinke (although there be many doers) yet scant one is to be found worthie amongst vs, for translating into our Countrie speach. Such a hard thing it is to bring matter out of any one language into another. And perhaps it may be that euen those who take themselues to bee much better learned than I am (as what is he that is not, hauing any name for learning at all ?) will finde it an harder peece of woorke than they thinke, euen to make Greeke speake Englishe, if they will make proofe thereof as I haue done. Whose labor and trauayle I woulde as gladly see, as they are lyke now to see mine, that such an Orator as this is, might bee so framed to speake our tongue, as none were able to amende him, and that he might be founde to be most like himselfe. The which enterprise if any might haue bene moste bolde to haue taken vpon him, Sir Iohn Cheeke was the man, of all that euer I knew, or doe yet know in Englande. Such acquaintance had he with this notable Orator, so gladly did he reade him, and so often : that I thinke there was neuer olde Priest more perfite in his Portreise, nor supersticious Monke in our Ladies Psalter as they call it, nor yet good Preacher in the Bible or testament, than this man was in Demosthenes. And great cause moued him so to be, for that he sawe him to be the perfitest Orator that euer wrate for these two thousand yeares almost by past (for so long it is since he was) and also for that he perceyued him to haue before his eyes in all his Orations the aduauncement of vertue as a thing chiefly to be sought for, togither with the honor and welfare of his countrie. Besides this, maister Cheekes iudgement was great in translating out of one tongue into an other, and better skill he had in our English speach to iudge of the Phrases and properties of wordes, and to diuide sentences : than any else had that I haue knowne. And often he woulde englyshe his matters out of the Latine or Greeke vpon the sodeyne, by looking of the booke onely without reading or construing any thing at all : An vsage right worthie and verie profitable for all men, aswell for the vnderstanding of the booke, as also for the aptnesse of framing the Authors meaning and bettering thereby their iudgement, and therewithall perfiting their tongue and vtterance of speach. Moreouer he was moued greatly to like Demosthenes aboue all others, for that he sawe him so familiarly applying himselfe to the sense and vnderstanding of the common people, that he sticked not to say, that none euer was more fitte to make an English man tell his tale praise worthily in an open hearing, either in Parlament or in Pulpit, or otherwise, than this onely Orator was. . . .

And although your honour hath no neede of these my doinges, for that the Greeke is so familiar vnto you, and that you also, as well as I, haue hearde Sir Iohn Cheeke read the same Orations at other times : yet I thinke for diuers causes I shoulde in right present vnto your honour this my traueyle the rather to haue it through your good liking and allowance, to be made common to many. First the sayd Sir Iohn Cheeke (whome I doe often name, for the honour and reuerence due of so worthie a man) was your brother in lawe [*Sir W. Cecil's first wife was Cheeke's sister*], your deare friende, your good admonisher, and teacher in your yonger yeares, to take that way of vertue, the fruite whereof you do feele and taste to your great ioy at this day, and shall for euer be remembered therefore" . . . *Ed.* 1570.

We may not wonder then ; if Ascham so affectionately refers to Cheke in this work ; as ' that Ientleman of worthie memorie, my dearest frend and teacher of all the poore learning I haue," *p.* 138.

[We would here add, out of the same *Epistle*, by way of parenthesis, Wilson's defence of Translations, which was possibly provoked by Ascham's remarks, at *p.* 127. " But such as are grieued with translated bokes, are lyke to them that eating fine Manchet, are angry with others that feede on Cheate breade. And yet God knoweth men would as gladly eate Manchet as they, if they had it. But all can not weare Veluet, or feede with the best, and therefore such are contented for necessities sake to weare our Countrie cloth, and to take themselues to hard fare, that can haue no better."]

7. We have noticed a few of the influences on Ascham in his earlier life; in order to understand his outlook on the Literature of his day; while—as he was growing from 48 to 53 years of age—he wrote this book. The Italian influence had come in like a flood after the publication of Tottel's Miscellany in June 1557. In his rejection of this influence, while he kept up with the classical learning of the time, we judge him to be a Scholar of Henry's time, surviving into the reign of Elizabeth. We do not allude to his Invective against *Italianated Englishmen*, for which he had doubtless adequate grounds : but to his shunning the airy lightsomeness of Italian poesy, which so much characterizes English Verse for the next forty years. Every one is entitled to a preference in such matters, and Ascham with others. Though he contended for English Iambics, he confessed he never had a "poeticall head." He owned to loving the Italian language next after Greek and Latin : but Fiction and Rhyme he could not abide. So we realize him as the strong plain Englishman of Henry's day, with his love for all field sports and for cock-fighting, his warm generous heart, his tolerant spirit, his thorough scholarship, his beautiful penmanship : a man to be loved and honoured.

8. Ascham's special craft was teaching the young, Latin and Greek. He had taught the Queen, as he tells us at *p.* 96 : and now read Greek with her, as she desired. Being thus about the Court, and the Court resting at Windsor on the 10th Dec. 1563 ; the officers in attendance dined together under the presidency of the Secretary of State. Of the Table Talk on that occasion and its results : Ascham's own account is the best : and need not be repeated here.

9. Looking within the book ; we see that begun in December 1563, it was prosecuted off and on for two years and a half, until Sir Richard Sackville's death in July 1566. It was then, for sorrow's sake, flung aside. 'Almost two yeares togither, this booke lay *scattered*, and neglected,' and then finished, so far as we now possess it, by the encouragement of Cecil, in the last six or eight months of Ascham's life. Ascham died 30 Dec : 1568.

If a guess might be hazarded : it would seem that the Author had but gathered the materials together, up to Sir Richard Sackville's death : and that he wove them together in their present form, after he resumed the book again. The allusion at *p.* 137, to the Queen's visit to Cambridge, in August 1564, as '*late* being there,' would show that that part was written about 1565 : while the phrase at *p.* 71, 'Syr Richard Sackuille, that worthy Ientleman, *of worthie memorie*, as I sayd in the *begynnynge*,' would proue that at least *The Præface* and the Invective against Italianated Englishmen were written after the resumption of the book in 1568 : and consequently that it was after then, that the work was finally planned. The first book was then completed, and the second far proceeded with, when Death parted for euer, the busy worker from his Book. This is also confirmed by Ascham's last letter to Sturm : which proves him to haue been intent on the work just before his decease.

10. Thanks to the editions of Upton and Bennet, *The Scholemaster* (which, like so many of the books of Elizabeth's time, had been quite forgotten in the previous sixteenth century) has obtained, for a hundred years or more, the reputation of an historic English work of general as well as of professional interest. With it, more than with any other of his works, is Ascham's name usually associated. As *Toxophilus* was the gift of his manhood towards the cultivation of the Body : so in this work—the legacy almost of his last hours—we inherit his ripest, his most anxious thought upon the Education of the Mind and Heart.

11. Among that first race of modern learned Englishmen, who fed and carried aloft the Lamp of Knowledge through all those changing and tempestuous times into the peaceful days of Elizabeth : none has become more famous than Roger Ascham : who, taught by the greatest English Teacher of his youth-tide, Sir John Cheeke : in due time became, to his undying delight, the Instructor of the most noble Scholar within the realm :—the Virgin Queen herself.

ROGER ASCHAM'S METHOD OF TEACHING LATIN.

1. That part of *The Scholemaster* which describes English life and manners of that age, is for us an heritage of authentic information : his Criticism of Ancient and Contemporary Latin writers, establishes a test of the Classical acumen of his time : but his system of teaching Latin—and *mutatis mutandis* other languages—deserves our study as a contribution in aid of Education, for all time.

2. We would wish to associate with this Reprint, an excellent book, *Essays on Educational Reformers*, by the Rev. R. H. Quick, M.A., London, 1868 : 7s. 6d, but worthy of being perpetually sold at a shilling as a companion volume to this reprint ; inasmuch as it is in some measure a continuation and completion of *The Scholemaster.* For in these Essays, Mr. Quick ably analyses and compares the successive systems of Instruction adopted by The Jesuits, Ascham, Montaigne, Ratich, Milton, Comenius, Locke, Rousseau, Basedow, Pestalozzi, Jacotot, and Herbert Spencer. We cannot therefore too strongly recommend the work to the attention of all those who desire to acquaint themselves with Modern Thought and Experiment in the Science and Art of Teaching.

3. Ascham's Method is avowedly based upon *B.I. c.* 34 of Cicero's *De Oratore*, of which the following is a translation : and more especially upon the latter portion of it. "But in my daily exercises I used, when a youth, to adopt chiefly that method which I knew that Caius Carbo, my adversary, generally practised ; which was, that, having selected some nervous piece of poetry, or read over such a portion of a speech as I could retain in my memory, I used to declaim upon what I had been reading in other words, chosen with all the judgment that I possessed. But at length I perceived that in that method there was this inconvenience, that Ennius, if I exercised myself on his verses, or Gracchus, if I laid one of his orations before me, had forestalled such words as were peculiarly appropriate to the subject, and such as were the most elegant and altogether the best ; so that, if I used the same words, it profited nothing ; if others, it was even prejudicial to me, as I habituated myself to use such as were less eligible. Afterwards I thought proper, and continued the practice at a rather more advanced age, to translate the orations of the best Greek orators ; by fixing upon which I gained this advantage, that while I rendered into Latin what I had read in Greek, I not only used the best words, and yet such as were of common occurrence, but also formed some words by imitation, which would be new to our countrymen, taking care, however, that they were unobjectionable." *Ed.* 1855.

4. Upon these hints, Ascham—after considering all possible means of teaching languages, which he there discusses in the second book—insisted upon *the exhaustive study of one or two books*, each to be of the highest excellence in its way.

In fact his system might be labelled as

The Double Translation of a Model Book.

Mr. Quick remarks, "There are three ways in which the model-book may be studied. 1st, It may be read through rapidly again and again, which was Ratich's plan and Hamilton's ; or, 2nd, each lesson may be thoroughly mastered, read in various ways a dozen times at the least, which was Ascham's plan ; or, 3rd, the pupil may begin always at the beginning, and advance a little further each time, which was Jacotot's plan," *p.* 215.

5. Ascham, at *p.* 94, quotes Pliny and Dionysius Halicarnasseus in support of his Method, in a passage we have not space to quote, but which is the key to his system. In the brief space that remains to us, we can but outline the process of study he laid down, commending the method to the careful consideration of all teachers.

PREPARATORY.

LEARNER. After the child hath learned perfectly the eight parts of speech : let him then learn the right joining together of substantives with adjectives, the noun with the verb, the relative with the antecedent, *p.* 25.

A. *DOUBLE TRANSLATION.*

The Model Book, to begin with, which Ascham recommended in his time was John Sturm's selection of Cicero's letters, for the capacity of children.

This work was first published at Strasburg in 1539, under the title or *Ciceronis Epistolæ Libri iv, puerili educationi confecti* ; and again in 1572.

I. *M A S T E R.* a. Let *him* teach the child, cheerfully and plainly, the *cause* and *matter* of the letter, *p.* 26.

  b. Then let *him* construe it into English, so often, as the child may *easily* carry away the understanding of it, *p.* 26.

  c. Let *him* parse it over perfectly, *p.* 26.

II. *L E A R N E R.* a. Let the child, by and bye, both conspire [*i.e.* combine] and parse it over again. So that it may *appear*, that the child doubteth in nothing that *his master taught him before, p.* 26.

  ∴ So far it is the Mind and Memory comprehending and reproducing the Oral Teaching.

  b. Then the child must take a paper book, and sitting in some place where no one shall prompt him, by himself, let him translate into English his former lesson, *p.* 26.

M A S T E R. c. Then shewing it to his master : let his master take from him his Latin book.

L E A R N E R. d. Then, pausing an hour at the least : let the child translate his own English into Latin, in another Paper Book.

III. *M A S T E R.* a. When the child bringeth it, turned into Latin ; let the Master, at the first, lead and teach his Scholer, to join the Rules of his Grammar Book, with the examples of his present lesson, until the Scholar, by himself, be able to fetch out of his Grammar, every Rule for every Example. So, as the Grammar book be ever in the Scholars hand, and also used of him *as a Dictionary*, for every present use, *p.* 26.

  b. The Master must *compare* the child's Retranslation with Cicero's book, and lay them both together, *p.* 26.

  Praising him where he doth well, either in choosing or true placing of Cicero's words.

  But if the child miss, either in forgetting a word, or in changing a good for a worse, or misordering the sentence . . . the master shall have good occasion to say. " N. [like M. or N. in the Catechism] Tully would have used such a word, not this. Tully would have placed this word here, not there : would have used this case, this number, this person, this degree, the gender : he would have used this mood, this tense, this simple rather than that compound ; this adverb here not there ; he would have ended the sentence with this verb, not with that noun or participle, &c.

  In these few lines, I have wrapped up the most tedious part of Grammar and also the ground of almost all the Rules . . . Which after this sort, the master shall teach without all error, and the scholar shall learn without great pain : the Master being lead by so sure a guide and the Scholar being brought into so plain and easy a way, *p.* 27.

Axiom. A child shall take more profit of two faults, gently warned of, then of four things rightly hit, *p.* 27.

  ∴ All this while, the child shall use to speak no Latin, *p.* 28.

With this way of good understanding the matter, plain construing, diligent parsing, daily translating, cheerfull admonishing, and heedfull amending of faults ; never leaving behind just praise for well doing : I would have the Scholar brought up : while he had read and translated over the first book of Cicero's Epistles chosen out by Sturm ; with a good piece of a Comedy of Terence [Terence at that time held a position in Latin Education, which has not since been maintained], *p.* 28.

B. *ANALYSIS.*

As you perceive your scholar to go better and better on away : first, with understanding his lesson more quickly, with passing more readily, with translating more speedily and perfectly than he was wont.

IV. *M A S T E R.* a. After, give him longer lessons to translate.

  b. Begin to teach him, both in NOUNS and VERBS ; what is *Proper* or *Literal* ? what is *Figurative* ? what is *Synonymous*, what is *Diverse*, which be *Opposites* : and which be the most notable *Phrases* in all his reading.

V. *L E A R N E R.* a. Your scholar, *after he hath done his Double translating*, let him write in a third Paper Book four of the fore-named six, diligently marked out of every lesson. As

| *Four* ` or else
three or two if
there be no
more. | { | *Proper.*
Figures.
Synonymes.
Differents.
Oposites.
Phrases. | If there be none
of these all
in some reading
yet omit not
the order
but write. | { | *Differents.* **None.**
Opposites. **None.**
&c. |

This diligent translating, joined with this heedful marking, in the foresaid
Epistles : and afterward in some plain Oration of Tully, as *pro Lege Manilia
pro Archaia Poeta*, or in those three *Ad Catum Cæsarem* shall work such **a**
right choice of words, so straight a framing of sentences, such a true judge-
ment, both to write skilfully and speak witty, as wise men shall **both praise**
and marvel at, *pp.* 29-31.

C. *READING AND A SECOND KIND OF TRANSLATION.*

After that your Scholar shall come indeed : first to a ready perfectness in
translating, then to a ripe and skilful choice in marking out his six points, *p.* 87.
VI. *L E A R N E R*. a. I would have him *read* now, a good deal now **at**
every lecture, these books, *p.* 88.
    [1.] Some book of Cicero, as the Third Book of Epistles chosen **out by**
        Sturm, *de Amicit., de Senect.* : or the first book *Ad Quint. frat.*
    [2.] Some Comedy of Terence or Plautus (But in Plautus, skilful choice
        must be used by the Master to train his scholar to a judgement, in
        perfecting, and cutting out over old and improper words).
    [3.] Cæsar's *Commentaries*, in which is seen the unspotted propriety of
        the Latin tongue ; even when it was at its acme.
    [4.] Some Orations of Livy, such as be both longest and plainest.
  b. He shall not now daily use translation : but only construe again and
parse where ye suspect is any need. Yet let him not omit in these books,
marking diligently and writing out orderly his six points.
VII. *M A S T E R*. a. For *translating*, use you yourself, every second **and**
third day, to choose out some Epistle *Ad Atticum*, some notable com-
monplace out of Cicero's Orations, or some other part of Tully, **by your**
discretion : *which your Scholar may not know where to find.*
    Translate it you yourself into plain natural English, and then give **it**
him to translate into Latin again : allowing him good space and time **to**
do it : both with diligent heed and good advisement.
    Here his wit will be new set on work ; his judgment for right choice,
truly tried ; his memory for sure retaining, better exercised than by
learning anything without the book. And here, how much he hath profited, shall plainly appear.
VIII. *M A S T E R*. a. When he bringeth it translated unto you, bring **you**
forth the place of Cicero. Lay them together. Compare the one with
the other. Commend his good choice and right placing of words. Show
his faults gently, but blame them not over sharply. For of such miss-
ings gently admonished of, proceedeth Glad and Good Heed-taking.
Of Good Heed-taking, springeth chiefly Knowledge, which after groweth
to perfectness : if this Order be diligently used by the Scholar **and gently**
handled by the Master, *p.* 88.

D. *A THIRD KIND OF TRANSLATION.*

When, by this diligent and speedy reading over those forenamed good
books of Cicero, Terence, Cæsar, and Livy : and by the second kind of
translating out of your English, time shall breed skill, and use shall bring
perfection : then you may try, if you will, your scholar, with the third kind
of translation. Although the two first ways, by mine opinion, be not only
sufficient of themselves, but also surer both for the Master's teaching and
Scholar's learning, than this third way is. Which is this.
IX. *M A S T E R*. Write you in *English*, some letter, as it were from him
to his father or to some other friend ; naturally, according to the disposi-
tion of the child : or some tale or fable, or plain narration. But yet use
you yourself such discretion for choice therein as the matter may be
within the compass, both for words and sentences, of his former learning.
X. *L E A R N E R*. Let him *translate* it into Latin again, abiding in such
place where no other scholar may prompt him.
And now take heed, lest your Scholar do not better in some point than **you**
yourself : except you have been diligently exercised in these kinds of translating before, *pp.* 89, 90.

BIBLIOGRAPHY.

THE SCHOLEMASTER.

* Editions not seen.

(a) Issues in the Author's lifetime.

None.

(b) Issues since the Author's death.

I. *As a separate publication.*

1. 1570. London. 1 vol. 4to. *Editio princeps.* See title on opposite page.
It was thus entered at Stationers Hall, early in 1570.
"Rd. of mʳ Daye for his lycense for printinge of a boke intituled the
schole mʳ of Wynsore made by mʳ Askecham" . . . . iijd.
Ext. of Regrs. ʊᵗ ᵗtat. Co. Ed. by J. P. Collier, i. 217. *Ed.* 1848.

2. 1571. London. The same title as No. 1, from which it differs in spelling
1 vol. 4to. and punctuation. Neither of these two first editions are to be
preferred to the other, as regards accuracy in these respects.

There are stated to be editions in 4to of *1572, *1573, *1579, *1583; but
there are no copies either in the British Museum or the Bodleian; neither
does Herbert quote them.

3. 1589. London. *The Scholemaster.* . . . As in No. 1. At London,
1 vol. 4to. Printed by ABELL IEFFES, *Anno* 1589.

∴ *Then the work as it were goes out of memory for 120 years.*

4. 1711. London. The Scholemaster : or a plain and perfect Way of teach-
1 vol. 8vo. ing Children to Understand, Write, and speak the *Latin
Tongue.* . . . Now Corrected, and Revised with an
Addition of *Explanatory Notes,* by the Reverend Mr. JAMES
UPTON, A.M., Rector of *Brimpton* in *Somersetshire* ; and late
Fellow of *King's* College in Cambridge.

5. 1743. London. The Scholemaster : shewing a Plain and Perfect Way
1 vol. 8vo. of Teaching the learned Languages. . . . Now revis'd a
second time, and much improved, by JAMES UPTON, A.M.,
Rector of *Monksilver* in *Somersetshire,* and late Fellow of
King's College in *Cambridge.* [A second Edition of No 4].

10. 1863. London. *The Scholemaster,* by Roger Ascham. Edited with
1 vol. 8vo. notes by JOHN E. B. MAYOR, M.A., Fellow of St. John's
College, Cambridge. [This is the best edition that has yet
appeared]. A reprint of No. **1** corrected by No. **2**.

12. 10 June 1870. London. *English Reprints* : see title at *p.* 1. A reprint
1 vol. 8vo. of No. **1,** collated by No. **2,** the important variations appear in [ ].

II. *With other works.*

6. 1771. London. The English Works of Roger Ascham. . . . With
1 vol. 4to. Notes and Observations, and the Author's Life. By JAMES
BENNET, Master of the Boarding-School at Hoddesdon in Hertfordshire. *The Schole Master* occupies *pp.* 187-347. [The
Dedication, and *Life* were by Dr. Johnson, who states that
Ascham 'was scarcely known as an author in his own language
till Mr. *Upton* published his *Scholemaster,' p.* xvi].

7. N. d. London. 1 vol. 4to. Another impression of No. **6**.

8. 1815. The English Works of Roger Ascham. A new Edition.
London. [Only 250 Copies printed. Ed. by J. G. COCHRANE]. Occupy-
1 vol. 8vo. ing *pp.* 183-333 is "*The Scholemaster.* Corrected and revised
with explanatory Notes, by the Rev. JAMES UPTON, A.M." :
This is therefore a Reprint of No. **8**.

9. N. d. 1 vol. 8vo. A reissue with a new title and without a date of No. **8**.

11. 1864-5. London. The whole works of Roger Ascham. Ed. by Rev.
Dr. Giles, formerly Fellow of C.C.C. Oxford. *The Scholemaster*
occupies ii-000. It is strange that after the appearance of Mr.
Mayor's Edition of the previous year, that this edition should
be 'a Reprint of No. **8,** which is itself a Reprint of 1743
No. **5**] collated with the earlier Editions,' and that it should *not*
have been wholly based on the original editions.

THE
SCHOLEMASTER

*Or plaine and perfite way of tea-
chyng children, to vnderstand, write, and
speake, in Latin tong, but specially purposed
for the priuate brynging vp of youth in Ientlemen and Noble mens houses, and commodious
also for all such, as haue forgot the Latin
tonge, and would, by themselues, without a Scholemaster, in short tyme,
and with small paines, recouer a
sufficient habilite, to vnderstand, write, and
speake Latin.*

¶ By Roger Afcham.

¶ *An.* 1 5 7 0.

AT LONDON.

Printed by Iohn Daye, dwelling
ouer Aldersgate.

¶ *Cum Gratia et Priuilegio Regiæ Maiestatis,
per Decennium.*

¶ **To the honorable Sir William**
Cecill Knight, principall Secretarie to
the Quenes moſt excellent Maieſtie.

Ondry and reaſonable be the cauſes why learned men haue vſed to offer and dedicate ſuch workes as they put abrode, to ſome ſuch perſonage as they thinke fitteſt, either in reſpect of abilitie of defenſe, or ſkill for iuge ment, or priuate regard of kindeneſſe and dutie. Euery one of thoſe conſiderations, Syr, moue me of right to offer this my late huſbands M. Aſchams worke vnto you. For well remembryng how much all good learnyng oweth vnto you for defenſe therof, as the Vniuerſitie of Cambrige, of which my ſaid late huſband was a member, haue in choſing you their worthy Chaunceller acknowledged, and how happily you haue ſpent your time in ſuch ſtudies and caried the vſe therof to the right ende, to the good ſeruice of the Quenes Maieſtie and your contrey to all our benefites, thyrdly how much my ſayd huſband was many wayes bound vnto you, and how gladly and comfortably he vſed in hys lyfe to recogniſe and report your goodneſſe toward hym, leauyng with me then hys poore widow and a great ſort of orphanes a good comfort in the hope of your good continuance, which I haue truly found to me and myne, and therfore do duely and dayly pray for you and yours: I could not

finde any man for whose name this booke was more agre able for hope [of] protection, more mete for submission to iudgement, nor more due for respect of worthynesse of your part and thankefulnesse of my husbandes and myne. Good I trust it shall do, as I am put in great hope by many very well learned that can well iudge therof. Mete therefore I compt it that such good as my husband was able to doe and leaue to the common weale, it should be receiued vnder your name, and that the world should owe thanke therof to you, to whom my husband the authour of it was for good receyued of you, most dutiefully bounden. And so besechyng you, to take on you the defense of this booke, to auaunce the good that may come of it by your allowance and furtherance to publike vse and benefite, and to accept the thankefull recognition of me and my poore children, trustyng of the continuance of your good memorie of M. Ascham and his, and dayly commendyng the prosperous estate of you and yours to God whom you serue and whoes you are, I rest to trouble you.

Your humble Margaret
Ascham.

·20· *A Præface to the*

Reader.

Hen the great plage was at London, the yeare 1 5 6 3. the Quenes
Maieſtie Queene *Elizabeth*, lay at
her Caſtle of Windſore : Where, vpon
the 10. day of December, it fortuned,
that in Sir *William Cicells* chamber,
hir Highneſſe Principall Secretarie,
there dined togither theſe perſon-
ages, M. Secretarie him ſelfe, Syr *William Peter*, Syr
J. Maſon, D. *Wotton*, Syr *Richard Sackuille* Treaſurer
of the Exchecker, Syr *Walter Mildmaye* Chauncellor
of the Exchecker, M. *Haddon* Maſter of Requeſtes,
M. *John Astley* Maſter of the Iewell houſe, M. *Bernard
Hampton*, M. *Nicaſius*, and *J.* Of which number, the
moſt part were of hir Maieſties moſt honourable priuie
Counſell, and the reaſt ſeruing hir in verie good place.
I was glad than, and do reioice yet to remember, that
my chance was ſo happie, to be there that day, in the
companie of ſo manie wiſe and good men togither, as
hardly than could haue beene pi[c]ked out againe, out
of all England beſide.

M. Secretarie hath this accuſtomed maner, though
his head be neuer ſo full of moſt weightie affaires of
the Realme, yet, at diner time he doth ſeeme to lay
them alwaies aſide : and findeth euer fitte occaſion to
taulke pleaſantlie of other matters, but moſt gladlie of
ſome matter of learning : wherein, he will curteſlie
heare the minde of the meaneſt at his Table.

Not long after our ſitting doune, I haue ſtrange

B

newes brought me, fayth M. Secretarie, this morning,

M. *Secreta-*   that diuerfe Scholers of Eaton, be runne
rie.   awaie from the Schole, for feare of beating.   Whereupon, M. Secretarie tooke occafion, to
wifhe, that fome more difcretion were in many
Scholemafters, in vfing correction, than commonlie
there is.   Who many times, punifhe rather, the weakenes of nature, than the fault of the Scholer.   Whereby,
many Scholers, that might elfe proue well, be driuen
to hate learning, before they knowe, what learning
meaneth : and fo, are made willing to forfake their
booke, and be glad to be put to any other kinde of
liuing.

M. *Peter.*   M. *Peter*, as one fomewhat feuere of
nature, faid plainlie, that the Rodde onelie, was the
fworde, that muft keepe, the Schole in obedience, and
M. *Wotton.*   the Scholer in good order.   M. *Wotton*, a
man milde of nature, with foft voice, and fewe wordes,
inclined to M. Secretaries iudgement, and faid, in mine
Ludus li-   opinion, the Scholehoufe fhould be in
terarum.   deede, as it is called by name, the houfe of
playe and pleafure, and not of feare and bondage :
Plato de   and as I do remember, fo faith *Socrates* in
Rep. 7.   one place of *Plato*.   And therefore, if a
Rodde carie the feare of a Sworde, it is no maruell, if
thofe that be fearefull of nature, chofe rather to forfake the Plaie, than to ftand alwaies within the feare
of a Sworde in a fonde mans handling.   M.
M. *Mason.*   *Mafon*, after his maner, was verie merie
with both parties, pleafantlie playing, both, with the
fhrewde touches of many courfte boyes, and with the
fmall difcretion of many leude Scholemafters.   M.
M. *Haddon.*   *Haddon* was fullie of M. *Peters* opinion,
and faid, that the beft Scholemafter of our time, was
the greateft beater, and named the Perfon.   Though,
The Author of   quoth I, it was his good fortune, to fend
this booke.   from his Schole, vnto the Vniuerfitie, one
of the beft Scholers in deede of all our time, yet wife
men do thinke, that that came fo to paffe, rather, by

the great towardnes of the Scholer, than by the great
beating of the Mafter: and whether this be true or no,
you your felfe are beft witnes. I faid fomewhat farder
in the matter, how, and whie, yong children, were foner
allured by loue, than driuen by beating, to atteyne
good learning: wherein I was the bolder to fay my
minde, bicaufe M. Secretarie curteflie prouoked me
thereunto: or elfe, in fuch a companie, and namelie
in his præfence, my wonte is, to be more willing, to
vfe mine eares, than to occupie my tonge.

Syr *Walter Mildmaye*, M. *Astley*, and the reft, faid
verie litle: onelie Syr *Rich. Sackuill*, faid nothing at
all. After dinner I went vp to read with the Queenes
Maieftie. We red than togither in the Greke tongue
as I well remember, that noble Oration Demost
of *Demosthenes* againft *Æfchines*, for his περὶ πα-
falfe dealing in his Ambaffage to king ραπρεσβ.
Philip of Macedonie. Syr *Rich. Sackuile* came
fone after: and finding me in hir Maie- Syr R.
fties priuie chamber, he tooke me by Sackuiles communication
the hand, and carying me to a windoe, with the Au-
faid, M. *Afcham*, I would not for a good thor of this booke.
deale of monie, haue bene, this daie, abfent from
diner. Where, though I faid nothing, yet I gaue as
good eare, and do confider as well the taulke, that
paffed, as any one did there. M. Secretarie faid very
wifely, and moft truely, that many yong wittes be
driuen to hate learninge, before they know what
learninge is. I can be good witnes to this my felfe:
For a fond Scholemafter, before I was fullie fourtene
yeare olde, draue me fo, with feare of beating, from
all loue of learninge, as nowe, when I know, what
difference it is, to haue learninge, and to haue litle, or
none at all, I feele it my greateft greife, and finde it
my greateft hurte, that euer came to me, that it was my
fo ill chance, to light vpon fo lewde a Scholemafter.
But feing it is but in vain, to lament thinges pafte, and
alfo wifdome to looke to thinges to cum, furely, God
willinge, if God lend me life, I will make this my mif-

hap, fome occafion of good hap, to litle *Robert Sack-uile* my fonnes fonne. For whofe bringinge vp, I would gladlie, if it fo pleafe you, vfe fpeciallie your good aduice. I heare faie, you haue a fonne, moch of his age : we wil deale thus togither. Point you out a Scholemafter, who by your order, fhall teache my fonne and yours, and for all the reft, I will prouide, yea though they three do coft me a couple of hundred poundes by yeare : and befide, you fhall finde me as faft a Frend to you and yours, as perchance any you haue. Which promife, the worthie Ientleman furelie kept with me, vntill his dying daye.

The cheife pointes of this booke. We had than farther taulke togither, of bringing vp of children : of the nature, of quicke, and hard wittes : of the right choice of a good witte : of Feare, and loue in teaching children. We paffed from children and came to yonge men, namely, Ientlemen : we taulked of their to moch libertie, to liue as they luft : of their letting loufe to fone, to ouermoch experience of ill, contrarie to the good order of many good olde common welthes of the Perfians and Grekes : of witte gathered, and good fortune gotten, by fome, onely by experience, without learning. And laftlie, he required of me verie earneft-lie, to fhewe, what I thought of the common goinge of Englifhe men into Italie. But, fayth he, bicaufe this place, and this tyme, will not fuffer fo long taulke, as thefe good matters require, therefore I pray you, at my requeft, and at your leyfure, put in fome order of writing, the cheife pointes of this our taulke, concern-ing, the right order of teachinge, and honeftie of liuing, for the good bringing vp of children and yong men. And furelie, befide contentinge me, you fhall both pleafe and profit verie many others. I made fome excufe by lacke of habilitie, and weakenes of bodie : well, fayth he, I am not now to learne, what you can do. Our deare frende, good M. *Goodricke*, whofe iudgement I could well beleue, did once for all, fatiffye me fullie therein. Againe, I heard you fay, not long agoe, that you may thanke Syr *John Cheke*, for all the learninge you haue : And I know verie well my felfe, that you did teach the Quene. And therefore feing God did fo bleffe you, to make you the Scholer of the beft Mafter, and alfo the Schole-mafter of the beft Scholer, that euer were in our tyme, furelie, you fhould pleafe God, benefite your countrie, and honeft your owne name, if you would take the paines, to impart to others, what you learned of foch a Mafter, and how ye taught fuch a fcholer. And, in vttering the ftuffe ye receiued of the one, in declaring the order ye tooke with the other, ye fhall neuer lacke, neither matter, nor maner, what to write, nor how to write in this kinde of Argument.

I beginning fome farther excufe, fodeinlie was called to cum to the Queene. The night following, I flept litle, my head was fo full of this our former taulke, and I fo mindefull, fomewhat to fatiffie the honeft re-queft of fo deare a frend. I thought to præpare fome litle treatife for a New yeares gift that Chriftmas. But, as it chanceth to bufie builders, fo, in building thys my poore Scholehoufe (the rather bicaufe the forme of it is fomewhat new, and differing from others) the worke rofe dailie higher and wider, than I thought it would at the beginninge.

And though it appeare now, and be in verie deede, but a fmall cotage, poore for the ftuffe, and rude for the workemanfhip, yet in going forward, I found the fite fo good, as I was lothe to giue it ouer, but the making fo coftlie, outreaching my habilitie, as many tymes I wifhed, that fome one of thofe three, my deare frendes, with full purffes, Syr *Tho. Smithe*, M. *Haddon*, or M. *Watfon*, had had the doing of it. Yet, neuertheleffe, I my felfe, fpending gladlie that litle, that I gatte at home by good Syr *Iohn Cheke*, and that that I bor-rowed abroad of my frend *Sturmius*, befide fomewhat that was left me in Reuerfion by my olde Mafters, *Plato*, *Aristotle*, and *Cicero*,

M. $\begin{cases} \textit{Smith.} \\ \textit{Haddon.} \\ \textit{Watson.} \end{cases}$

Syr *I. Cheke.*
I. Sturminus
Plato.
Aristotle.
Cicero.

I haue at laſt patched it vp, as I could, and as you
ſee.   If the matter be meane, and meanly handled, I
pray you beare, both with me, and it : for neuer worke
went vp in worſe wether, with mo lettes and ſtoppes,
than this poore Scholehouſe of mine.   Weſtminſter
Hall can beare ſome witneſſe, beſide moch weakenes
of bodie, but more trouble of minde, by ſome ſoch
ſores, as greue me to toche them my ſelfe, and therefore I purpoſe not to open them to others.   And, in
middes of outward iniuries, and inward cares, to encreaſe them withall, good Syr *Rich. Sack-*
Syr *R.*   *uile* dieth, that worthie Ientleman : That
Sackuill.
earneſt fauorer and furtherer of Gods true Religion :
That faithfull Seruitor to his Prince and Countrie : A
louer of learning, and all learned men : Wiſe in all
doinges : Curteſſe to all perſons : ſhewing ſpite to
none : doing good to many : and as I well found, to
me ſo faſt a frend, as I neuer loſt the like before.
Whan he was gone, my hart was dead.   There was
not one, that woare a blacke gowne for him, who
caried a heuier hart for him, than I.   Whan he was
gone, I caſt this booke awaie : I could not looke vpon
it, but with weping eyes, in remembring him, who was
the onelie ſetter on, to do it, and would haue bene,
not onelie a glad commender of it, but alſo a ſure and
certaine comfort, to me and mine, for it.   Almoſt two
yeares togither, this booke lay ſcattered, and neglected,
and had bene quite giuen ouer of me, if the goodneſſe
of one had not giuen me ſome life and ſpirite againe.
God, the mouer of goodneſſe, proſper alwaies him and
his, as he hath many times comforted me and mine,
and, I truſt to God, ſhall comfort more and more.   Of
whom, moſt iuſtlie I may ſaie, and verie oft, and alwaies gladlie, I am wont to ſay, that ſweete verſe of
Sophocles, ſpoken by *Oedipus* to worthie *Theſeus.*

Soph. in   ἔχω, [γὰρ ἅ'] χω διὰ σε, κοὐκ ἄλλον βροτῶν.
Oed. Col.

Thys hope hath helped me to end this booke : which,
if he allowe, I ſhall thinke my labours well imployed,

and fhall not moch æfteme the mifliking of any others. And I truft, he fhall thinke the better of it, bicaufe he fhall finde the beft part thereof, to cum out of his Schole, whom he, of all men loued and liked beft.

Yet fome men, frendly enough of nature, but of fmall iudgement in learninge, do thinke, I take to moch paines, and fpend to moch time, in fettinge forth thefe childrens affaires. But thofe good men were neuer brought vp in *So-crates* Schole, who faith plainlie, that no man goeth about a more godlie purpofe, than he that is mindfull of the good bring-ing vp, both of hys owne, and other mens children.

Therfore, I truft, good and wife men, will thinke well of this my doing. And of other, that thinke otherwife, I will thinke my felfe, they are but men, to be pardoned for their follie, and pitied for their ignoraunce.

Plato in initio Theagis.
οὐ γὰρ ἔστι περὶ ὅτου θειοτέρου ἄνθρωπος ἂν βουλεύσαιτο, ἢ περὶ παι-δείας, καὶ τῶν αὑτοῦ, καὶ τῶν οἰκείων.

In writing this booke, I haue had earneft refpecte to three fpeciall pointes, trothe of Religion, honeftie in liuing, right order in learning. In which three waies, I praie God, my poore children may diligently waulke : for whofe fake, as nature would, and reafon required, and neceffitie alfo fomewhat compelled, I was the willinger to take thefe paines.

For, feing at my death, I am not like to leaue them any great ftore of liuing, therefore in my life time, I thought good to bequeath vnto them, in this litle booke, as in my Will and Teftament, the right waie to good learning : which if they followe, with the feare of God, they fhall verie well cum to fufficiencie of liuinge.

I wifbe alfo, with all my hart, that yong M. *Rob. Sackuille,* may take that fructe of this labor, that his worthie Grauntfather purpofed he fhould haue done : And if any other do take, either proffet, or pleafure hereby, they haue caufe to thanke M. *Robert Sackuille,* for whom fpeciallie this my Scholemafter was prouided.

And one thing I would haue the Reader confider in readinge this booke, that bicaufe, no Scholemafter hath charge of any childe, before he enter into hys Schole, therefore I leauing all former care, of their good bringing vp, to wife and good Parentes, as a matter not belonging to the Scholemafter, I do appoynt thys my Scholemafter, than, and there to begin, where his office and charge beginneth. Which charge lafteth not long, but vntill the Scholer be made hable to go to the Vniuerfitie, to procede in Logike, Rhetoricke, and other kindes of learning.

Yet if my Scholemafter, for loue he beareth to hys Scholer, fhall teach hym fomewhat for hys furtherance, and better iudgement in learning, that may ferue him feuen yeare after in the Vniuerfitie, he doth hys Scholer no more wrong, nor de-ferueth no worfe name thereby, than he doth in London, who fellinge filke or cloth vnto his frend, doth giue him better meafure, than either hys pro-mife or bargaine was.

Farewell in Chrift.

The first booke for the youth.

Fter the childe hath learned perfitlie the eight partes of speach, let him then learne the right ioyning togither of substantiues with adiectiues, the nowne with the verbe, the relatiue with the antecedent. And in learninge farther hys Syntaxis, by mine aduice, he shall not vse the common order in common scholes, for making of latines: wherby, the childe commonlie learneth, first, an euill choice of wordes, (and right choice of wordes, saith *Cæsar*, is the *Cic.* de Cla. or. foundation of eloquence) than, a wrong placing of wordes: and lastlie, an ill framing of the sentence, with a peruerse iudgement, both of wordes and sentences. These faultes, taking once roote in yougthe, be neuer, or hardlie, pluckt away in age. Moreouer, there is no one thing, that hath more, either dulled the wittes, or taken Making of Latines marreth Children. awaye the will of children from learning, then the care they haue, to satiffie their masters, in making of latines.

For, the scholer, is commonlie beat for the making, when the master were more worthie to be beat for the mending, or rather, marring of the same: The master many times, being as ignorant as the childe, what to saie properlie and fitlie to the matter.

Two scholemasters haue set forth in print, either of them a booke, of soch kinde of latines, *Horman. Whittington.* *Horman* and *Whittington.*

A childe shall learne of the better of them, that, which an other daie, if he be wise, and cum to iudgement, he must be faine to vnlearne againe.

There is a waie, touched in the firſt booke of
De Or.   *Cicero De Oratore*, which, wiſelie brought
into ſcholes, truely taught, and conſtantly vſed, would
not onely take wholly away this butcherlie feare in
making of latines, but would alſo, with eaſe and pleaſure, and in ſhort time, as I know by good experience,
worke a true choice and placing of wordes, a right
ordering of ſentences, an eaſie vnderſtandyng of the
tonge, a readines to ſpeake, a facultie to write, a true
iudgement, both of his owne, and other mens doinges,
what tonge ſo euer he doth vſe.

The waie is this.   After the three Concordances
learned, as I touched before, let the maſter read vnto
hym the Epiſtles of *Cicero*, gathered togither and
choſen out by *Sturmius*, for the capacitie of children.

Firſt, let him teach the childe, cherefullie and plainlie,
The order of   the cauſe, and matter of the letter: then, let
teaching.   him conſtrue it into Engliſhe, ſo oft, as the
childe may eaſilie carie awaie the vnderſtanding of it:
Laſtlie, parſe it ouer perfitlie.   This done thus, let
the childe, by and by, both conſtrue and parſe it
ouer againe: ſo, that it may appeare, that the childe
douteth in nothing, that his maſter taught him before.   After this, the childe muſt take a paper booke,
and fitting in ſome place, where no man ſhall prompe
him, by him ſelf, let him tranſlate into Engliſhe his
Two paper   former leſſon.   Then ſhewing it to his
bokes.   maſter, let the maſter take from him his
latin booke, and pauſing an houre, at the leaſt, than
let the childe tranſlate his owne Engliſhe into latin
againe, in an other paper booke.   When the childe
bringeth it, turned into latin, the maſter muſt compare
it with *Tullies* booke, and laie them both togither: and
where the childe doth well, either in choſing, or true
Children learne   placing of *Tullies* wordes, let the maſter
by prayse.   praiſe him, and ſaie here ye do well.   For I
aſſure you, there is no ſuch whetſtone, to ſharpen a good
witte and encourage a will to learninge, as is praiſe.

But if the childe miſſe, either in forgetting a worde,

or in chaunging a good with a worfe, or mifordering the fentence, I would not haue the mafter, either froune, or chide with him, if the childe haue done his diligence, and vfed no trewandfhip therein.   For I know by good experience, that a childe fhall take more profit of two fautes, ientlie warned of, then of foure thinges, rightly hitt.   For than, the mafter fhall haue good occafion to faie vnto him. N. *Tullie* would haue vfed fuch a worde, not this : *Tullie* would haue placed this word here, not there : would haue vfed this cafe, this number, this perfon, this degree, this gender : he would haue vfed this moode, this tens, this fimple, rather than this compound : this aduerbe here, not there : he would haue ended the fentence with this verbe, not with that nowne or participle. etc.

Ientleness in teaching.

In thefe fewe lines, I haue wrapped vp, the moft tedious part of Grammer : and alfo the ground of almoft all the Rewles, that are fo bufilie taught by the Mafter, and fo hardlie learned by the Scholer, in all common Scholes : which after this fort, the mafter fhall teach without all error, and the fcholer fhall learne without great paine : the mafter being led by fo fure a guide, and the fcholer being brought into fo plaine and eafie a waie.   And therefore, we do not contemne Rewles, but we gladlie teach Rewles : and teach them, more plainlie, fenfiblie, and orderlie, than they be commonlie taught in common Scholes.   For whan the Mafter fhall compare *Tullies* booke with his [the] Scholers tranflation, let the Mafter, at the firft, lead and teach his Scholer, to ioyne the Rewles of his Grammer booke, with the examples of his prefent leffon, vntill the Scholer, by him felfe, be hable to fetch out of his Grammer, euerie Rewle, for euerie Example : So, as the Grammer booke be euer in the Scholers hand, and alfo vfed of him, as a Dictionarie, for euerie prefent vfe.   This is a liuely and perfite waie of teaching of Rewles : where the common waie, vfed in common Scholes, to read the Grammer alone

by it ſelfe, is tedious for the Maſter, hard for the
Scholer, colde and vncumfortable for them bothe.

Let your Scholer be neuer afraide, to aſke you any
dou[b]t, but vſe diſcretlie the beſt allurements ye can,
to encorage him to the ſame : leſt, his ouermoch hear-
inge of you, driue him to ſeeke ſome miſorderlie ſhifte :
as, to ſeeke to be helped by ſome other booke, or
to be prompted by ſome other Scholer, and ſo goe
aboute to beg[u]ile you moch, and him ſelfe more.

With this waie, of good vnderſtanding the ma[t]ter,
plaine conſtruinge, diligent parſinge, dailie tranſlat-
inge, cherefull admoniſhinge, and heedefull amendinge
of faultes : neuer leauinge behinde iuſte praiſe for
well doinge, I would haue the Scholer brought vp
withall, till he had red, and tranſlated ouer ye firſt booke
of Epiſtles choſen out by *Sturmius*, with a good peece
of a Comedie of *Terence* alſo.

All this while, by mine aduiſe, the childe ſhall vſe
to ſpeake no latine : For, as *Cicero* ſaith in like matter,
Latin speak- with like wordes, *loquendo, male loqui
yng. diſcunt.* And, that excellent learned man,
G. Budæus. *G. Budæus*, in his Greeke Commentaries,
ſore complaineth, that whan he began to learne the
latin tonge, vſe of ſpeaking latin at the table, and elſe-
where, vnaduiſedlie, did bring him to ſoch an euill
choice of wordes, to ſoch a crooked framing of ſentences, that no one thing did hurt or hinder him more,
all the daies of his life afterward, both for redineſſe in
ſpeaking, and alſo good iudgement in writinge.

In very deede, if children were brought vp, in ſoch
a houſe, or ſoch a Schole, where the latin tonge were
properlie and perſitlie ſpoken, as *Tib.* and *Ca. Gracci*
were brought vp, in their mother *Cornelias* houſc,
ſurelie, than the dailie vſe of ſpeaking, were the beſt
and readieſt waie, to learne the latin tong. But now,
commonlie, in the beſt Scholes in England, for wordes,
right choice is ſmallie regarded, true proprietrie whollie
neglected, confuſion is brought in, barbariouſneſſe is
bred up ſo in yong wittes, as afterward they be, not
onelie marde for ſpeaking, but alſo corrupted in iudge-

ment : as with moch adoe, or neuer at all, they be
brought to right frame againe.

Yet all men couet to haue their children fpeake latin :
and fo do I verie earneftlie too. We bothe, haue one
purpofe : we agree in defire, we wifh one end : but we
differ fomewhat in order and waie, that leadeth rightlie
to that end. Other would haue them fpeake at all
aduentures : and, fo they be fpeakinge, to fpeake, the
Mafter careth not, the Scholer knoweth not, what.
This is, to feeme, and not to bee : except it be, to be
bolde without fhame, rafhe without fkill, full of wordes
without witte. I wifh to haue them fpeake fo, as it
may well appeare, that the braine doth gouerne the
tonge, and that reafon leadeth forth the taulke. *Socrates* doctrine is true in *Plato,* and well *Plato.*
marked, and truely by *Horace* in *Arte Horat.*
Poetica, that, where fo euer knowledge doth accom-
panie the witte, there beft vtterance doth alwaies awaite
vpon the tonge : For, good vnderftanding muft firft
be bred in the childe, which, being nurifhed   Much writyng
with fkill, and vfe of writing (as I will teach breedeth ready
more largelie hereafter) is the onelie waie speakyng.
to bring him to iudgement and readineffe in fpeakinge :
and that in farre fhorter time (if he followe conftantlie
the trade of this lit[t]le leffon) then he fhall do, by
common teachinge of the common fcholes in England.

But, to go forward, as you perceiue, your fcholer to
goe better and better on awaie, firft, with vnderftanding his leffon more quicklie, with parfing more readelie,
with tranflating more fpedelie and perfitlie then he
was wonte, after, giue him longer leffons to tranflate :
and withall, begin to teach him, both in nownes, and
verbes, what is *Proprium,* and what is   The second
Tranflatum, what *Synonymum,* what *Di-* degree and
uerfum, which be *Contraria,* and which be order in
moft notable *Phrafes* in all his lecture.   teachyng.

As :

   Proprium.   { *Rex Sepultus est*
          { *magnifice.*

Tranſlatum.	{ *Cum illo principe,* *ſepulta est et gloria* *et Salus Re[i]publicæ.*
Synonyma.	{ *Enſis, Gladius.* *Laudare, prædicare.*
Diuerſa.	{ *Diligere, Amare.* *Calere, Exardeſcere* *Inimicus, Hostis.*
Contraria.	{ *Acerbum et luctuoſum* *bellum.* *Dulcis et læta* *Pax.*
Phraſes.	{ *Dare verba.* *abjicere obedientiam.*

Your ſcholer then, muſt haue the third paper **booke:**
The thyrd paper boke. in the which, after he hath done his double
tranſlation, let him write, after this ſort
foure of theſe forenamed ſixe, diligentlie marked out
of euerie leſſon.

Quatuor.	{ *Propria.* *Tranſlata.* *Synonyma.* *Diuerſa.* *Contraria.* *Phraſes.*

Or elſe, three, or two, if there be no moe: and if
there be none of theſe at all in ſome lecture, yet not
omitte the order, but write theſe.

{ *Diuerſa nulla.*
Contraria nulla. etc.

This diligent tranſlating, ioyned with this heedefull
marking, in the foreſaid Epiſtles, and afterwarde in

fome plaine Oration of *Tullie*, as, *pro lege Manil: pro Archia Poeta*, or in thofe three *ad. C. Cæf*: fhall worke foch a right choife of wordes, fo ftreight a framing of fentences, foch a true iudgement, both to write fkilfullie, and fpeake wittlelie, as wife men fhall both praife, and maruell at.

If your fcholer do miffe fometimes, in marking rightlie thefe forefaid fixe thinges, chide not haftelie: for that fhall, both dull his witte, and dif- Ientlenes in corage his diligence: but monifh him gen- teaching. telie: which fhall make him, both willing to amende, and glad to go forward in loue and hope of learning.

I haue now wifhed, twife or thrife, this gentle nature, to be in a Scholemafter: And, that I haue done fo, neither by chance, nor without fome reafon, I will now declare at large, why, in mine opinion, Loue. loue is fitter then feare, ientlenes better Feare. then beating, to bring vp a childe rightlie in learninge.

With the common vfe of teaching and beating in common fcholes of England, I will not greatlie Common contend: which if I did, it were but a fmall Scholes. grammaticall controuerfie, neither belonging to herefie nor treafon, nor greatly touching God nor the Prince: although in very deede, in the end, the good or ill bringing vp of children, doth as much ferue to the good or ill feruice, of God, our Prince, and our whole countrie, as any one thing doth befide.

I do gladlie agree with all good Scholemafters in thefe pointes: to haue children brought to good perfitnes in learning: to all honeftie in maners: to haue all fau[l]tes rightlie amended: to haue euerie vice feuerelie corrected: but for the order and waie that leadeth rightlie to thefe pointes, we fomewhat differ. For commonlie, many fcholemafters, fome, as Sharpe I haue feen, moe, as I haue heard tell, Scholemasters. be of fo crooked a nature, as, when they meete with a hard witted fcholer, they rather breake him, than bowe him, rather marre him, then mend him. For whan the fcholemafter is angrie with fome other

matter, then will he foneſt faul to beate his ſcholer:
and though he him ſelfe ſhould be puniſhed for his
folie, yet muſt he beate ſome ſcholer for his pleaſure:
though there be no cauſe for him to do ſo, nor yet
fault in the ſcholer to deſerue ſo.   Theſe ye will ſay,
be fond ſcholemaſters, and fewe they be, that be found
to be ſoch.   They be fond in deede, but ſurelie ouermany ſoch be found euerie where.   But this will I
ſay, that euen the wiſeſt of your great
beaters, do as oft puniſhe nature, as they
do correcte faultes.   Yea, many times, the better nature, is ſorer puniſhed: For, if one, by quicknes of
witte, take his leſſon readelie, an other, by hardnes of
witte, taketh it not ſo ſpeedelie: the firſt is alwaies
commended, the other is commonlie puniſhed: whan
a wiſe ſcholemaſter, ſhould rather diſcretelie conſider
the right diſpoſition of both their natures, and not
ſo moch wey what either of them is able to do now,
as what either of them is likelie to do
hereafter.   For this I know, not onelie
by reading of bookes in my ſtudie, but alſo by
experience of life, abrode in the world, that thoſe,
which be commonlie the wiſeſt, the beſt learned, and
beſt men alſo, when they be olde, were neuer commonlie the quickeſt of witte, when they were yonge.
The cauſes why, amongeſt other, which be many, that
moue me thus to thinke, be theſe fewe, which I will
recken.   Quicke wittes commonlie, be apte to take,
vnapte to keepe: ſoone hote and deſirous of this and
that: as colde and ſone wery of the ſame againe:
more quicke to enter ſpedelie, than hable to pearſe
farre: euen like ouer ſharpe tooles, whoſe edges be
verie ſoone turned.   Soch wittes delite them ſelues in
eaſie and pleaſant ſtudies, and neuer paſſe farre forward in hie and hard ſciences.   And therefore the quickeſt wittes commonlie may proue the beſt Poetes, but
not the wiſeſt Orators: readie of tonge to ſpeak boldlie, not deepe of iudgement, either for good
counſell or wiſe writing.   Alſo, for maners

Nature
puniſhed.

Quicke wittes
for learnyng.

Quicke wittes,
for maners and
lyfe.

and life, quicke wittes commonlie, be, in defire, newfangle[d], in purpofe, vnconftant, light to promife any thing, readie to forget euery thing : both bene- fite and iniurie : and therby neither faft to frend, nor fearefull to foe : inquifitiue of euery trifle, not fecret in greateft affaires : bolde, with any perfon : bufie, in euery matter : fo[o]thing, foch as be prefent : nipping any that is abfent : of nature alfo, alwaies, flattering theii betters, enuying their equals, defpifing their inferiors : and, by quicknes of witte, verie quicke and readie, to like none fo well as them felues.

Moreouer commonlie, men, very quicke of witte, be alfo, verie light of conditions : and thereby, very readie of difpofition, to be caried ouer quicklie, by any light cumpanie, to any riot and vnthriftines when they be yonge : and therfore feldome, either honeft of life, or riche in liuing, when they be olde. For, quicke in witte, and light in maners, be, either feldome troubled, or verie fone we[e]ry, in carying a verie heuie purfe. Quicke wittes alfo be, in moft part of all their doinges, ouer quicke, haftie, rafhe, headie, and brainficke. Thefe two laft wordes, Headie, and Brainficke, be fitte and proper wordes, rifing naturallie of the matter, and tearmed aptlie by the condition, of ouer moch quickenes of witte. In yougthe alfo they be, readie fcoffers, priuie mockers, and euer ouer light and mer[r]y. In aige, fone teftie, very wafpifhe, and alwaies ouer miferable : and yet fewe of them cum to any great aige, by reafon of their mifordered life when they were yong : but a greate deale fewer of them cum to fhewe any great countenance, or beare any great authoritie abrode in the world, but either liue obfcurelie, men know not how, or dye obfcurelie, men marke not whan. They be like trees, that fhewe forth, faire bloffoms and broad leaues in fpring time, but bring out fmall and not long lafting fruite in harueft time : and that onelie foch, as fall, and rotte, before they be ripe, and fo, neuer, or feldome, cum to any good at all. For this ye fhall finde moft true by experience, that amongeft a number of quicke wittes in youthe, fewe be found, in the end, either verie fortunate for them felues, or verie profitable to ferue the common wealth, but decay and vanifh, men know not which way : except a very fewe, to whom peraduenture blood and happie parentage, may perchance purchace a long ftanding vpon the ftage. The which felicitie, becaufe it commeth by others procuring, not by their owne deferuinge, and ftand by other mens feete, and not by their own, what owtward brag fo euer is borne by them, is in deed, of it felfe, and in wife mens eyes, of no great eftimation.

Some wittes, moderate enough by nature, be many *Som sciences* tymes marde by ouer moch ftudie and vfe *hurt mens wits,* of fome fciences, namelie, Muficke, Arith*and mar mens* metick, and Geometrie. Thies fciences, *maners.* as they fharpen mens wittes ouer moch, fo they change mens maners ouer fore, if they be not moderatlie mingled, and wifelie applied to fom good vfe of life. *Mathematicall* Marke all Mathematicall heades, which be *heades.* onely and wholy bent to thofe fciences, how folitarie they be themfelues, how vnfit to liue with others, and how vnapte to ferue in the world. This is not onelie knowen now by common experience, but vttered long before by wife mens Iudgement and fen*Galen.* tence. *Galene* faith, moch Mufick mar*Plato.* reth mens maners : and *Plato* hath a notable place of the fame thing in his bookes *de Rep.* well marked alfo, and excellentlie tranflated by *Tullie* himfelf. Of this matter, I wrote once more at large, xx. yeare a go, in my booke of fhoting : now I thought but to touch it, to proue, that ouer moch quicknes of witte, either giuen by nature, or fharpened by ftudie, doth not commonlie bring forth, eyther greateft learning, beft maners, or happieft life in the end.

Contrariewife, a witte in youth, that is not ouer *Hard wits in* dulle, heauie, knottie and lumpifhe, but *learning.* hard, rough, and though fomwhat ftaffifhe, as *Tullie* wifheth *otium, quietum, non languidum* : and *negotium cum labore, non cum periculo,* fuch a witte I

say, if it be, at the firſt well handled by the mother,
and rightlie ſmo[o]thed and wrought as it ſhould, not
ouer[t]whartlie, and againſt the wood, by the ſcholemaſter, both for learning, and hole courſe of liuing,
proueth alwaies the beſt. In woode and ſtone, not
the ſofteſt, but hardeſt, be alwaies apteſt, for portra-
ture, both faireſt for pleaſure, and moſt durable for
proffit. Hard wittes be hard to receiue, but ſure to
keepe : painefull without werineſſe, hedefull without
wauering, conſtant without newfanglenes : bearing
heauie thinges, thoughe not lightlie, yet willinglie ;
entring hard thinges, though not eaſelie, yet depelie ;
and ſo cum to that perfitnes of learning in the ende,
that quicke wittes, ſeeme in hope, but do not in deede,
or elſe verie ſeldome, euer attaine vnto. Hard wits
Alſo, for maners and life, hard wittes com- in maners
monlie, ar[e] hardlie caried, either to deſire and lyfe.
euerie new thing, or elſe to maruell at euery ſtrange
thinge : and therefore they be carefull and diligent in
their own matters, not curious and buſey in other mens
affaires : and ſo, they becum wiſe them ſelues, and alſo
ar[e] counted honeſt by others. They be graue, ſtedfaſt,
ſilent of tong, ſecret of hart. Not haſtie in making,
but conſtant in ke[e]ping any promiſe. Not raſhe in
vttering, but war[y]e in conſidering euery matter : and
therby, not quicke in ſpeaking, but deepe of iudgement, whether they write, or giue counſell in all
waightie affaires. And theis be the men, that becum
in the end, both moſt happie for themſelues, and alwaiſe beſt eſtemed abrode in the world.

I haue bene longer in deſcribing, the nature, the
good or ill ſucceſſe, of the quicke and hard witte, than
perchance ſom will thinke, this place and The best wittes
matter doth require. But my purpoſe was driuen from
hereby, plainlie to vtter, what iniurie is other liuyng.
offered to all learninge, and to the common welthe
alſo, firſt, by the fond father in choſing, but chieflie by
the lewd ſcholemaſter in beating and driuing away the
beſt natures from learning. A childe that is ſtill, ſilent,

conſtant, and ſomwhat hard of witte, is either neuer
choſen by the father to be made a ſcholer, or elſe,
when he commeth to the ſchole, he is ſmally regarded,
little looked vnto, he lacketh teaching, he lacketh co-
raging, he lacketh all thinges, onelie he neuer lacketh
beating, nor any word, that may moue him to hate
learninge, nor any deed that may driue him from
learning, to any other kinde of liuing.

And when this ſadde natured, and hard witted
Hard wits
proue best in
euery kynde
of lyfe. child, is bette from his booke, and becum-
meth after eyther ſtudent of the common
lawe, or page in the Court, or ſeruingman,
or bound prentice to a merchant, or to ſom handie-
crafte, he proueth in the ende, wiſer, happier and
many tymes honeſter too, than many of theis quick
wittes do, by their learninge.

Learning is, both hindred and iniured to[o], by the ill
choice of them, that ſend yong ſcholers to the vniuerſities. Of whom muſt nedes cum all oure Diuines,
Lawyers, and Phyſicions.

Thies yong ſcholers be choſen commonlie, as yong
The ill choice
of wittes for
learnyng. apples be choſen by children, in a faire
garden about *S. Iames* tyde: a childe will
choſe a ſweeting, becauſe it is preſentlie
faire and pleaſant, and refuſe a Runnet, becauſe it is
than grene, hard, and ſowre, whan the one, if it be
eaten, doth breed, both wormes and ill humors: the
other if it ſtand his tyme, be ordered and kepte as it
ſhould, is holſom of it ſelf, and helpeth to the good
digeſtion of other meates: Sweetinges, will receyue
wormes, rotte, and dye on the tree, and neuer or
feldom cum to the gathering for good and laſting
ſtore.

For verie greaſe of hearte I will not applie the ſimilitude: but hereby, is plainlie ſeen, how learning is
robbed of hir beſt wittes, firſt by the greate beating,
and after by the ill choſing of ſcholers, to go to the
vniuerſities. Whereof cummeth partelie, that lewde
and ſpitefull prouerbe, ſounding to the great hurte of

learning, and fhame of learned men, that, the greateft
Clerkes be not the wifeft men.

And though I, in all this difcourfe, feem plainlie to
prefer, hard and roughe wittes, before quicke and light
wittes, both for learnyng and maners, yet am I not
ignorant that fom quicknes of witte, is a finguler gifte
of God, and fo moft rare emonges men, and namelie
fuch a witte, as is quicke without lightnes, fharpe without brittlenes, defirous of good thinges without newfanglenes, diligent in painfull thinges without werifom‧
nes, and conftant in good will to do all thinges well,
as I know was in Syr *Iohn Cheke*, and is in 'fom, that
yet liue, in whome all theis faire qualities of witte ar[e]
fullie mette togither.

But it is notable and trewe, that *Socrates* faith in
Plato to his frende *Crito*. That, that *Plato. in*
number of men is feweft, which far ex- *Critone.*
cede, either in good or ill, in wifdom or folie, but the
meane betwixt both, be the greateft num- Verie good or
ber : which he proueth trewe in diuerfe verie ill men,
other thinges : as in greyhoundes, emonges number.
which fewe are found, exceding greate, or exceding
litle, exceding fwift, or exceding flowe : And therfore, I fpeaking of quick and hard wittes, I ment,
the common number of quicke and hard wittes,
emonges the which, for the moft parte, the hard witte,
proueth manie times, the better learned, wifer and
honefter man : and therfore, do I the more lament,
that foch wittes commonlie be either kepte from learning, by fond fathers, or be[a]t[e] from learning by lewde
fcholemafters.

And fpeaking thus moche of the wittes of children
for learning, the opportunitie of the place, Horsemen be
and goodnes of the matter might require wiser in know-
to haue here declared the moft fpeciall Colte, than
notes of a good witte for learning in a Scholemasters
childe, after the maner and cuftume of a knowledge of
good horfman, who is fkilfull, to know, a good witte.
and hable to tell others, how by certein fure fignes, a

man may choiſe a colte, that is like to proue an other
day, excellent for the ſaddle.   And it is pit[t]ie, that
commonlie, more care is had, yea and that emonges
A good Rider   verie wiſe men, to finde out rather a cun
better reward-   nynge man for their horſe, than a cunnyng
ed than a good
Scholemaster.   man for their children.   They ſay nay in
worde, but they do ſo in dede.   For, to the one, they will
gladlie giue a ſtipend of 200. Crounes by [the] yeare,
and loth to offer to the other, 200. ſhillinges.   God, that
ſitteth in heauen laugheth their choice to ſkorne, and
Horse well   rewardeth their liberalitie as it ſhould : for
broken, chil-   he ſuffereth them, to haue, tame and well
dren ill taught.   ordered horſe, but wilde and vnfortunate
Children : and therfore in the ende they finde more plea
ſure in their horſe, than comforte in their children.

But concerning the trewe notes of the beſt wittes
for learning in a childe, I will reporte, not myne own
opinion, but the very iudgement of him, that was
counted the beſt teacher and wiſeſt man that learning
Plato in 7   maketh mention of, and that is *Socrates* in
de Rep.   *Plato*, who expreſſeth orderlie thies ſeuen
plaine notes to choiſe a good witte in a child for
learninge.

Trewe notes of a
good witte.

1 Εὐφυής.
2 Μνήμων.
3 Φιλομαθής.
4 Φιλόπονος.
5 Φιλήκοος.
6 Ζητητικὸς.
7 Φιλέπαινος.

And bicauſe I write Engliſh, and to Engliſhemen, I
will plainlie declare in Engliſhe both, what thies wordes
of *Plato* meane, and how aptlie they be linked, and
how orderlie they fol[l]ow one an other.

1. Εὐφυής.

Witte.   Is he, that is apte by goodnes of witte,
Will.   and appliable by readines of will, to learning, hauing all other qualities of the minde and partes

of the bodie, that muſt an other day ſerue learning, not
tro[u]bled, mangled, and halfed, but ſounde, whole, full,
and hable to do their office : as, a tong, *The tong.*
not ſtamering, or ouer hardlie drawing forth wordes,
but plaine, and redie to deliuer the meaning of the
minde : a voice, not ſofte, weake, piping, *The voice.*
womanniſhe, but audible, ſtronge, and manlike : a
countenance, not weriſhe and crabbed, but *Face.*
faire and cumlie : a perſonage, not wretched and
deformed, but taule and goodlie : for *Stature.*
ſurelie a cumlie countenance, with a goodlie ſtature,
geueth credit to learning, and authoritie *Learnyng*
to the perſon : otherwiſe commonlie, either *ioyned with
a cumlie*
open contempte, or priuie diſſauour doth *personage.*
hurte, or hinder, both perſon and learning. And, euen
as a faire ſtone requireth to be ſette in the fineſt gold,
with the beſt workmanſhyp, or elſe it leſeth moch of the
Grace and price, euen ſo, excellencye in learning, and
namely Diuinitie, ioyned with a cumlie perſonage, is a
meruelous Iewell in the world. And how can a
cumlie bodie be better employed, than to ſerue the
faireſt exerciſe of Goddes greateſt gifte, and that is
learning. But commonlie, the faireſt bodies, ar[e] be-
ſtowed on the fouleſt purpoſes. I would it were not
ſo : and with examples herein I will not medle : yet I
wiſhe, that thoſe ſhold, both mynde it, and medle with
it, which haue moſt occaſion to looke to it, as good
and wiſe fathers ſhold do, and greateſt authoritie to
amend it, as good and wiſe magiſtrates ought to do :
And yet I will not let, openlie to lament the vnfortunate caſe of learning herein.

For, if a father haue foure ſonnes, three faire and
well formed both mynde and bodie, the *Deformed*
fourth, wretched, laine, and deformed, his *creatures*
choice ſhalbe, to put the worſt to learning, *commonlie set
to learnyng.*
as one good enoughe to becum a ſcholer.
I haue ſpent the moſt parte of my life in the Vniuerſitie, and therfore I can beare good witnes that
many fathers commonlie do thus : wherof, I haue hard

many wiſe, learned, and as good men as euer I knew, make great, and oft complainte : a good horſeman will choiſe no ſoch colte, neither for his own, nor yet for his maſters ſadle. And thus moch of the firſt note.

2. Μνήμων.

Memorie. Good of memorie, a ſpeciall parte of the firſt note εὐφνής, and a mere benefite of nature : yet it is ſo neceſſarie for learning : as *Plato* maketh it a ſeparate and perſite note of it ſelfe, and that ſo princi- pall a note, as without it, all other giftes of nature do **Aul. Gel.** ſmall feruice to learning, *Afranius*, that olde Latine Poete maketh Memorie the mother of learning and wiſedome, ſaying thus.

Vſus me genuit, Mater peperit memoria, and though it be the mere gifte of nature, yet is memorie well preſerued by vſe, and moch encreaſed by order, as our **Three ſure** ſcholer muſt learne an other day in the **ſignes of a** Vniuerſitie : but in a childe, a good me- **good me-** morie is well known, by three properties : **morie.** that is, if it be, quicke in receyuing, ſure in keping, and redie in deliuering forthe againe.

3. Φιλομαθής.

Giuen to loue learning : for though a child haue all the giftes of nature at wiſhe, and perfection of memorie at will, yet if he haue not a ſpeciall loue to learning, he ſhall neuer attaine to moch learning. And therfore *Iſocrates*, one of the nobleſt ſcholemaſters, that is in memorie of learning, who taught Kinges and Princes, as *Halicarnaſſæus* writeth, and out of whoſe ſchole, as *Tullie* ſaith, came forth, mo noble Capitanes, mo wiſe Councelors, than did out of *Epeius* horſe at *Troie*. This *Iſocrates*, I ſay, did cauſe to be written, at the entrie of his ſchole, in golden letters, this golden ſentence, ἐὰν ἦς φιλομαθής, ἔση πολυμαθής which excellentlie ſaid in *Greeke*, is thus rudelie in Engliſhe, if thou loueſt learning, thou ſhalt attayne to moch learning.

4 Φιλόπονος.

Is he, that hath a luft to labor, and a will to take paines. For, if a childe haue all the benefites of nature, with perfection of memorie, loue, like, and praife learning neuer fo moch, yet if he be not of him felfe painfull, he fhall neuer attayne vnto it. And yet where loue is prefent, labor is feldom abfent, and namelie in ftudie of learning, and matters of the mynde : and therfored id *Ifocrates* rightlie iudge, that if his fcholer were φῖλομαθής he cared for no more. *Ariftotle,* variing from *Ifocrates* in priuate affaires of life, but agreing with *Ifocrates* in common iudgement of learning, for loue and labor in learning, is of the fame opinion, vttered in thefe wordes, in his Rhetorike *ad Theodecten.* Li-   2 Rhet. ad bertie kindleth loue : Loue refufeth no labor :   Theod. and labor obteyneth what fo euer it feeketh. And yet neuerthelesse, Goodnes of nature may do little good : Perfection of memorie, may ferue to fmall vfe : All loue may be employed in vayne : Any labor may be fone graualed, if a man truft alwaies to his own finguler witte, and will not be glad fomtyme to heare, take aduife, and learne of an other : And therfore doth *Socrates* very notablie adde the fifte note.

5 Φιλήκοος.

He, that is glad to heare and learne of an other. For otherwife, he fhall fticke with great troble, where he might go eafelie forwarde : and alfo catche hardlie a verie litle by his owne toyle, whan he might gather quicklie a good deale, by an others mans teaching. But now there be fome, that haue great loue to learning, good luft to labor, be willing to learne of others, yet, either of a fonde fhamefaftnes, or elfe of a proud folie, they dare not, or will not, go to learne of an nother : And therfore doth *Socrates* wifelie adde the fixte note of a good witte in a childe for learning, and that is.

6 Ζητητικός.

He, that is naturallie bold to aſke any queſtion, deſirous to ſearche out any dou[b]te, not aſhamed to learne of the meaneſt, not affraide to go to the greateſt, vntill he be perfitelie taught, and fullie ſatiſſiede.   The ſeuenth and laſt poynte is.

7 Φιλέπαινος.

He, that loueth to be praiſed for well doing, at his father, or maſters hand.   A childe of this nature, will earneſtlie loue learnyng, gladlie labor for learning, willinglie learne of other, boldlie aſke any dou[b]te.   And thus, by *Socrates* iudgement, a good father, and a wiſe ſcholemaſter, ſhold choſe a childe to make a ſcholer of, that hath by nature, the foreſayd perfite qualities, and cumlie furniture, both of mynde and bodie, hath memorie, quicke to receyue, ſure to keape, and readie to deliuer : hath loue to learning : hath luſt to labor : hath deſire to learne of others : hath boldnes to aſke any queſtion : hath mynde holie bent, to wynne praiſe by well doing.

The two firſte poyntes be ſpeciall benefites of nature : which neuertheleſſe, be well preſerued, and moch encreaſed by good order.   But as for the fiue laſte, loue, labor, gladnes to learne of others, boldnes to aſke dou[b]tes, and will to wynne praiſe, be wonne and maintened by the onelie wiſedome and diſcretion of the ſcholemaſter.   Which fiue poyntes, whether a ſcholemaſter ſhall work ſo[o]ner in a childe, by fearefull beating, or curteſe handling, you that be wiſe, iudge.

Yet ſome men, wiſe in deede, but in this matter, more by ſeueritie of nature, than any wiſdome at all, do laugh at vs, when we thus wiſhe and reaſon, that yong children ſhould rather be allured to learning by ientilnes and loue, than compelled to learning, by beating and feare : They ſay, our reaſons ſerue onelie to breede forth talke, and paſſe a waie tyme, but we neuer ſaw good ſcholemaſter do ſo, nor neuer red of wiſe man that thought ſo.

Yes forfothe : as wife as they be, either in other mens opinion, or in their owne conceite, I will bring the contrarie iudgement of him, who, they them felues fhall confefle, was as wife as they are, or elfe they may be iuftlie thought to haue fmall witte at all : and that is *Socrates*, whofe iudgement in *Plato* is plainlie this in thefe *Plato* in 7. de Rep. wordes : which, bicaufe they be verie notable, I will recite them in his owne tonge, οὐδὲν μάθημα μετὰ δουλείας χρὴ μανθάνειν· οἱ μὲν γὰρ τοῦ σώματος πόνοι βίᾳ πονούμενοι χεῖρον οὐδέν τὸ σῶμα ἀπερνάξονται; ψυχῇ δε, βίαιον οὐδὲν ἔμμονον μάθημα: in Englifhe thus, No learning ought to be learned with bondage: For, bodelie labors, wrought by compulfion, hurt not the bodie : but any learning learned by compulfion, tarieth not long in the mynde: And why? For what foeuer the mynde doth learne vnwillinglie with feare, the fame it doth quicklie forget without care. And left proude wittes, that loue not to be contraryed, but haue luft to wrangle or trifle away troth, will fay, that *Socrates* meaneth not this of childrens teaching, but of fom other higher learnyng, heare, what *Socrates* in the fame place doth more plainlie fay : μὴ τοίνυν βίᾳ ; ὦ ἄριστε, τοὺς παῖδας ἐν τοῖς μαθήμασιν, ἀλλὰ παίζοντας τρέφε, that is to fay, and therfore, my deare frend, bring not vp your children in learning by compulfion and feare, but by playing and pleafure. And you, that do read *Plato*, as ye fhold, do well perceiue, that thefe be no The right readyng of *Plato*. Queftions afked by *Socrates*, as doutes, but they be Sentences, firft affirmed by *Socrates*, as mere trothes, and after, giuen forth by *Socrates*, as right Rules, moft neceffarie to be marked, and fitte to be folowed of all them, that would haue children taughte, as they fhould. And in this counfell, iudgement, and authoritie of *Socrates* I will repofe my felfe, vntill I meete with a man of the contrarie mynde, whom I may iuftlie take to be wifer, than I thinke *Socrates* was. Fonde fcholemafters, neither can vnderftand, nor will folow this good counfell of *Socrates*, Yong Ientlemen, be wifelier taught to ryde, by but wife ryders, in their office, can and will *common ryders, than to learne, by common Scholemasters.* do both : which is the onelie cauſe, that commonly, the yong ientlemen of England, go ſo vnwillinglie to ſchole, and run ſo faſt to the ſtable : For in verie deede fond ſcholemaſters, by feare, do beate into them, the hatred of learning, and wiſe riders, by ientle allurementes, do breed vp in them, the loue of riding.   They finde feare, and bondage in ſcholes, They feele libertie and freedome in ſtables : which cauſeth them, vtterlie to abhor[r]e the one, and moſt gladlie to haunt the other. And I do not write this, that in exhorting to the one, I would diſſuade yong ientlemen from the other : yea I am ſorie, with all my harte, that they be giuen no *Ryding.*   more to riding, then they be : For, of all outward qualities, to ride faire, is moſt cumelie for him ſelfe, moſt neceſſarie for his contrey, and the greater he is in blood, the greater is his praiſe, the more he doth exce[e]de all other therein.   It was one of the three excellent praiſes, amongeſt the noble ientlemen the old *Perſians*, Alwaiſe to ſay troth, to ride faire, and ſhote well : and ſo it was engrauen vpon *Darius* tumbe, as *Strabo.* 15.   *Strabo* beareth witneſſe.

> *Darius the king, lieth buried here,*
> *Who in riding and ſhoting had neuer peare.*

But, to our purpoſe, yong men, by any meanes, leeſing the loue of learning, whan by tyme they cum to their owne rule, they carie commonlie, from the ſchole with them, a perpetuall hatred of their maſter, and a continuall contempt of learning.   If ten Ientlemen be aſked, why they forget ſo ſone in Court, that which they were learning ſo long in ſchole, eight of them, or let me be blamed, will laie the fault on their ill handling, by their ſcholemaſters.

Cuſpinian doth report, that, that noble Emperor *Maximilian*, would lament verie oft, his miſſortune herein.

Paſtime.   Yet, ſome will ſay, that children of na
Learnyng.   ture, loue paſtime, and miſlike learning :

bicaufe, in their kinde, the one is eafie and pleafant,
the other hard and werifon : which is an opinion not
fo trewe, as fome men weene : For, the matter lieth
not fo much in the difpofition of them that be yong, as
in the order and maner of bringing vp, by them that
be old, nor yet in the difference of learnyng and paftime.
For, beate a child, if he daunce not well, and cherifh
him, though he learne not well, ye fhall haue him, vn-
willing to go to daunce, and glad to go to his booke.
Knocke him alwaies, when he draweth his fhaft ill, and
fauo[u]r him againe, though he fau[l]t at his booke, ye
fhall haue hym verie loth to be in the field, and verie
willing to be in the fchole. Yea, I faie more, and not
of my felfe, but by the iudgement of thofe, from whom
few wifemen will gladlie diffent, that if euer the nature
of man be giuen at any tyme, more than other, to receiue goodnes, it is, in innocencie of yong yeares,
before, that experience of euill, haue taken roote in
hym. For, the pure cleane witte of a fweete yong
babe, is like the neweft wax, moft hable to receiue the
beft and fayreft printing : and like a new bright filuer
difhe neuer occupied, to receiue and kepe cleane, anie
good thyng that is put into it.

And thus, will in children, wifelie |Will.⎫
wrought withall, maie eafelie be won   ⎬in children.
to be verie well willing to learne. And
witte in children, by nature, namelie |Witte⎭
memorie, the onely keie and keper of all learning, is
readieft to receiue, and fureft to kepe anie maner of
thing, that is learned in yougth: This, lewde and learned,
by common experience, know to be moft trewe. For
we remember nothyng fo well when we be olde, as
thofe things which we learned when we were yong :
And this is not ftraunge, but common in all natures
workes. Euery man fees, (as I fayd be-   Yong yeares
fore) new wax is beft for printyng : new   aptest for
claie, fitteft for working : new fhorne wo[o]ll,   learnyng.
apteft for fone and fureft dying : new frefh flefh, for
good and durable falting. And this fimilitude is not

rude, nor borowed of the larder houſe, but out of his
ſcholehouſe, of whom, the wiſeſt of **England**, neede not
be aſhamed to learne.   Yong Graftes grow not onelie
foneſt, but alſo faireſt, and bring alwayes forth the beſt
and ſweeteſt frute: yong whelpes learne eaſelie to carie:
yong Popingeis learne quicklie to ſpeake : And ſo, to
be ſhort, if in all other thinges, though they lacke
reaſon, ſens, and life, the ſimilitude of youth is fitteſt
to all goodneſſe, ſurelie nature, in mankinde, is moſt
beneficiall and effectuall in this behalfe.

Therfore, if to the goodnes of nature, be ioyned the
wiſedome of the teacher, in leading yong wittes into a
right and plaine waie of learnyng, ſurelie, children,
kept vp in Gods feare, and gouerned by his grace,
maie moſt eaſelie be brought well to ſerue God, and
contrey both by vertue and wiſedome.

But if will, and witte, by farder age, be once allured
from innocencie, delited in vaine ſightes, fil[l]ed with
foull taulke, crooked with wilfulneſſe, hardned with
ſtubburneſſe, and let louſe to diſobedience, ſurelie it is
hard with ientleneſſe, but vnpoſſible with ſeuere crueltie,
to call them backe to good frame againe.   For, where
the one, perchance maie bend it, the other ſhall ſurelie
breake it : and ſo in ſtead of ſome hope, leaue an
aſſured deſperation, and ſhameleſſe contempt of all

Xen. 1. Cyri   goodneſſe, the fardeſt pointe in all miſchief,
Pæd.   as *Xenophon* doth moſt trewlie and moſt
wittelie marke.

Therfore, to loue or to hate, to like or contemne, to
plie this waie or that waie to good or to bad, ye ſhall
haue as ye vſe a child in his youth.

And one example, whether loue or feare doth worke
more in a child, for vertue and learning, I will gladlie
report : which maie be h[e]ard with ſome pleaſure, and
folowed with more profit.   Before I went into *Germanie,* I came to Brodegate in Le[i]ceſterſhire, to take
Lady Iane   my leaue of that noble Ladie *Iane Grey,* to
Grey.   whom I was exceding moch beholdinge.
Hir parentes, the Duke and Duches, with all the

houſhold, Gentlemen and Gentlewomen, were hunt-
inge in the Parke : I founde her, in her Chamber,
readinge *Phædon Platonis* in Greeke, and that with as
moch delite, as ſom ientlemen wold read a merie tale
in *Bocaſe.* After ſalutation, and dewtie done, with
ſom other taulke, I aſked hir, whie ſhe wold leeſe ſoch
paſtime in the Parke ? ſmiling ſhe anſwered me : I
wiſſe, all their ſporte in the Parke is but a ſhadoe to
that pleaſure, that I find in *Plato* : Alas good folke,
they neuer felt, what trewe pleaſure ment.   And howe
came you Madame, quoth I, to this deepe knowledge
of pleaſure, and what did chieflie allure you vnto it :
ſeinge, not many women, but verie fewe men haue
atteined thereunto.   I will tell you, quoth ſhe, and
tell you a troth, which perchance ye will meruell at.
One of the greateſt benefites, that euer God gaue me,
is, that he ſent me ſo ſharpe and ſeuere Parentes, and
ſo ientle a ſcholemaſter.   For when I am in preſence
either of father or mother, whether I ſpeake, kepe
ſilence, ſit, ſtand, or go, eate, drinke, be merie, or ſad,
be ſowyng, plaiyng, dauncing, or doing anie thing els,
I muſt do it, as it were, in ſoch weight, meſure, and
number, euen ſo perfitelie, as God made the world, or
elſe I am ſo ſharplie taunted, ſo cruellie threatened,
yea preſentlie ſome tymes, with pinches, nippes, and
bobbes, and other waies, which I will not name, for
the honor I beare them, ſo without meaſure miſordered,
that I thinke my ſelfe in hell, till tyme cum, that I
muſt go to *M. Elmer,* who teacheth me ſo ientlie, ſo
pleaſantlie, with ſoch faire allurementes to learning,
that I thinke all the tyme nothing, whiles I am with
him.   And when I am called from him, I fall on
weeping, becauſe, what ſoeuer I do els, but learning,
is ful of grief, trouble, feare, and whole miſliking vnto
me : And thus my booke, hath bene ſo moch my
pleaſure, and bringeth dayly to me more pleaſure and
more, that in reſpect of it, all other pleaſures, in very
deede, be but trifles and troubles vnto me.   I remember this talke gladly, both bicauſe it is ſo worthy

of memorie, and bicauſe alſo, it was the laſt talke that
euer I had, and the laſt tyme, that euer I ſaw that
noble and worthie Ladie.

I could be ouer long, both in ſhewinge iuſt cauſes,
and in recitinge trewe examples, why learning ſhold
be taught, rather by loue than feare. He that wold
ſee a perfite diſcourſe of it, let him read that learned
treateſe, which my frende *Ioan. Sturmius*
wrote *de inſtitutione Principis*, to the Duke
of *Cleues*.

*Sturmius.
de Inſt. Princ.*

The godlie counſels of *Salomon* and
Ieſus the ſonne of *Sirach*, for ſharpe kepinge
in, and bridleinge of youth, are ment rather,
for fatherlie correction, then maſterlie beating, rather
for maners, than for learninge: for other places, than
for ſcholes. For God forbid, but all euill touches,
wantonnes, lyinge, pickinge, ſlouthe, will, ſtubburn-
neſſe, and diſobedience, ſhold be with ſharpe chaſtiſe-
ment, daily cut away.

*Qui parcit
virgæ, odit
filium.*

This diſcipline was well knowen, and diligentlie vſed,
among the *Græcians*, and old *Romanes*, as doth
appeare in *Ariſtophanes*, *Iſocrates*, and *Plato*, and alſo
in the Comedies of *Plautus*: where we ſee that
children were vnder the rule of three perſones: *Præcep-
tore, Pædagogo, Parente*: the ſcholemaſter
taught him learnyng withall ientlenes: the
Gouernour corrected his maners, with
moch ſharpeneſſe: The father, held the ſterne
of his whole obedience: And ſo, he that vſed to
teache, did not commonlie vſe to beate, but remitted
that ouer to an other mans charge. But what ſhall
we ſaie, when now in our dayes, the ſcholemaſter is
vſed, both for *Præceptor* in learnyng, and *Pædagogus* in
maners. Surelie, I wold he ſhold not confound their
offices, but diſcretelie vſe the dewtie of both ſo, that
neither ill touches ſhold be left vnpuniſhed, nor
ientle[ne]ſſe in teaching anie wiſe omitted. And he
ſhall well do both, if wiſelie he do appointe diuerſitie of
tyme, and ſeparate place, for either purpoſe: vſing

1. Scholemaster.
2. Gouernour.
3. Father.

alwaife foch difcrete moderation, as the fcholehoufe fhould be counted a fanctuarie against feare : and verie well learning, a common perdon for ill doing, if the fault, of it felfe be not ouer heinous.

And thus the children, kept vp in Gods feare, and preferued by his grace, finding paine in ill doing, and pleafure in well ftudiyng, fhold eafelie be brought to honeftie of life, and perfitenes of learning, the onelie marke, that good and wife fathers do wifhe and labour, that their children, fhold moft bufelie, and carefullie fhot at.

There is an other difcommoditie, befides crueltie in fcholemafters in beating away the loue of learning from children, which hindreth learning and vertue, and good bringing vp of youth, and namelie yong ientlemen, verie moch in England. This fault is cleane contrary to the firft. I wifhed before, to haue loue of learning bred vp in children : I wifhe as moch now, to haue yong men brought vp in good order of liuing, and in fome more feuere difcipline, then commonlie they be. We haue lacke in England of foch good order, as the old noble *Perfians* fo carefullie vfed : whofe children, to the age of xxi. yeare, were brought vp in learnyng, and exercifes of labor, and that in foch place, where they fhould, neither fee that was vncumlie, nor heare that was vnhoneft. Yea, a yong ientlemen was neuer free, to go where he would, and do what he lifte him felf, but vnder the kepe, and by the counfell, of fome graue gouernour, vntill he was, either maryed, or cal[le]d to beare fome office in the common wealth.

And fee the great obedience, that was vfed in old tyme to fathers and gouernours. No fonne, were he neuer fo old of yeares, neuer fo great of birth, though he were a kynges fonne, might not mary, [might marry] but by his father and mothers alfo confent. *Cyrus* the great, after he had conquered *Babylon*, and fubdewed

Riche king *Cræſus* with whole *Aſia minor*, cummyng
tryumphantlie home, his vncle *Cyaxeris* offered him
his daughter to wife.   *Cyrus* thanked his vncle, and
praiſed the maide, but for mariage he anſwered him
with thies wiſe and ſweete wordes, as they be vttered

Xen. 8. Cyri by *Xenophon*, ὦ κυαξάρη, τό τε γένος
Ped.   ἐπαινῶ καὶ τὴν παῖδα καὶ τὰ δῶρα· βούλομαι
δέ, ἔφη, σὺν τῇ τοῦ πατρὸς γνώμῃ καὶ τῇ τῆς μητρὸς ταυτά
σοι συναινέσαι, &c., that is to ſay: Vncle *Cyaxeris*, I
commend the ſtocke, I like the maide, and I allow
well the dowrie, but (ſayth he) by the counſell and
conſent of my father and mother, I will determine
farther of thies matters.

Strong *Samſon* alſo in Scripture ſaw a maide that
liked him, but he ſpake not to hir, but went home to
his father, and his mother, and deſired both father and
mother to make the mariage for him.   Doth this
modeſtie, doth this obedience, that was in great kyng
Cyrus, and ſtoute *Samſon*, remaine in our yongmen at
this daie? no ſurelie : For we liue not longer after
them by tyme, than we liue farre different from them
by good order.   Our tyme is ſo farre from that old
diſcipline and obedience, as now, not onelie yong
ientlemen, but euen verie girles dare without all feare,
though not without open ſhame, where they liſt, and
how they liſt, marie them ſelues in ſpite of father,
mother, God, good order, and all.   The cauſe of this
euill is, that youth is leaſt looked vnto, when they ſtand
[in] moſt neede of good kepe and regard.   It auail-
eth not, to ſee them well taught in yong yeares, and
after whan they cum to luſt and youthfull dayes, to
giue them licence to liue as they luſt them ſelues.
For, if ye ſuffer the eye of a yong Ientleman, once to
be entangled with vaine ſightes, and the eare to be
corrupted with fond or filthie taulke, the mynde ſhall
quicklie fall ſeick, and ſone vomet and caſt vp, all the
holeſome doctrine, that he receiued in childhoode,
though he were neuer ſo well brought vp before.   And
being ons [once] inglutted with vanitie, he will ſtreight

way loth all learning, and all good counfell to the
fame.   And the parentes for all their great coft and
charge, reape onelie in the end, the fru[i]te of grief and
care.

   This euill, is not common to poore men, Great mens
as God will haue it, but proper to riche sonnes worst
and great mens children, as they deferue brought vp.
it.   In deede from feuen, to feuentene, yong ientlemen commonlie be carefullie enough brought vp : But
from feuentene to feuen and twentie (the moft dangerous tyme of all a mans life, and moft flipperie to ftay
well in) they haue commonlie the reigne of all licens
in their owne hand, and fpeciallie foch as Wise men fond
do liue in the Court.   And that which is fathers.
moft to be merueled at, commonlie, the wifeft and alfo
beft men, be found the fondeft fathers in this behalfe.
And if fom good father wold feick fome remedie
herein, yet the mother (if the houfe hold of our Lady)
had rather, yea, and will to, haue her fonne cunnyng
and bold, in making him to lyue trimlie when he is
yong, than by learning and trauell, to be able to ferue
his Prince and his contrie, both wifelie in peace, and
ftoutelie in warre, whan he is old.

   The fault is in your felues, ye noble Meane mens
men[s] fonnes, and therefore ye deferue the sonnes come
greater blame, that commonlie, the meaner to great
authoritie.
mens children, cum to be, the wifeft councellours, and
greateft doers, in the weightie affaires of this Realme.
And why ? for God will haue it fo, of his prouidence :
bicaufe ye will haue it no otherwife, by your negligence.

   And God is a good God, and wifeft in all his doinges,
that will place vertue, and difplace vice, Nobilitie within thofe kingdomes, where he doth go- out wisedome.
uerne.   For he knoweth, that Nobilitie, without vertue and wifedome, is bloud in deede, but bloud trewelie, without bones and finewes : and fo of it felfe,
without the other, verie weeke to beare the burden of
weightie affaires.

The greateſt ſhippe in deede commonlie carieth the greateſt burden, but yet alwayes with the greateſt ieoperdie, not onelie for the perſons and goodes com-

Nobilitie with wiſedome.

mitted vnto it, but euen for the ſhyppe it ſelfe, except it be gouerned, with the greater wiſdome.

But Nobilitie, gouerned by learning and wiſedome,

Nobilite with { Wiſedome. / out wiſedome.

is in deede, moſt like a faire ſhippe, hauyng tide and winde at will, vnder the reule of a ſkilfull maſter : whan contrarie wiſe, a ſhippe, carried, yea with the hieſt

tide and greateſt winde, lacking a ſkilfull maſter, moſt commonlie, doth either, ſinck it ſelfe vpon ſandes, or breake it ſelfe vpon rockes. And euen ſo, how manie

Vaine pleaſure, and ſtoute wilfulnes, two greateſt enemies to Nobilitie.

haue bene, either drowned in vaine pleaſure, or ouerwhelmed by ſtout wilfulneſſe, the hiſtories of England be able to aſſourde ouer many examples vnto vs. Therfore,

ye great and noble mens children, if ye will haue rightfullie that praiſe, and enioie ſurelie that place, which your fathers haue, and elders had, and left vnto you, ye muſt kepe it, as they gat it, and that is, by the onelie waie, of vertue, wiſedome and worthineſſe.

For wiſedom, and vertue, there be manie faire examples in this Court, for yong Ientlemen to fo[l]low. But they be, like faire markes in the feild, out of a mans reach, to far of, to ſhote at well. The beſt and worthieſt men, in deede, be ſomtimes ſeen, but ſeldom taulked withall : A yong Ientleman, may ſomtime knele to their perſon, ſmallie vſe their companie, for their better inſtruction.

But yong Ientlemen are faine commonlie to do in the Court, as yong Archers do in the feild : that is to take ſoch markes, as be nie them, although they be

Ill companie marreth youth.

neuer ſo foule to ſhote at. I meene, they be driuen to kepe companie with the worſte : and what force ill companie hath, to corrupt good wittes, the wiſeſt men know beſt.

And not ill companie onelie, but the ill opinion alſo of the moſt part, doth moch harme, and namelie of thoſe, which ſhold be wiſe in the trewe decyphring, of the good diſpoſition of nature, of cumlineſſe in Courtlie maners, and all right doinges of men. *The Court iudgeth worst of the best natures in youth.*

But error and phantaſie, do commonlie occupie, the place of troth and iudgement. For, if a yong ientleman, be demeure and ſtill of nature, they ſay, he is ſimple and lacketh witte : if he be baſhefull, and will ſoone bluſhe, they call him a babiſhe and ill brought vp thyng, when *Xenophon* doth preciſelie note in *Cyrus*, that his baſhfulnes in youth, *Xen. in* 1. *Cyr. Pæd.* was ye verie trewe ſigne of his vertue and ſtoutnes after : If he be innocent and ignorant of ill, they ſay, he is rude, and hath no grace, ſo vngraciouſlie do ſom graceleſſe men, miſuſe the faire and godlie word G R A C E. *The Grace in Courte.*

But if ye would know, what grace they meene, go, and looke, and learne emonges them, and ye ſhall ſee that it is : Firſt, to bluſh at nothing. And bluſhyng in youth, ſayth *Ariſtotle* is nothyng els, but feare to do ill : which feare beyng once luſtely fraid away from youth, then foloweth, to dare do any miſchief, to contemne ſtoutly any goodneſſe, to be buſie in euery matter, to be ſkilfull in euery thyng, to acknowledge no ignorance at all. To do thus in Court, is counted of ſome, the chief and greateſt grace of all : and termed by the name of a vertue, called Corage and boldneſſe, whan *Craſſus* in *Cic.* 3. *de Or.* Cicero teacheth the cleane contrarie, and that moſt wittelie, ſaying thus : *Audere, cum bonis etiam rebus coniunĉlum, per ſeipſum eſt magnopere fugiendum.* Which is to ſay, to be bold, yea in a good matter, is for it ſelf, greatlie to be exchewed. *Grace of Courte.* *Boldnes, yea in a good matter, not to be praised.*

Moreouer, where the ſwing goeth, there to follow, fawne, flatter, laugh and lie luſtelie at other mens liking. To face, ſtand formeſt, ſhoue backe : and to the meaner man, or vnknowne in the *More Grace of Courte.*

Court, to ſeeme ſomwhat ſolume, coye, big, and dangerous of looke, taulk, and anſwere : To thinke well of
him ſelfe, to be luſtie in contemning of others, to haue
ſome trim grace in a priuie mock. And in greater
preſens, to beare a braue looke: to be warlike, though
he neuer looked enimie in the face in warre : yet ſom
warlike ſigne muſt be vſed, either a ſlouinglie buſking,
or an ouerſtaring frounced hed, as though out of euerie
heeres toppe, ſhould ſuddenlie ſtart out a good big
othe, when nede requireth. Yet praiſed be God, England hath at this time, manie worthie Capitaines and good ſouldiours, which be in
deede, ſo honeſt of behauiour, ſo cumlie
of conditions, ſo milde of maners, as they may be
examples of good order, to a good ſort of others,
which neuer came in warre. But to retorne, where I
left : In place alſo, to be able to raiſe taulke, and
make diſcourſe of euerie riſhe : to haue a verie good
will, to heare him ſelfe ſpeake : To be ſeene in Palm-
eſtrie, wherby to conueie to chaſt eares,
ſom fond or filthie taulke :

Men of warre, best of conditions.

Palmistrie.

And, if ſom Smithfeild Ruffian take vp, ſom ſtrange
going : ſom new mowing with the mouth : ſom wrinch-
yng with the ſhoulder, ſom braue prouerbe : ſom freſh
new othe, that is not ſtale, but will rin [run] round in the
mouth : ſom new diſguiſed garment, or deſperate hat,
fond in facion, or gauriſh in colour, what ſoeuer it coſt,
how ſmall ſoeuer his liuing be, by what ſhift ſoeuer it
be gotten, gotten muſt it be, and vſed with the firſt, or
els the grace of it, is ſtale and gone : ſom part of this
graceleſſe grace, was diſcribed by me, in a little rude
verſe long ago.

> To laughe, to lie, to flatter, to face :
> Foure waies in Court to win men grace.
> If thou be thrall to none of theiſe,
> Away good Peek goos, hens Iohn Cheeſe :
> Marke well my word, and marke their dede,
> And thinke this verſe part of thy Creed.

Would to God, this taulke were not trewe, and that

fom **mens** doinges were not thus · I write not to hurte any, but to proffit fom : to accufe none, but to monifh foch, who, allured by ill counfell, and folowing ill example, contrarie to their good bringyng vp, and againft their owne good nature, yeld ouermoch to thies folies and faultes : I know many feruing men, of good order, and well ftaide : And againe, I heare faie, there be fom feruing men do but ill feruice to their yong mafters. Yea, rede *Terence* and *Plaut[us]*. aduifedlie ouer, and ye fhall finde in thofe two wife writers, almoft in euerie no vnthriftie yong man, that is not brought there vnto, by the fotle inticement of fom lewd feruant. And euen now in our dayes *Getæ* and *Daui*, *Gnatos* and manie bold bawdie *Phormios* to, be preafing in, to pratle on euerie ftage, to medle in euerie matter, whan honeft *Parmenos* fhall not be hard, but beare fmall fwing with their mafters. Their companie, their taulke, their ouer great experience in mifchief, doth eafelie corrupt the beft natures, and beft brought vp wittes.

> Councell.
> Ill {
> Company.
>
> Seruinge men.
> *Terentius.*
> *Plautus.*
>
> commedie,
> Serui corruptelæ iuuenum.
>
> Multi Getæ
> pauci
> Parmenones.

But I meruell the leffe, that thies miforders be emonges fom in the Court, for commonlie in the contrie alfo euerie where, innocencie is gone : Bafhfulneffe is banifhed : moch prefumption in yougthe : fmall authoritie in aige : Reuerence is neglected : dewties be confounded : and to be fhorte, difobedience doth ouerflowe the bankes of good order, almofte in euerie place, almofte in euerie degree of man.

> Miforders in
> the countrey.

Meane men haue eies to fee, and caufe to lament, and occafion to complaine of thies miferies : but other haue authoritie to remedie them, and will do fo to, whan God fhall think time fitte. For, all thies miforders, be Goddes iufte plages, by his fufferance, brought iuftelie vpon vs, for our finnes, which be infinite in nomber, and horrible in deede, but namelie, for the

greate abhominable ſin of vnkindneſſe : but what vnkindneſſe ? euen ſuch vnkindneſſe as was
in the Iewes, in contemninge Goddes voice,
in ſhrinking from his woorde, in wiſhing
backe againe for *Ægypt*, in committing aduoultrie
and hordom, not with the women, but with the doctrine of Babylon, did bring all the plages, deſtructions,
and Captiuities, that fell ſo ofte and horriblie, vpon
Iſraell.

Contempt of Gods trewe Religion.

We haue cauſe alſo in England to beware of vnkindneſſe, who haue had, in ſo fewe yeares, the Candel of
Goddes worde, ſo oft lightned, ſo oft put out, and yet will
venture by our vnthankfulneſſe in doctrine
and ſinfull life, to leeſe againe, lighte,
Candle, Candleſticke and all.

Doctrina Mores.

God kepe vs in his feare, God grafte in vs the trewe
knowledge of his woorde, with a forward will to folowe
it, and ſo to bring forth the ſweete fruites of it, and
then ſhall he preſerue vs by his Grace, from all maner
of terrible dayes.

The remedie of this, doth not ſtand onelie, in making good common lawes for the hole
Realme, but alſo, (and perchance cheiflie) in obſeruing
priuate diſcipline euerie man carefullie in
his own houſe : and namelie, if ſpeciall
regard be had to yougth : and that, not ſo much, in
teaching them what is good, as in keping
them from that, that is ill.

Publicæ Leges.

Domestica disciplina.

Cognitio boni.

Therefore, if wiſe fathers, be not as well ware in
weeding from their Children ill thinges,
and ill companie, as they were before, in
graftinge in them learninge, and prouiding for them
good ſcholemaſters, what frute, they ſhall reape of all
their coſte and care, common experience doth tell.

Ignoratio mali.

Here is the place, in yougthe is the time whan ſom
ignorance is as neceſſarie, as moch knowledge : and not in matters of our dewtie
towardes God, as ſom wilful wittes willinglie againſt their owne knowledge, perniciouſlie againſte

Some ignor-ance, as good as knowledge.

their owne confcience, haue of late openlie taught.
In deede *S. Chryfoftome*, that noble and *Chrisost. de*
eloquent Doctor, in a fermon *contra fatum*, *Fato.*
and the curious ferchinge of natiuities, doth wifelie faie,
that ignorance therein, is better than knowledge : But
to wring this fentence, to wrefte thereby out of mens
handes, the knowledge of Goddes doctrine, is without
all reafon, againft common fence, contrarie to the
iudgement alfo of them, which be the difcreteft men,
and beft learned, on their own fide.   I know, *Iu-*
lianus Apoftata did fo, but I neuer hard or *Iulia. Apostat.*
red, that any auncyent father of the primitiue chirch
either thought or wrote fo.

But this ignorance in yougthe, which I   *Innocency in*
fpake on, or rather this fimplicitie, or moft   *youth.*
trewlie, this innocencie, is that, which the noble
Perfians, as wife *Xenophon* doth teftifie, were fo carefull,
to breede vp their yougth in.   But Chriftian fathers
commonlie do not fo.   And I will tell you a tale, as
moch to be mifliked, as the *Perfians* example is to be
folowed.

This laft fomer, I was in a Ientlemans houfe : where
a yong childe, fomewhat paft fower yeare   *A childe ill*
olde, cold in no wife frame his tonge, to   *brought vp.*
faie, a litle fhorte grace : and yet he could roundlie
rap out, fo manie vgle othes, and thofe of the neweft
facion, as fom good man of fourefcore yeare olde hath
neuer hard named before : and that which was moft
deteftable of all, his father and mother   *Ill Parentes.*
wold laughe at it.   I moche doubte, what comforte,
an other daie, this childe fhall bring vnto them.   This
Childe vfing moche the companie of feruinge men, and
geuing good eare to their taulke, did eafelie learne,
which he fhall hardlie forget, all [the] daies of his life
hereafter : So likewife, in the Courte, if a yong Ientleman
will ventur[e] him felf into the companie of Ruffians, it
is ouer great a ieopardie, left, their facions, maners,
thoughtes, taulke and deedes, will verie fone, be euer
like.   The confounding of companies, breedeth con-

Ill companie. fuſion of good maners both in the Courte, and euerie where elſe.

And it maie be a great wonder, but a greater ſhame, to vs Chriſtian men, to vnderſtand, what a heithen Iſocrates.   writer, *Iſocrates*, doth leaue in memorie of writing, concerning the care, that the noble Citie of *Athens* had, to bring vp their yougthe, in honeſt companie, and vertuous diſcipline, whoſe taulke in Greke, is, to this effect, in Engliſhe.

"The Citie, was not more carefull, to ſee their Chil-
In Orat   "dren well taughte, than to ſee their yong
Ariopag.   "men well gouerned : which they brought
" to paſſe, not ſo much by common lawe, as by priuate
" diſcipline.   For, they had more regard, that their
" yougthe, by good order ſhold not offend, than how,
" by lawe, they might be puniſhed : And if offenſe
" were committed, there was, neither waie to hide it,
" neither hope of pardon for it.   Good natures, were
" not ſo moche openlie praiſed as they were ſecretlie
" marked, and watchfullie regarded, leſt they ſhould
" leaſe the goodnes they had.   Therefore in ſcholes of
" ſinging and dauncing, and other honeſt exerciſes,
" gouernours were appointed, more diligent to ouerſee
" their good maners, than their maſters were, to teach
" them anie learning.   It was ſom ſhame to a yong
" man, to be ſeene in the open market : and if for
" buſineſſe, he paſſed throughe it, he did it, with a
" meruelous modeſtie, and baſhefull facion.   To eate,
" or drinke in a Tauerne, was not onelie a ſhame, but
" alſo puniſhable, in a yong man.   To contrarie, or to
" ſtand in termes with an old man, was more heinous,
" than in ſom place, to rebuke and ſcolde with his
" owne father : with manie other mo good orders, and
faire diſciplines, which I referre to their reading, that
haue luſt to looke vpon the deſcription of ſuch a
worthie common welthe.

Good sede,   And to know, what worthie frute, did
worthie frute.   ſpring of ſoch worthie ſeade, I will tell yow
the moſt meruell of all, and yet ſoch a trothe, as no

man fhall denie it, except fuch as be ignorant in
knowledge of the beft ftories.

Athens, by this difcipline and good ordering of
yougthe, did breede vp, within the circu[i]te *Athenes.*
of that one Citie, within the compas of one hondred
yeare, within the memorie of one mans life, fo manie
notable Capitaines in warre, for worthineffe, wifdome
and learning, as be fcarfe matchable no *Roma.*
not in the ftate of Rome, in the compas of thofe
feauen hondred yeares, whan it florifhed mofte.

And bicaufe, I will not onelie faie it, but alfo proue
it, the names of them be thefe. *Miltiades,* The noble
Themiftocles, Xantippus, Pericles, Cymon, Capitaines of
Alcybiades, Thrafybulus, Conon, Iphicrates, Athens.
Xenophon, Timotheus, Theopompus, Demetrius, and diuers other mo : of which euerie one, maie iuftelie be
fpoken that worthie praife, which was geuen to *Scipio
Africanus,* who, *Cicero* douteth, whether he were, more
noble Capitaine in warre, or more eloquent and wife
councelor in peace. And if ye beleue not me, read
diligentlie, *Æmilius Probus* in Latin, and *Æmil. Probus.*
Plutarche in Greke, which two, had no *Plutarchus.*
caufe either to flatter or lie vpon anie of thofe which
I haue recited.

And befide nobilitie in warre, for excellent and
matchles mafters in all maner of learninge, The learned of
in that one Citie, in memorie of one aige, Athenes.
were mo learned men, and that in a maner altogether,
than all tyme doth remember, than all place doth
affourde, than all other tonges do conteine. And I
do not meene of thofe Authors, which, by iniurie of
tyme, by negligence of men, by crueltie of fier and
fworde, be loft, but euen of thofe, which by Goddes
grace, are left yet vnto us : of which I thank God,
euen my poor ftudie lacketh not one. As, in Philofophie, *Plato, Ariftotle, Xenophon, Euclide,* and *Theo-
phraft* : In eloquens and Ciuill lawe, *Demofthenes,
Æfchines, Lycurgus, Dinarchus, Demades, Ifocrates,
Ifæus, Lyfias, Antifthenes, Andocides* : In hiftories, *He·*

rodotus, Thucydides, Xenophon: and which we lacke, to our great loſſe, *Theopompus* and *Eph[orus]*: In Poetrie, *Æſchylus, Sophocles, Euripides, Ariſtophanes*, and ſome-what of *Menander, Demoſthenes* ſiſter[s] ſonne.

Now, let Italian, and Latin it ſelf, Spaniſhe, French, Douch, and Engliſhe bring forth their lern-ing, and recite their Authors, *Cicero* onelie excepted, and in one or two moe in Latin, they be all patched cloutes and ragges, in compariſon of faire wouen broade cloathes. And trewelie, if there be any good in them, it is either lerned, borowed, or ſtolne, from ſome one of thoſe worthie wittes of *Athens*.

Learnyng, chiefly con-teined in the Greke, and in no other tong.

The remembrance of ſoch a common welthe, vſing ſoch diſcipline and order for yougthe, and thereby bringing forth to their praiſe, and leauing to vs for our example, ſuch Capitaines for warre, ſoch Councel-ors for peace, and matcheles maſters, for all kinde of learninge, is pleaſant for me to recite, and not irkſum, I truſt, for other to heare, except it be ſoch, as make neither counte of vertue nor learninge.

And whether, there be anie ſoch or no, I can not well tell: yet I heare ſaie, ſome yong Ien-tlemen of oures, count it their ſhame to be counted learned: and perchance, they count it their ſhame, to be counted honeſt alſo, for I heare ſaie, they medle as litle with the one, as with the other. A mer-uelous caſe, that Ientlemen ſhold ſo be aſhamed of good learning, and neuer a whit aſhamed of ill maners: ſoch do laie for them, that the Ientlemen of France do ſo: which is a lie, as God will haue it. *Langæus,* and *Bellæus* that be dead, and the noble *Vidam* of Chartes, that is aliue, and infinite mo in France, which I heare tell of, proue this to be moſt falſe. And though ſom, in France, which will nedes be Ientlemen, whether men will or no, and haue more ientleſhipe in their hat, than in their hed, be at deedlie feude, with both learning and honeſtie, yet I beleue, if that noble Prince, king *Francis* the firſt were

Contemners of learnyng.

Ientlemen of France.

aliue, they fhold haue, neither place in his Courte, nor penfion in his warres, if he had knowledg of them. This opinion is not

Franciscus 1. Nobilis. Francorum Rex.

French, but plaine Turckifhe: from whens, fom French fetche moe faultes, than this: which, I praie God, kepe out of England, and fend alfo thofe of oures better mindes, which bend them felues againfte vertue and learninge, to the contempte of God, difhonor of their contrie, to the hurt of manie others, and at length, to the greateft harme, and vtter deftruction of themfelues.

Some other, hauing better nature, but leffe witte, (for ill commonlie, haue ouer moch witte) do not vtterlie difpraife learning, but they faie, that without learning, common expcrience, knowledge of all facions, and haunting all

Experience without learnyng.

companies, fhall worke in yougthe, both wifdome, and habilitie, to execute anie weightie affaire. Surelie long experience doth proffet moch, but mofte, and almoft onelie to him (if we meene honeft affaires) that is diligentlie before inftructed with preceptes of well doinge. For good precepts of learning, be the eyes of the minde, to looke wifelie before a man, which waie to go right, and which not.

Learning teacheth more in one yeare than experience in twentie: And learning

Learnyng. Experience.

teacheth fafelie, when experience maketh mo miferable then wife. He hafardeth fore, that waxeth wife by experience. An vnhappie Mafter he is, that is made cunning by manie fhippe wrakes: A miferable merchant, that is neither riche or wife, but after fom bankroutes. It is coftlie wifdom, that is bought by experience. We know by experience it felfe, that it is a meruelous paine, to finde oute but a fnort waie, by long wandering. And furelie, he that wold proue wife by experience, he maie be wittie in deede, but euen like a fwift runner, that runneth faft out of his waie, and vpon the night, he knoweth not whither. And verilie they be feweft of number, that be happie or wiſe by vnlearned experience.   And looke well vpon the former life of thoſe fewe, whether your example be old or yonge, who without learning haue gathered, by long experience, a litle wiſdom, and ſom happines : and whan you do conſider, what miſcheife they haue committed, what dangers they haue eſcaped (and yet **xx.** for one, do periſhe in the aduenture) than thinke well with your ſelfe, whether ye wold, that your owne ſon, ſhould cum to wiſdom and happines, by the waie of ſoch experience or no.

Syr *Roger Chamloe.*   It is a notable tale, that old Syr *Roger Chamloe,* ſometime cheife Iuſtice, wold tell of him ſelfe.   When he was Auncient in Inne of Courte, certaine yong Ientlemen were brought before him, to be corrected for certaine miſorders : And one of the luſtieſt ſaide : Syr, we be yong ientlemen, and wiſe men before vs, haue proued all facions, and yet thoſe haue done full well : this they ſaid, becauſe it was well knowen, that Syr *Roger* had bene a good feloe in his yougth.   But he aunſwered them verie wiſelie.   In deede ſaith he, in yougthe, I was, as you ar[e] now : and I had twelue feloes like vnto my ſelf, but not one of them came to a good ende.   And therfore, folow not my example in yougth, but folow my councell in aige, if euer ye thinke to cum to this place, or to thies yeares, that I am cum vnto, leſſe ye meete either with pouer- tie or Tiburn in the way.

Experience.   Thus, experience of all facions in yougthe, beinge, in profe, alwaiſe daungerous, in iſſhue, ſeldom lucklie, is a waie, in deede, to ouermoch know- ledge, yet vſed commonlie of ſoch men, which be either caried by ſom curious affection of mynde, or driuen by ſom hard neceſſitie of life, to haſard the triall of ouer manie perilous aduentures.

Erasmus.   *Eraſmus* the honour of learning of all oure time, ſaide wiſelie that experience is the common Experience, the ſcholehouſe of Foles, and ill men. ſcholehouſe of foles, and ill men : Men, of witte and honeſtie, be otherwiſe inſtructed. For there be, that kepe them out of fier,

and yet was neuer burned : That beware of water, and
yet was neuer nie drowninge : That hate harlottes,
and was neuer at the ſtewes : That abhorre falſhode,
and neuer brake promis themſelues.

But will ye ſee, a fit Similitude of this aduentured
experience. A Father, that doth let louſe his ſon, to
all experiences, is moſt like a fond Hunter, that letteth
ſlippe a whelpe to the hole herde. Twentie to one,
he ſhall fall vpon a raſcall, and let go the faire game.
Men that hunt ſo, be either ignorant perſones, preuie
ſtealers, or night walkers.

Learning therefore, ye wiſe fathers, and good bringing vp, and not blinde and dangerous experience, is
the next and readieſt waie, that muſt leede your Children, firſt, to wiſdom, and than to worthineſſe, if euer
ye purpoſe they ſhall cum there.

And to ſaie all in ſhorte, though I lacke   How experi-
Authoritie to giue counſell, yet I lacke not   ence may
proffet.
good will to wiſſhe, that the yougthe in England,
ſpeciallie Ientlemen, and namelie nobilitie, ſhold be
by good bringing vp, ſo grounded in iudgement of
learninge, ſo founded in loue of honeſtie, as, whan
they ſho[u]ld be called forthe to the execution of great
affaires, in ſeruice of their Prince and co[u]ntrie, they
might be hable, to vſe and to order, all experiences,
were they good were they bad, and that, according to
the ſquare, rule, and line, of wiſdom, learning, and
vertue.

And, I do not meene, by all this my   Diligente
taulke, that yong Ientlemen, ſhould al-   learninge ought
to be ioyned
waies be poring on a booke, and by vſing   with pleaſant
good ſtudies, ſhold leaſe honeſt pleaſure,   paſtimes,
and haunt no good paſtime, I meene no-   namelie in a
Ientleman.
thing leſſe : For it is well knowne, that I both like and
loue, and haue alwaies, and do yet ſtill vſe, all exerciſes and paſtimes, that be fitte for my nature and
habilitie. And beſide naturall diſpoſition, in iudgement, alſo, I was neuer, either Stoick in doctrine, or
Anabaptiſt in Religion to miſlik a merie, pleaſant,

and plaifull nature, if no outrage be committed, againſt lawe, me[a]ſure, and good order.

Therefore, I wo[u]ld wiſhe, that, beſide ſome good time, fitlie appointed, and conſtantlie kepte, to encreaſe by readinge, the knowledge of the tonges and learning, yong ientlemen ſhold vſe, and delite in all Courtelie

Learnyng ioyned with paſtimes. exerciſes, and Ientlemanlike paſtimes. And good cauſe whie : For the ſelf ſame noble Citie of Athenes, iuſtlie commended of me before, did wiſelie and vpon great conſideration, appoint, the Muſes, *Apollo*, and *Pallas*, to be patrones

Muſæ. of learninge to their yougthe. For the Muſes, beſides learning, were alſo Ladies of dauncinge,

Apollo. mirthe and miniſtrelſie : *Apollo*, was god of ſhooting, and Author of cunning playing vpon Inſtru-

Pallas. mentes : *Pallas* alſo was Laidie miſtres in warres. Wherbie was nothing elſe ment, but that learninge ſhold be alwaiſe mingled, with honeſt mirthe, and cumlie exerciſes : and that warre alſo ſhold be gouerned by learning, and moderated by wiſdom, as did well appeare in thoſe Capitaines of *Athenes* named by me before, and alſo in *Scipio* and *Cæſar* the two Diamondes of Rome.

And *Pallas*, was no more feared, in weering *Ægida*,

Learning rewleth both warre and peace. than ſhe was praiſed, for choſing *Oliua* : whereby ſhineth the glory of learning, which thus, was Gouernour and Miſtres, in the noble Citie of *Athenes*, both of warre and peace.

Therefore, to ride cumlie : to run faire at the tilte or ring : to plaie at all weapones : to ſhote faire in bow, or ſurelie in gon : to vaut luſtely : to runne : to

The paſtimes that be fitte for Courtlie Ientlemen. leape : to wreſtle : to ſwimme : To daunce cumlie : to ſing, and playe of inſtrumentes cunnyngly : to Hawke : to hunte : to playe at tennes, and all paſtimes generally, which be ioyned with labor, vſed in open place, and on the day light, conteining either ſome fitte exerciſe for warre, or ſome pleaſant paſtime for peace, be not onelie cumlie and decent, but alſo verie neceſſarie, for a Courtlie Ientleman to vſe.

But, of all kinde of paftimes, fitte for a Ientleman, I
will, godwilling, in fitter place, more at large, declare
fullie, in my booke of the Cockpitte: which The Cokpitte.
I do write, to fatiffie fom, I truft, with fom reafon,
that be more curious, in marking other mens doinges, than carefull in mendyng their owne faultes.
And fom alfo will nedes bufie them felues in meruel-
ing, and adding thereunto vnfrendlie taulke, why I, a
man of good yeares, and of no ill place, I thanke God
and my Prince, do make choife to fpend foch tyme in
writyng of trifles, as the fchole of fhoting, the Cockpitte, and this booke of the firft Principles of Grammer,
rather, than to take fome weightie matter in hand,
either of Religion, or Ciuill difcipline.

Wife men I know, will well allow of my choife
herein : and as for fuch, who haue not witte of them
felues, but muft learne of others, to iudge right of mens
doynges, let them read that wife Poet   A booke of
Horace in his *Arte Poetica*, who willeth   lofty title, bear-
wifemen to beware, of hie and loftie Titles.   ouer great a
For, great fhippes, require coftlie tackling,   promife.
and alfo afterward dangerous gouernment: Small boates,
be neither verie chargeable in makyng, nor verie oft in
great ieoperdie : and yet they cary many tymes, as
good and coftlie ware, as greater veffels do.   A meane
Argument, may eafelie beare, the light The right
burden of a fmall farte, and haue alwaife choife, to chose
a fitte Argument
at hand, a ready excufe for ill handling : to write vpon.
And, fome praife it is, if it fo chaunce, to be better in
deede, than a man dare venture to feeme.   A hye
title, doth charge a man, with the heauie burden, of to
great a promife : and therefore fayth *Horace* verie
wittelie, that, that Poete was a verie foole,   *Hor. in Arte*
that began hys booke, with a goodlie verfe   *Poet.*
in deede, but ouer proude a promife.

Fortunam Priami cantabo et nobile bellum,

And after, as wifelie.

Quantò rectiùs hic, qui nil molitur ineptè etc.

E

Homers wisdom in choice of his Argument. Meening *Homer*, who, within the compaſſe of a ſmal Argument, of one harlot, and of one good wife, did vtter ſo much learning in all kinde of ſciences, as, by the iudgement of *Quintilian*, he deſerueth ſo hie a praiſe, that no man yet deſerued to ſit in the ſecond degree beneth him. And thus moch out of my way, concerning my purpoſe in ſpending penne, and paper, and tyme, vpon trifles, and namelie to aunſwere ſome, that haue neither witte nor learning, to do any thyng them ſelues, neither will nor honeſtie, to ſay well of other.

The Cortegian, an excellent booke for a ientleman. To ioyne learnyng with cumlie exerciſes, *Conto Baldeſœr Castiglione* in his booke, *Cortegiane*, doth trimlie teache : which booke, aduiſedlie read, and diligentlie folowed, but one yeare at home in England, would do a yong ientleman more good, I wiſſe, then three yeares trauell abrode ſpent in *Italie*. And I meruell this booke, is no more read in the Court, than it is, ſeyng it is ſo well tranſlated into Engliſh by a worthie Ientleman

Syr *Tho. Hobbie.* Syr *Th. Hobbie*, who was many wayes well furniſhed with learnyng, and very expert in knowledge of diuers tonges.

Examples better than preceptes. And beſide good preceptes in bookes, in all kinde of tonges, this Court alſo neuer lacked many faire examples, for yong ientlemen to folow : And ſurelie, one example, is more valiable, both to good and ill, than xx. preceptes written in bookes : and ſo *Plato*, not in one or two, but diuerſe places, doth plainlie teach.

King *Ed.* 6. If kyng *Edward* had liued a litle longer, his onely example had breed ſoch a raſe of worthie learned ientlemen, as this Realme neuer yet did affourde.

The yong Duke of Suffolke. *L. H. Martreuers.* And, in the ſecond degree, two noble Primeroſes of Nobilitie, the yong Duke of Suffolke, and Lord *H. Matreuers*, were ſoch two examples to the Court for learnyng, as our tyme may rather wiſhe than looke for agayne.

At Cambrige alfo, in S. Iohns Colledge, in my tyme, I do know, that, not fo much the good ftatutes, as two Ientlemen, of worthie memorie Syr *Iohn Cheke*, and Doctour *Readman*, by

Syr John Cheke.

their onely example of excellency in learnyng, of godnes in liuyng, of diligence in ftudying, of councell in exhorting, of [by] good order in all thyng,

D. Readman.

did breed vp, fo many learned men, in that one College of S. Iohns, at one time, as I beleue, the whole Vniuerfitie of *Louaine*, in many yeares, was neuer able to afford.

Prefent examples of this prefent tyme, I lift not to the touch : yet there is one example, for all Ientlemen of this Court to fol[l]ow, that

Queene Elisabeth.

may well fatiffie them, or nothing will ferue them, nor no example moue them, to goodnes and learning.

It is your fhame, (I fpeake to you all, you yong Ientlemen of England) that one mayd[e] fhould go beyond you all, in excellencie of learnyng, and knowledge of diuers tonges. Pointe forth fix of the beft giuen Ientlemen of this Court, and all they together, fhew not fo much good will, fpend not fo much tyme, beftow not fo many houres, dayly, orderly, and conftantly, for the increafe of learning and knowledge, as doth the Queenes Maieftie her felfe. Yea I beleue, that befide her perfit readines, in *Latin, Italian, French*, and *Spanifh*, fhe readeth here now at Windfore more Greeke euery day, than fome Prebendarie of this Chirch doth read *Latin* in a whole weeke. And that which is moft praife worthie of all, within the walles of her priuie chamber, fhe hath obteyned that excellencie of learnyng, to vnderftand, fpeake, and write, both wittely with head, and faire with hand, as fcarce one or two rare wittes in both the Vniuerfities haue in many yeares reached vnto. Amongeft all the benefites yat God hath bleffed me with all, next the knowledge of Chriftes true Religion, I counte this the greateft, that it pleafed God to call me, to be one poore minifter in fettyng for

ward theſe excellent giftes of learnyng in this moſt
excellent Prince.   Whoſe onely example, if the
reſt of our nobilitie would folow, than might England be, for learnyng and wiſedome in
nobilitie, a ſpectacle to all the world
beſide.   But ſee the miſhap of men : The
beſt examples haue neuer ſuch forſe to moue to any
goodnes, as the bad, vaine, light and fond, haue to all
ilnes.

Ill Examples haue more force, then good examples.

And one example, though out of the compas of
learning, yet not out of the order of good maners, was
notable in this Courte, not fullie xxiiij. yeares a go,
when all the actes of Parlament, many good Procla-
mations, diuerſe ſtrait commaundementes, ſore puniſhment openlie, ſpeciall regarde priuatelie, cold not do ſo
moch to take away one miſorder, as the example of
one big one of this Courte did, ſtill to kepe vp the
ſame : The memorie whereof, doth yet remaine, in a
common prouerbe of Birching lane.

Take hede therfore, ye great ones in ye Court, yea
though ye be ye greateſt of all, take hede,
what ye do, take hede how ye liue.   For
as you great ones vſe to do, ſo all meane
men loue to do.   You be in deed, makers
or marrers, of all mens maners within the
Realme.   For though God hath placed yow, to be
cheife in making of lawes, to beare greateſt authoritie,
to commaund all others : yet God doth order, that all
your lawes, all your authoritie, all your commaundementes, do not halfe ſo moch with meane men, as doth
your example and maner of liuinge.   And
for example euen in the greateſt matter,
if yow your ſelues do ſerue God gladlie and orderlie
for conſcience ſake, not coldlie, and ſomtyme for
maner ſake, you carie all the Courte with yow, and
the whole Realme beſide, earneſtlie and orderlie to do
the ſame.   If yow do otherwiſe, yow be the onelie
authors, of all miſorders in Religion, not onelie to the
Courte, but to all England beſide.   Infinite ſhall be

Great men in Court, by their example, make or marre, all other mens maners.

Example in Religion.

made cold in Religion by your example, that neuer
were hurt by reading of bookes.

And in meaner matters, if three or foure great ones
in Courte, will nedes outrage in apparell, Example in
in huge hofe, in monft[e]rous hattes, in apparell.
gaurifhe colers, let the Prince Proclame, make Lawes,
order, punifhe, commaunde euerie gate in London dailie
to be watched, let all good men befide do euerie where
what they can, furelie the miforder of apparell in mean
men abrode, fhall neuer be amended, except the greateft
in Courte will order and mend them felues firft. I
know, fom greate and good ones in Courte, were
authors, that honeft Citizens in London, fhoulde
watche at euerie gate, to take mifordered perfones in
apparell. I know, that honeft Londoners did fo :
And I fawe, which I fawe than, and reporte now with
fome greife, that fom Courtlie men were offended with
thefe good men of London. And that, which greued
me moft of all, I fawe the verie fame tyme, for all theis
good orders, commaunded from the Courte and exe-
cuted in London, I fawe I fay, cum out Masters, Vshers,
of London, euen vnto the prefence of the and Scholers of
Prince, a great rable of meane and light fense.
perfons, in apparell, for matter, againft lawe, for making, againft order, for facion, namelie hofe, fo without
all order, as he thought himfelfe moft braue, that durft
do moft in breaking order and was moft monfterous in
miforder. And for all the great commaundementes,
that came out of the Courte, yet this bold miforder,
was winked at, and borne withall, in the Courte. I
thought, it was not well, that fom great ones of the
Court, durft declare themfelues offended, with good
men of London, for doinge their dewtie, and the good
ones of the Courte, would not fhew themfelues offended,
with the ill men of London, for breaking good order.
I fownde thereby a fayinge of *Socrates* to be moft trewe
that ill men be more haftie, than good men be forwarde,
to profecute their purpofes, euen as Chrift himfelfe
faith, of the Children of light and darknes.

Beſide apparell, in all other thinges to, not ſo moch, good lawes and ſtrait commaundementes as the example and maner of liuing of great men, doth carie all meane men euerie where, to like, and loue, and do, as they do.   For if but two or three noble men in the Court, *Example in* wold but beginne to ſhoote, all yong *shootyng.* Ientlemen, the whole Court, all London, the whole Realme, would ſtraight waie exerciſe ſhooting.

What praiſe ſhold they wynne to themſelues, what commoditie ſhold they bring to their contrey, that would thus deſerue to be pointed at: Beholde, there goeth, the author of good order, the guide of good men.   I cold ſay more, and yet not ouermoch.   But perchance, ſom will ſay, I haue ſtepte to farre, out of my ſchole, into the common welthe, from teaching a *Written not* yong ſcholer, to moniſhe greate and noble *for great men,* men : yet I truſt good and wiſe men will *but for great* thinke and iudge of me, that my minde *mens children.* was, not ſo moch, to be buſie and bold with them, that be great now, as to giue trewe aduiſe to them, that may be great hereafter.   Who, if they do, as I wiſhe them to do, how great ſo euer they be now, by blood and other mens meanes, they ſhall be-cum a greate deale greater hereafter, by learninge, vertue, and their owne deſertes : which is trewe praiſe, right worthines, and verie Nobilitie in deede.   Yet, if ſom will needes preſſe me, that I am to bold with great men, and ſtray to farre from my matter, I will anſwere *Ad Philip.*   them with *S. Paul, ſiue per contentionem, ſiue quocunque modo, modò Chriſtus prædicetnr, etc.* euen ſo, whether in place, or out of place, with my matter, or beſide my matter, if I can hereby either prouoke the good, or ſtaye the ill, I ſhall thinke my writing herein well imployed.

But, to cum downe, from greate men, and hier matters, to my litle children, and poore ſchoolehouſe againe, I will, God willing, go forwarde orderlie, as I purpoſed, to inſtructe Children and yong men, both for learninge and maners.

Hitherto, I haue ſhewed, what harme, ouermoch

feare bringeth to children: and what hurte, ill companie, and ouermoch libertie breedeth in yougthe:
meening thereby, that from feauen yeare olde, to
feauentene, loue is the beft allurement to learninge:
from feauentene to feauen and twentie, that wife men
fhold carefullie fee the fteppes of yougthe furelie ftaide
by good order, in that moft flipperie tyme: and fpeciallie in the Courte, a place moft dangerous for yougthe
to liue in, without great grace, good regarde, and diligent looking to.

Syr *Richard Sackuile*, that worthy Ientleman of
worthy memorie, as I fayd in the begynnynge, in the
Queenes priuie Chamber at Windefore, Trauelling
after he had talked with me, for the right into Italie.
choice of a good witte in a child for learnyng, and of
the trewe difference betwixt quicke and hard wittes, of
alluring yong children by ientlenes to loue learnyng,
and of the fpeciall care that was to be had, to keepe
yong men from licencious liuyng, he was moft earneft
with me, to haue me fay my mynde alfo, what I thought,
concernyng the fanfie that many yong Ientlemen of
England haue to trauell abroad, and namely to lead a
long lyfe in Italie. His requeft, both for his authoritie,
and good will toward me, was a fufficient commaunde-
ment vnto me, to fatiffie his pleafure, with vtteryng
plainlie my opinion in that matter. Syr quoth I, I
take goyng thither, and liuing there, for a yonge ientleman, that doth not goe vnder the ke[e]pe and garde of
fuch a man, as both, by wifedome can, and authoritie
dare rewle him, to be meruelous dangerous. And
whie I faid fo than, I will declare at large now: which
I faid than priuatelie, and write now openlie, not bicaufe I do contemne, either the knowledge of ftrange
and diuerfe tonges, and namelie the Italian The Italian
tonge, which next the Greeke and Latin tong.
tonge, I like and loue aboue all other: or elfe bicaufe
I do defpife, the learning that is gotten, or the experience that is gathered in ftrange contries: or for any
priuate malice that beare to Italie: which Italia.

Roma.   contrie, and in it, namelie Rome, I haue alwayes fpeciallie honored: bicaufe, tyme was, whan Italie and Rome, haue bene, to the greate good of vs that now liue, the beft breeders and bringers vp, of the worthieft men, not onelie for wife fpeakinge, but alfo for well doing, in all Ciuill affaires, that euer was in the worlde. But now, that tyme is gone, and though the place remayne, yet the olde and prefent maners, do differ as farre, as blacke and white, as vertue and vice. Vertue once made that contrie Miftres ouer all the worlde. Vice now maketh that contrie flaue to them, that before, were glad to ferue it. All man feeth it: They themfelues confeffe it, namelie foch, as be beft and wifeft amongeft them. For finne, by luft and vanitie, hath and doth breed vp euery where, common contempt of Gods word, priuate contention in many families, open factions in euery Citie: and fo, makyng them felues bonde, to vanitie and vice at home, they are content to beare the yoke of feruyng ftraungers abroad. *Italie* now, is not that *Italie,* that it was wont to be: and therfore now, not fo fitte a place, as fome do counte it, for yong men to fetch either wifedome or honeftie from thence. For furelie, they will make other but bad Scholers, that be fo ill Mafters to them felues. Yet, if a ientleman will nedes trauell into *Italie,* he fhall do well, to looke on the life, of the wifeft traueller, that euer traueled thether, fet out by the wifeft writer, that euer fpake with tong, Gods doctrine onelie excepted: and that is *Vlyffes* in

Vlysses.   *Homere.*   *Vlyffes,* and his trauell, I wifhe
Homere.   our trauelers to looke vpon, not fo much to feare them, with the great daungers, that he many tymes fuffered, as to inftruct them, with his excellent wifedome, which he alwayes and euerywhere vfed. Yea euen thofe, that be learned and wittie trauelers, when they be difpofed to prayfe traueling, as a great commendacion, and the beft Scripture they haue for it, they gladlie recite the third verfe of *Homere,* in his firft booke of *Odyffea,* conteinyng a great prayfe of

Vlyſſes, for the witte he gathered, and wiſe- ὀδυς, α.
dome he vſed in trauelling.

Which verſe, bicauſe, in mine opinion, it was not
made at the firſt, more naturallie in *Greke* by *Homere*,
nor after turned more aptelie into *Latin* by *Horace*,
than it was a good while ago, in Cambrige, tranſlated into Engliſh, both plainlie for the ſenſe, and
roundlie for the verſe, by one of the beſt Scholers, that
euer S. Iohns Colledge bred, *M. Watſon*, myne old
frend, ſomtime Biſhop of Lincolne, therefore, for their
ſake, that haue luſt to ſee, how our Engliſh tong, in
auoidyng barbarous ryming, may as well receiue, right
quantitie of ſillables, and trewe order of verſifiyng (of
which matter more at large hereafter) as either *Greke*
or *Latin*, if a cunning man haue it in [the] handling,
I will ſet forth that one verſe in all three tonges, for
an Example to good wittes, that ſhall delite in like
learned exerciſe.

Homerus.

πολλῶν δ' ἀνθρώπων ἴδεν ἄστεα καὶ νόον ἔγνω.

Horatius.

Qui mores hominum multorum vidit et vrbes.

M. Watson.

All trauellers do gladly report great prayſe of Vlyſſes,
For that he knew many mens maners, and ſaw many Cities.

And yet is not *Vlyſſes* commended, ſo much, nor
ſo oft, in *Homere*, bicauſe he was ⎫   ⎧ πολύτροπος
πολύτροπος, that is, ſkilfull in many ⎪ *Vlyss* ⎨
mens manners and facions, as bi- ⎪   ⎩ πολύμητις
cauſe he was πολύμητις, that is, wiſe ⎭
in all purpoſes, and war[y]e in all places : which wiſedome
and warenes will not ſerue neither a tra- *Pallas* from
ueler, except *Pallas* be alwayes at his heauen.
elbow, that is Gods ſpeciall grace from heauen, to kepe
him in Gods feare, in all his doynges, in all his ieorneye.

For, he ſhall not alwayes in his abſence out of Eng-
Alcynous. δδ. 2. land, light vpon the ientle *Alcynous*, and
walke in his faire gardens full of all
harmeleſſe pleaſures : but he ſhall ſome-
tymes, fall, either into the handes of ſome
Cyclops. δδ. 1. cruell *Cyclops*, or into the lappe of ſome
Calypſo. δδ. ε. wanton and dalying Dame *Calypſo* : and
ſo ſuffer the danger of many a deadlie
Denne, not ſo full of perils, to diſtroy
the body, as, full of vayne pleaſures, to
poyſon the mynde. Some *Siren* ſhall
Sirenes. ſing him a ſong, ſweete in tune, but
δδ. μ. ſownding in the ende, to his vtter de-
Scylla. ſtruction. If *Scylla* drowne him not,
Caribdis *Carybdis* may fortune ſwalow hym.
Circes. δδ. κ. Some *Circes* ſhall make him, of a plaine
Engliſh man, a right *Italian*. And at length to hell, or
to ſome helliſh place, is he likelie to go : from whence
is hard returning, although one *Vlyſſes*, and that by
δδ. λ. *Pallas* ayde, and good counſell of *Tireſias*
once eſcaped that horrible Den of deadly darkenes.

Therfore, if wiſe men will nedes ſend their ſonnes
into *Italie*, let them do it wiſelie, vnder the kepe and
garde of him, who, by his wiſedome and honeſtie, by
his example and authoritie, may be hable to kepe them
ſafe and ſound, in the feare of God, in Chriſtes trewe Religion, in good order and honeſtie of liuyng : except they
will haue them run headling [headlong], into ouermany
ieoperdies, as *Vlyſſes* had done many tymes, if *Pallas*
had not alwayes gouerned him : if he had not vſed, to
δδ. μ. ſtop his eares with waxe : to bind him ſelfe
δδ. κ. to the maſt of his ſhyp : to feede dayly, vpon
Moly Herba. that ſwete herbe *Moly* with the bla[c]ke roote
and white floore, giuen vnto hym by Mercurie, to auoide
all inchantmentes of *Circes*. Wherby, the Diuine Poete
Homer ment couertlie (as wiſe and Godlym en do iudge)
that loue of honeſtie, and hatred of ill, which *Dauid*
Pſal. 33. more plainly doth call the feare of God :
the onely remedie agaynſt all inchantementes of ſinne.

I know diuerſe noble perſonages, and many worthie

Ientlemen of England, whom all the *Siren* fonges of *Italie*, could neuer vntwyne from the mafte of Gods word : nor no inchantment of vanitie, ouerturne them, from the feare of God, and loue of honeftie.

But I know as many, or mo, and fome, fometyme my deare frendes, for whofe fake I hate going into that countrey the more, who, partyng out of England feruent in the loue of Chriftes doctrine, and well furnifhed with the feare of God, returned out of *Italie* worfe tranfformed, than euer were any in *Circes* Court.   I know diuerfe, that went out of England, men of innocent life, men of excellent learnyng, who returned out of *Italie*, not onely with worfe manners, but alfo with leffe learnyng : neither fo willing to liue orderly, nor yet fo hable to fpeake learnedlie, as they were at home, before they went abroad.   And why?   *Plato*, yat wife writer, and worthy traueler him felfe, telleth the caufe why.   He went into *Sicilia*, a countrey, no nigher *Italy* by fite of place, than *Italie* that is now, is like *Sicilia* that was then, in all corrupt maners and licencioufnes of life.   *Plato* found in *Sicilia*, euery Citie full of vanitie, full of factions, euen as *Italie* is now.   And as *Homere*, like a learned Poete, doth feyne, that *Circes*, by pleafant inchantmentes, did turne men into beaftes, fome into Swine, fom in Affes, fome into Foxes, fome into Wolues etc. euen fo, *Plato*, like a wife Philofopher, doth plainelie declare, that pleafure, by licenti- Plat. ad Dionys. Epist. 3.
ous vanitie, that fweet and perilous poyfon of all youth, doth ingender in all thofe that yeld vp themfelues to her, foure notorious properties.

1. λήθην
2. δυσμαθῐαν
3. ἀφροσύνην
4. ὕβριν.

The fruits ot vayne pleasure.

The firft, forgetfulnes of all good thinges learned before: the fecond, dulnes to receyue either learnyng or honeftie euer after: the third, a mynde embracing lightlie the worfe opinion, and baren of difcretion to make

Causes why men returne out of Italie, lesse learned and worse manered.

trewe difference betwixt good and ill, betwixt troth, and vanitie, the fourth, a proude difdainfulnes of other *Homer* and good men, in all honeſt matters. *Homere* *Plato* ioyned and *Plato*, haue both one meanyng, looke and expounded. both to one end.   For, if a man inglutte himſelf with A Swyne. vanitie, or walter in filthines like a Swyne, all learnyng, all goodnes, is fone forgotten : Than, An Aſſe. quicklie fhall he becum a dull Aſſe, to vnderſtand either learnyng or honeſtie : and yet fhall A Foxe. he be as futle as a Foxe, in breedyng of mifchief, in bringyng in miforder, with a bufie head, a difcourfing tong, and a factious harte, in euery priuate affaire, in all matters of ſtate, with this pretie propertie, ἀφροσύνη, always glad to commend the worfe partie, Quid, et vnde. and euer ready to defend the falſer opinion. And why ?   For, where will is giuen from goodnes to vanitie, the mynde is fone caryed from right iudgement to any fond opinion, in Religion, in Philofophie, or any other kynde of learning.   The fourth fruite of ὕβρις. vaine pleaſure, by *Homer* and *Platos* iudgement, is pride in them ſelues, contempt of others, the very badge of all thoſe that ſerue in *Circes* Court. The true meenyng of both *Homer* and *Plato*, is plainlie declared in one ſhort ſentence of the holy Prophet of Hieremas God *Hieremie*, crying out of the vaine and 4. Cap. vicious life of the *Ifraelites*.   This people (fayth he) be fooles and dulhedes to all goodnes, but fotle, cunning and bolde, in any mifchiefe. etc.

The true medecine againſt the inchantmentes of *Circes*, the vanitie of licencious pleaſure, the inticementes of all finne, is, in *Homere*, the herbe *Moly*, with the blacke roote, and white flooer, fower at the Heſiodus de firſt, but fweete in the end : which, *Heſiodus* virtute. termeth the ſtudy of vertue, hard and irkfome in the beginnyng, but in the end, eaſie and pleaſant.   And that, which is moſt to be marueled at, the diuine Poete Homerus diui- *Homere* fayth plainlie that this medicine nus Poeta. againſt finne and vanitie is not found out by man, but giuen and taught by God.   And for fome [ones] fake, that will haue delite to read that fweete and Godlie

Verſe, I will recite the very wordes of *Homere* and alſo
turne them into rude Engliſh metre.

$$\chi\alpha\lambda\epsilon\pi\grave{o}\nu \; \delta\grave{\epsilon} \; \tau' \; \acute{o}\rho\acute{\upsilon}\sigma\sigma\epsilon\iota\nu$$
$$\grave{\alpha}\nu\delta\rho\acute{\alpha}\sigma\iota \; \gamma\epsilon \; \theta\nu\eta\tau o\~{\imath}\sigma\iota, \; \theta\epsilon o\grave{\iota} \; \delta\acute{\epsilon} \; \pi\acute{\alpha}\nu\tau\alpha \; \delta\acute{\upsilon}\nu\alpha\nu\tau\iota.$$

In Engliſh thus.

No mortall man, with ſweat of browe, or toile of minde,
But onely God, who can do all, that herbe doth finde.

Plato alſo, that diuine Philoſopher, hath many **Godly**
medicines agaynſt the poyſon of vayne pleaſure, in
many places, but ſpecially in his Epiſtles to *Dioniſius*
the tyrant of *Sicilie*: yet agaynſt thoſe, Plat. ad. Dio.
that will nedes becum beaſtes, with ſeruyng of
Circes, the Prophet *Dauid,* crieth moſt loude, *Nolite*
fieri ſicut eques et mulus : and by and by Psal. 32.
giueth the right medicine, the trewe herbe *Moly, In*
camo et freno maxillas eorum conſtringe, that is to ſay,
let Gods grace be the bitte, let Gods feare be the bridle,
to ſtay them from runnyng headlong into vice, and to
turne them into the right way agayne. *Dauid* in the
ſecond Pſalme after, giueth the ſame medi- Psal. 33.
cine, but in theſe plainer wordes, *Diuerte à malo et fac*
bonum. But I am affraide, that ouer many of our
trauelers into *Italie,* do not exchewe the way to *Circes*
Court : but go, and ryde, and runne, and flie thether,
they make great haſt to cum to her : they make great
ſute to ſerue her : yea, I could point out ſome with my
finger, that neuer had gone out of England, but onelie
to ſerue *Circes,* in *Italie.* Vánitie and vice, and any
licence to ill liuyng in England was counted ſtale and
rude vnto them. And ſo, beyng Mules and Horſes
before they went, returned verie Swyne and Aſſes home
agayne : yet euerie where verie Foxes with as ſuttle
and buſie heades ; and where they may, verie Woolues,
with cruell malicious hartes. A maruelous A trewe Pic-
monſter, which, for filthines of liuyng, for ture of a knight
dulnes to learning him ſelfe, for wilineſſe of Circes Court.
in dealing with others, for malice in hurting without
cauſe, ſhould carie at once in one bodie, the belie of
a Swyne, the head of an Aſſe, the brayne of a Foxe,

the wombe of a wolfe.   If you thinke, we iudge amiſſe,
and write to ſore againſt you, heare, what the *Italian*
The Italians iudgement of Englishmen brought vp in Italie. ſayth of the Engliſh Man, what the maſter reporteth of the ſcholer: who vttereth playnlie, what is taught by him, and what learned by you, ſaying, *Engleſe Italianato e vn diabolo incarnato,* that is to ſay, you remaine men in ſhape and facion, but becum deuils in life and condition.   This is not, the opinion of one, for ſome priuate ſpite, but the iudgement of all, in a common Prouerbe, which riſeth, of that learnyng, and thoſe maners, which
The Italian diffameth them ſelfe, to shame the Englishe man. you gather in *Italie*: a good Scholehouſe of wholeſome doctrine, and worthy Maſters of commendable Scholers, where the Maſter had rather diffame hym ſelfe for hys teachyng, than not ſhame his Scholer for his learnyng. A good nature of the maiſter, and faire conditions of the ſcholers.   And now choſe you, you *Italian* Engliſhe men, whether you will be angrie with vs, for calling you monſters, or with the *Italianes*, for callyng you deuils, or elſe with your owne ſelues, that take ſo much paines, and go ſo farre, to make your ſelues both.   If ſome yet do not well vnderſtand, what is an Engliſh man Italianated, I will plainlie tell him.   He, that by
An English man Italianated. liuing, and traueling in *Italie*, bringeth home into England out of *Italie*, the Religion, the learning, the policie, the experience, the maners of *Italie*.   That is to ſay, for Religion, Papiſtrie or worſe: for learnyng, leſſe commonly than they caried out with them: for pollicie, a factious hart, a diſcourſing head, a mynde to medle in all mens matters: for experience, plentie of new miſchieues neuer knowne in England before: for maners, varietie of vanities,

and chaunge of filthy lyuing.   Theſe be the inchantementes of *Circes*, brought out of *Italie*, to marre mens maners in England; much, by example of ill life, but more by preceptes of fonde

bookes, of late tranflated out of *Italian*
into Englifh, fold in euery fhop in Lon-
don, commended by honeft titles the fo[o]ner to corrupt
honeft maners : dedicated ouer boldlie to vertuous and
honourable perfonages, the eafielier to beg[u]ile fimple
and innocent wittes.   It is pitie, that thofe,
which haue authoritie and charge, to allow and
diffalow bookes to be printed, be no more circumfpect
herein, than they are.   Ten Sermons at Paules Croffe
do not fo moch good for mouyng men to trewe doctrine, as one of thofe bookes do harme, with inticing
men to ill liuing.   Yea, I say farder, thofe bookes,
tend not fo moch to corrupt honeft liuing, as they do,
to fubuert trewe Religion.   Mo Papiftes be made, by
your mer[r]y bookes of *Italie*, than by your earneft bookes
of *Louain*.   And bicaufe our great Phificians, do winke
at the matter, and make no counte of this fore, I,
though not admitted one of their felowfhyp, yet hauyng
bene many yeares a prentice to Gods trewe Religion,
and truft to continewe a poore iorney man therein all
dayes of my life, for the dewtie I owe, and loue I beare,
both to trewe doctrine, and honeft liuing, though I
haue no authoritie to amend the fore my felfe, yet I
will declare my good will, to difcouer the fore to others.

S. Paul faith, that fectes and ill opinions,   Ad Gal. 5.
be the workes of the flefh, and frutes of finne, this is
fpoken, no more trewlie for the doctrine, than fenfiblie
for the reafon.   And why?   For, ill doinges, breed
ill thinkinges.   And of corrupted maners, fpryng peruerted iudgementes.   And how?   there be in man
two fpeciall thinges :   Mans | Voluntas⎫   ⎧Bonum.
will, mans mynde.   Where | ⎬Refpicit⎨
will inclineth to goodnes, the | Mens ⎭   ⎩Verum.
mynde is bent to troth : Where will is caried from
goodnes to vanitie, the mynde is fone drawne from
troth to falfe opinion.   And fo, the readieft way to
entangle the mynde with falfe doctrine, is firft to in-
tice the will to wanton liuyng.   Therfore, when the
bufie and open Papiftes abroad, could not, by their
contentious bookes, turne men in England faft enough,

from troth and right iudgement in doctrine, than the
sutle and secrete Papiſtes at home, procured
bawdie bookes to be tranſlated out of the
Italian tonge, whereby ouer many yong willes and
wittes allured to wantonnes, do now boldly contemne
all ſeuere bookes that ſounde to honeſtie and godlines.
In our forefathers tyme, whan Papiſtrie, as a ſtandyng
poole, couered and ouerflowed all England, fewe
bookes were read in our tong, ſauyng certaine bookes
Cheualrie, as they ſayd, for paſtime and pleaſure, which,
as ſome ſay, were made in Monaſteries, by idle Monkes,
or wanton Chanons: as one for example, *Morte Ar-*
Morte Arthur.   *thure*: the whole pleaſure of which booke
ſtandeth in two ſpeciall poyntes, in open mans ſlaughter,
and bold bawdrye: In which booke thoſe be counted
the nobleſt Knightes, that do kill moſt men without any
quarrell, and commit fowleſt aduoulter[i]es by ſutleſt
ſhiftes: as Sir *Launcelote*, with the wife of king *Arthure*
his maſter: Syr *Triſtram* with the wife of king *Marke*
his vncle: Syr *Lamerocke* with the wife of king *Lote*,
that was his own aunte.   This is good
ſtuffe, for wiſe men to laughe at, or honeſt
men to take pleaſure at.   Yet I know, when Gods
Bible was baniſhed the Court, and *Morte Arthure* receiued into the Princes chamber.   What toyes, the
dayly readyng of ſuch a booke, may worke in the will
of a yong ientleman, or a yong mayde, that liueth
welthelie and idlelie, wiſe men can iudge, and honeſt
men do pitie.   And yet ten *Morte Arthures* do not the
tenth part ſo much harme, as one of theſe bookes,
made in *Italie*, and tranſlated in England.
They open, not fond and common wayes
to vice, but ſuch ſubtle, cunnyng, new, and diuerſe
ſhiftes, to cary yong willes to vanitie, and yong wittes
to miſchief, to teach old bawdes new ſchole poyntes,
as the ſimple head of an Engliſhman is not hable to
inuent, nor neuer was hard of in England before, yea
when Papiſtrie ouerflowed all.   Suffer theſe bookes to
be read, and they ſhall ſoone diſplace all bookes of
godly learnyng.   For they, carying the will to vanitie

and marryng good maners, ſhall eaſily
corrupt the mynde with ill opinions, and
falſe iudgement in doctrine : firſt, to thinke nothyng
of God hym ſelfe, one ſpeciall pointe that is to be
learned in *Italie,* and *Italian* bookes. And
that which is moſt to be lamented, and
therfore more nedefull to be looked to, there be moe
of theſe vngratious bookes ſet out in Printe within theſe
fewe monethes, than haue bene ſene in England many
ſcore yeare[s] before. And bicauſe our Engliſh men
made *Italians* can not hurt, but certaine perſons, and in
certaine places, therfore theſe *Italian* bookes are made
Engliſh, to bryng miſchief enough openly and boldly, to
all ſtates great and meane, yong and old, euery where.

And thus yow ſee, how will intiſed to wantonnes,
doth eaſelie allure the mynde to falſe opinions : and
how corrupt maners in liuinge, breede falſe iudgement
in doctrine : how ſinne and fleſhlines, bring forth ſectes
and hereſies : And therefore ſuffer not vaine bookes to
breede vanitie in mens willes, if yow would haue
Goddes trothe take roote in mens myndes.

That Italian, that firſt inuented the Italian Prouerbe
againſt our Engliſhe men Italianated, ment no more
their vanitie in liuing, than their lewd opinion in Religion. For, in calling them Deuiles, he   The Italian
carieth them cleane from God : and yet   prouerbe
he carieth them no farder, than they wil-   expounded.
linglie go themſelues, that is, where they may freely
ſay their mindes, to the open contempte of God and
all godlines, both in liuing and doctrine.

And how ? I will expreſſe how, not by a Fable of
Homere, nor by the Philoſophie of *Plato,* but by a
plaine troth of Goddes word, ſenſiblie vttered by *Dauid*
thus. Thies men, *abhominabiles faƈti in ſtudijs ſuis,*
thinke verily, and ſinge gladlie the verſe before, *Dixit
inſipiens in Corde ſuo, non eſt Deus :* that is *Psa.* 14.
to ſay, they geuing themſelues vp to vanitie, ſhakinge
of the motions of Grace, driuing from them the feare
of God, and running headlong into all ſinne, firſt,
luſtelie contemne God, than ſcornefullie mocke his

worde, and alfo fpitefullie hate and hurte all well willers
thereof.   Than they haue in more reuerence, the
triumphes of Petrarche : than the Genefis of Mofes :
They make more account of *Tullies* offices, than *S.
Paules* epiftles : of a tale in *Bocace*, than a ftorie of the
Bible.   Than they counte as Fables, the holie mifteries
of Chriftian Religion.   They make Chrift and his Gofpell, onelie ferue Ciuill pollicie : Than neyther Religion
cummeth amiffe to them : In tyme they be Promoters
of both openlie : in place againe mockers of both priuilie, as I wrote oncein a rude ryme.

Now new, now olde, now both, now neither,
To ſerue the worldes courſe, they care not with whether.

For where they dare, in cumpanie where they like,
they boldlie laughe to fcorne both proteftant and Pap-
ift.   They care for no fcripture : They make no counte
of generall councels : they contemne the confent of
the Chirch : They paffe for no Doctores : They
mocke the Pope : They raile on *Luther* : They allow
neyther fide : They like none, but onelie themfelues :
The marke they fhote at, the ende they looke for, the
heauen they defire, is onelie, their owne prefent pleafure, and priuate proffit : whereby, they plainlie declare,
of whofe fchole, of what Religion they be : that is,
Epicures in liuing, and ἄθεοι in doctrine : this laft
worde is no more vnknowne now to plaine Englifhe
men, than the Perfon was vnknown fomtyme in England, vntill fom[e] Englifhe man tooke peines to fetch
that deuelifh opinion out of Italie.   Thies men, thus

The Italian
Chirche in
London.

Italianated abroad, can not abide our
Godlie Italian Chirch at home : they be
not of that Parifh, they be not of that felowfhyp : they like not yat preacher : they heare not
his fermons : Excepte fometymes for companie, they
cum thither, to heare the Italian tongue naturally
fpoken, not to hear Gods doctrine trewly preached.

And yet, thies men, in matters of Diuinitie, openlie
pretend a great knowledge, and haue priuately to them
felues, a verie compendious vnderftanding of all, which
neuertheles they will vtter when and where they lifte :

And that is this : All the mifteries of *Mofes*, the whole
lawe and Cerimonies, the Pfalmes and Prophetes,
Chrift and his Gofpell, G O D and the Deuill, Heauen
and Hell, Faith, Confcience, Sinne, Death, and all
they fhortlie wrap vp, they quickly expounde with this
one halfe verfe of *Horace.*

Credat Iudæus Appella.

Yet though in Italie they may freely be of no Religion, as they are in Englande in verie deede to, neuertheleffe returning home into England they muft
countenance the profeffion of the one or the other,
howfoeuer inwardlie, they laugh to fcorne both. And
though, for their priuate matters they can follow, fawne,
and flatter noble Perfonages, contrarie to them in all
refpectes, yet commonlie they allie them- Papiftrie and
felues with the worft Papiftes, to whom impietie
agree in three
they be wedded, and do well agree togither opinions.
in three proper opinions : In open contempte of
Goddes worde : in a fecret fecuritie of finne : and in
a bloodie defire to haue all taken away, by fword and
burning, that be not of their faction. They that do
read, with indifferent iudgement, *Pygius* and *Pigius.*
Machiauel, two indifferent Patriarches of *Machiauelus.*
thies two Religions, do know full well what I fay trewe.

Ye fee, what manners and doctrine, our Englifhe
men fetch out of Italie : For finding no other there,
they can bring no other hither. And therefore, manie
godlie and excellent learned Englifhe men, Wise and hon-
not manie yeares ago, did make a better est trauelers.
choice, whan open crueltie draue them out of this
contrie, to place themfelues there, where Chriftes doctrine, the feare of God, punifhment of finne, *Germanie.*
and difcipline of honeftie, were had in fpeciall regarde.

I was once in Italie my felfe : but I thanke *Venice.*
God, my abode there, was but ix. dayes : And yet I fawe in
that lit[t]le tyme, in one Citie, more libertie to finne, than
euer I h[e]ard tell of in our noble Citie of *London.*
London in ix. yeare. I fawe, it was there, as free to finne,
not onelie without all punifhment, but alfo without any
mans marking, as it is free in the Citie of London, to

choſe, without all blame, whether a man luſt to weare
Shoo or Pantocle. And good cauſe why: For being
vnlike in troth of Religion, they muſt nedes be vnlike
in honeſtie of liuing. For bleſſed be Chriſt, in our Citie
Seruice of God in England. of London, commonlie the commande-
mentes of God, be more diligentlie taught,
and the ſeruice of God more reuerentlie vſed, and that
daylie in many priuate mens houſes, than they be in
Seruice of God in Italie. Italie once a weeke in their common
Chirches. where, maſking Ceremonies, to
delite the eye, and vaine ſoundes, to pleaſe the eare,
do quite thruſt out of the Chirches, all ſeruice of God
The Lord Maior of London. in ſpirit and troth. Yea, the Lord Maior of
London, being but a Ciuill officer, is com-
monlie for his tyme, more diligent, in puniſhing ſinne,
the bent enemie againſt God and good order, than all
The Inquiſitors in Italie the bloodie Inquiſitors in Italie be in ſea-
uen yeare. For, their care and charge is,
not to puniſh ſinne, not to amend manners, not to
purge doctrine, but onelie to watch and ouerſee that
Chriſtes trewe Religion ſet no ſure footing, where the
Pope hath any Iuriſdiction. I learned, when I was at
An vngodlie pollicie. *Venice*, that there it is counted good pollicie, when there be foure or fiue brethren
of one familie, one, onelie to marie: and all the reſt,
to waulter, with as litle ſhame, in open lecherie, as
Swyne do here in the common myre. Yea, there be as
fayre houſes of Religion, as great prouiſion, as diligent
officers, to kepe vp this miſorder, as Bridewell is, and
all the Maſters there, to kepe downe miſorder. And
therefore, if the Pope himſelfe, do not onelie graunt
pardons to furder thies wicked purpoſes abrode in
Italie, but alſo (although this preſent Pope, in the beginning, made ſom ſhewe of miſliking thereof) aſſigne
both meede and merite to the maintenance of ſtewes
and brothelhouſes at home in Rome, than let wiſe men
thinke Italie a ſafe place for holſom doctrine, and
godlie manners, and a fitte ſchole for yong ientlemen
of England to be brought vp in.

Our Italians bring home with them other faulteſ

from Italie, though not fo great as this of Religion, yet a great deale greater, than many good men well beare. For commonlie they cum home, common contemners of mariage and readie per-fuaders of all other to the fame: not becaufe they loue virginitie, nor yet becaufe they hate prettie yong virgines, but, being free in Italie, to go whither fo euer luft will cary them, they do not like, that lawe and honeftie fhould be foch a barre to their like libertie at home in England. And yet they be, the greateft makers of loue, the daylie daliers, with fuch pleafant wordes, with fuch fmilyng and fecret countenances, with fuch fignes, tokens, wagers, purpofed to be loft, before they were purpofed to be made, with bargaines of wearing colours, floures, and herbes, to breede oc-cafion of ofter meeting of him and her, and bolder talking of this and that, etc. And although I haue feene fome, innocent of ill, and ftayde in all honeftie, that haue vfed thefe thinges without all harme, without all fufpicion of harme, yet thefe knackes were brought firft into England by them, that learned them before in *Italie* in *Circes* Court: and how Courtlie curteffes fo euer they be counted now, yet, if the meaning and maners of fome that do vfe them, were fomewhat amended, it were no great hurt, neither to them felues, nor to others.

An other propertie of this our Englifh *Italians* is, to be meruelous fingular in all their matters: Singular in knowledge, ignorant of nothyng: So fingular in wife-dome (in their owne opinion) as fcarfe they counte the beft Counfellor the Prince hath, comparable with them: Common difcourfers of all matters: bufie fearchers of moft fecret affaires: open flatterers of great men: priuie miflikers of good men: Faire fpeakers, with fmiling countenances, and much curteffie openlie to all men. Ready ba[c]kbiters, fore nippers, and fpitefull reporters priuilie of good men. And beyng brought vp in *Italie*, in fome free Citie, as all Cities be there: where a man may freelie difcourfe againft what he will, againft whom he luft: againft any Prince, agaynft any gouernement, yea againft God him

Contempt of mariage.

felfe, and his whole Religion : where he muſt be, either
Guelphe or *Gibiline,* either *French* or *Spaniſh* : and alwayes compelled to be of ſome partie, of ſome faction,
he ſhall neuer be compelled to be of any Religion :
And if he medle not ouer much with Chriſtes true Religion, he ſhall haue free libertie to embrace all Religions, and becum, if he luſt at once, without any let or
puniſhment, Iewiſh, Turkiſh, Papiſh, and Deuilliſh.

A yong Ientleman, thus bred vp in this goodly ſchole,
to learne the next and readie way to ſinne, to haue a buſie
head, a factious hart, a talkatiue tonge, fed with diſcourſing of factions : led to contemne God and his Religion, ſhall cum home into England, but verie ill taught,
either to be an honeſt man him ſelf, a quiet ſubiect to his
Prince, or willyng to ſerue God, vnder the obedience of
trewe doctrine, or with in the order of honeſt liuing.

I know, none will be offended with this my generall
writing, but onelie ſuch, as finde them ſelues giltie
priuatelie therin : who ſhall haue a good leaue to be
offended with me, vntill they begin to amende them
ſelues.   I touch not them that be good : and I ſay to
litle of them that be nought.   And ſo, though not
enough for their deſeruing, yet ſufficientlie for this
time, and more els when, if occaſion ſo require.

And thus farre haue I wandred from my firſt purpoſe of teaching a child, yet not altogether out of the
way, bicauſe this whole taulke hath tended to the
onelie aduancement of trothe in Religion, an honeſtie
of liuing : and hath bene wholie within the compaſſe
of learning and good maners, the ſpeciall pointes belonging in the right bringing vp of youth.

But to my matter, as I began, plainlie and ſimplie
with my yong Scholer, ſo will I not leaue him, God
willing, vntill I haue brought him a perfite Scholer out
of the Schole, and placed him in the Vniuerſitie, to becum a fitte ſtudent, for Logicke and Rhetoricke : and ſo
after to Phiſicke, Law, or Diuinitie, as aptnes of nature,
aduiſe of frendes, and Gods diſpoſition ſhall lead him.

The ende of the firſt booke.

Fter that your fcholer, as I fayd before, fhall cum in deede, firft, to a readie perfitnes in tranflating, than, to a ripe and fkilfull choice in markyng out hys fixe pointes, as

1. *Proprium.*
2. *Tranflatum.*
3. *Synonynum.*
4. *Contrarium.*
5. *Diuerfum.*
6. *Phrafes.*

Than take this order with him : Read dayly vnto him, fome booke of *Tullie*, as the third *Cicero.* booke of Epiftles chofen out by *Sturmius, de Amicitia, de Senectute*, or that excellent Epiftle conteinyng almoft the whole firft booke *ad Q. fra* : fome Comedie of *Terence* or *Plautus* : but in *Plautus*, fkilfull *Terentius.* choice muft be vfed by the mafter, to traine *Plautus.* his Scholler to a iudgement, in cutting out perfitelie ouer old and vnproper wordes : *Cæf.* *Iul. Cæsar.* *Commentaries* are to be read with all curiofitie, in fpecially without all exception to be made either by frende or foe, is feene, the vnfpotted proprietie of the Latin tong, euen whan it was, as the *Grecians* fay, in ἀκμὴ, that is, at the hieft pitch of all perfiteneffe : or fome Orations of *T. Liuius*, fuch as be both longeft and *T. Liuius.* plaineft.

Thefe bookes, I would haue him read now, a good deale at euery lecture : for he fhall not now vfe da[i]lie tranflation, but onely conftrue againe, and parfe, where

ye ſuſpect is any nede : yet, let him not omitte in theſe
bookes, his former exerciſe, in marking diligently, and
writyng orderlie out his ſix pointes. And for tranſlating, vſe you your ſelfe, euery ſecond or thyrd day, to
choſe out, ſome Epiſtle *ad Atticum,* ſome notable common place out of his Orations, or ſome other part of
Tullie, by your diſcretion, which your ſcholer may not
know where to finde : and tranſlate it you your ſelfe,
into plaine naturall Engliſh, and than giue it him to
tranſlate into Latin againe : allowyng him good ſpace
and tyme to do it, both with diligent heede, and
good aduiſement. Here his witte ſhalbe new ſet on
worke : his iudgement, for right choice, trewlie tried :
his memorie, for ſure reteyning, better exerciſed, than
by learning, any thing without the booke : and here,
how much he hath proffited, ſhall plainly appeare.
Whan he bringeth it tranſlated vnto you, bring you
forth the place of *Tullie* : lay them together : compare
the one with the other : commend his good choice,
and right placing of wordes : Shew his faultes iently,
but blame them not ouer ſharply : for, of ſuch miſſings,
ientlie admoniſhed of, proceedeth glad and good heed
taking : of good heed taking, ſpringeth chiefly knowledge, which after, groweth to perfitneſſe, if this order,
be diligentlie vſed by the ſcholer and iently handled
by the maſter : for here, ſhall all the hard pointes of
Grammer, both eaſely and ſurelie be learned vp :
which, ſcholers in common ſcholes, by making of
Latines, be groping at, with care and feare, and yet in
many yeares, they ſcarce can reach vnto them. I remember, whan I was yong, in the North, they went to
the Grammer ſchole, litle children : they came from
thence great lubbers : alwayes learning, and litle pro-
fiting : learning without booke, euery thing, vnderſtandyng with in the booke, little or nothing. Their
whole knowledge, by learning without the booke, was
tied onely to their tong and lips, and neuer aſcended
vp to the braine and head, and therfore was ſone
ſpitte out of the mouth againe : They were, as men,

always goyng, but euer out of the way: and why?
For their whole labor, or rather great toyle without
order, was euen vaine idleneffe without proffit. In deed,
they tooke great paynes about learning: but employed
fmall labour in learning : Whan by this way prefcribed
in this booke, being ftreight, plaine, and eafie, the
fcholer is always laboring with pleafure, and euer
going right on forward with proffit: Always laboring
I fay, for, or he haue conftrued, parced, twife tranflated
ouer by good aduifement, marked out his fix pointes
by fkilfull iudgement, he fhall haue neceffarie occafion,
to read ouer euery lecture, a dofen tymes, at the leaft.
Which, bicaufe he fhall do always in order, he fhall
do it always with pleafure : And pleafure allureth
loue : loue hath luft to labor : labour always obtein-
eth his purpofe, as moft trewly, both *Ariftotle* in his
Rhetoricke and *Oedipus* in *Sophocles* do teach,
faying, πᾶν γὰρ ἐκπονόυμενον ἅλιϲκε. *et cet.* Rhet. 2
and this oft reading, is the verie right In Oedip. Tyr.
folowing, of that good Counfell, which Epift. lib. 7.
Plinie doth geue to his frende *Fufcus*, faying, *Multum,
non multa.* But to my purpofe againe:

Whan, by this diligent and fpedie reading ouer,
thofe forenamed good bokes of *Tullie, Terence, Cæfar*
and *Liuie*, and by this fecond kinde of tranflating out
of your Englifh, tyme fhall breed fkill, and vfe fhall
bring perfection, than ye may trie, if you will, your
fcholer, with the third kinde of tranflation : although
the two firft wayes, by myne opinion, be, not onelie
fufficent of them felues, but alfo furer, both for the
Mafters teaching, and fcholers learnyng, than this third
way is : Which is thus. Write you in Englifh, fome
letter, as it were from him to his father, or to fome
other frende, naturallie, according to the difpofition of
the child, or fome tale, or fable, or plaine narration,
according as *Aphthonius* beginneth his exercifes of
learning, and let him tranflate it into Latin againe,
abiding in foch place, where no other fcholer may
prompe him. But yet, vfe you your felfe foch difcre-

tion for choice therein, as the matter may be within
the compas, both for wordes and sentences, of his
former learning and reading.   And now take heede,
left your fcholer do not better in fome point, than you
your felfe, except ye haue bene diligentlie exercifed
in thefe kindes of tranflating before :

I had once a profe hereof, tried by good experience,
by a deare frende of myne, whan I came firft from
Cambrige, to ferue the Queenes Maieftie, than Ladie
Elizabeth, lying at worthie Sir *Ant. Denys* in Chefton.
Iohn Whitneye, a yong ientleman, was my bedfeloe,
who willyng by good nature and prouoked by mine
aduife, began to learne the Latin tong, after the order
declared in this booke.   We began after Chriftmas : I
read vnto him *Tullie de Amicitia*, which he did euerie
day twife tranflate, out of Latin into Englifh, and out
of Englifh into Latin agayne.   About S. Laurence
tyde after, to proue how he proffited, I did chofe out
Torquatus taulke *de Amicitia*, in the lat[t]er end of the
firft booke *de finib.* becaufe that place was, the fame in
matter, like in wordes and phrafes, nigh to the forme
and facion of fentences, as he had learned before in
de Amicitia.   I did tranflate it my felfe into plaine
Englifh, and gaue it him to turne into Latin : Which
he did, fo choiflie, fo orderlie, fo without any great
miffe in the hardeft pointes of Grammer, that fome, in
feuen yeare in Grammer fcholes, yea, and fome in the
Vniuerfities to, can not do halfe fo well.   This worthie
yong Ientleman, to my greateft grief, to the great
lamentation of that whole houfe, and fpeciallie to that
moft noble Ladie, now Queene *Elizabeth* her felfe,
departed within few dayes, out of this world.

And if in any caufe a man may without offence of
God fpeake fomewhat vngodlie, furely, it was fome
grief vnto me, to fee him hie fo haftlie to God, as he
did.   A Court, full of foch yong Ientlemen, were
rather a Paradife than a Court vpon earth.   And
though I had neuer Poeticall head, to make any verfe,
in any tong, yet either loue, or for[r]ow, or both, did
wring out of me than, certaine carefull thoughtes of

my good will towardes him, which in my m[o]urning for him, fell forth, more by chance, than either by skill or vse, into this kinde of misorderlie meter.

Myne owne Iohn Whitney, now farewell, now death doth
    parte vs twaine,
No death, but partyng for a while, whom life shall
    ioyne agayne.
Therfore my hart cease sighes and sobbes, cease for[r]owes
    seede to sow,
Wherof no gaine, but greater grief, and hurtfull care
    may grow.   *[lent,*
Yet, whan I thinke vpon soch giftes of grace as God him
My losse, his gaine, I must a while, with ioyfull teares
    lament.
Yong yeares to yelde soch frute in Court, where seede of
    vice is sowne.   *[knowne.*
Is sometime read, in some place seene, amongst vs seldom
His life he ledde, Christes lore to learne, with [w]ill to
    worke the same.
He read to know, and knew to liue, and liued to praise
    his name.
So fast to frende, so foe to few, so good to euery wight,
I may well wishe, but scarcelie hope, agayne to haue in sight.
The greater ioye his life to me, his death the greater payne:
His life in Christ so surelie set, doth glad my hearte
    agayne :   *[care,*
His life so good, his death better, do mingle mirth with
My spirit with ioye, my flesh with grief, so deare a
    frend to spare.
Thus God the good, while they be good, doth take, and
    leaues vs ill,
That we should mend our sinfull life, in life to tary still.
Thus, we well left, be better rest, in heauen to take his place,
That by like life, and death, at last, we may obteine like grace.
Myne owne Iohn Whiteney agayne fairewell, a while
    thus parte in twaine,
Whom payne doth part in earth, in heauen great ioye
    shall ioyne agayne.

In this place, or I procede farder, I will now declare, by whofe authoritie I am led, and by what reafon I am moued, to thinke, that this way of d[o]uble tranflation out of one tong into an other, in either onelie, or at leaft chiefly, to be exercifed, fpeciallie of youth, for the ready and fure obteining of any tong.

There be fix wayes appointed by the beft learned men, for the learning of tonges, and encreace of eloquence, as

1. *Tranflatio linguarum.*
2. *Paraphrafis.*
3. *Metaphrafis.*
4. *Epitome.*
5. *Imitatio.*
6. *Declamatio.*

All theis be vfed, and commended, but in order, and for refpectes : as perfon, habilitie, place, and tyme fhall require. The fiue laft, be fitter, for the Mafter, than the fcholer : for men, than for children : for the vniuerfities, rather than for Grammer fcholes : yet neuerthelefle, which is, fitteft in mine opinion, for our fchole, and which is, either wholie to be refufed, or partlie to be vfed for our purpofe, I will, by good authoritie, and fome reafon, I truft perticularlie of euerie one, and largelie enough of them all, declare orderlie vnto you.

¶ *Tranflatio Linguarum.*

Tranflation, is eafie in the beginning for the fcholer, and bringeth all[fo]moch learning and great iudgement to the Mafter. It is moft common, and moft commendable of all other exercifes for youth : moft common, for all your conftructions in Grammer fcholes, be nothing els but tranflations : but becaufe they be not double tranflations, as I do require, they bring forth but fimple and fingle commoditie, and bicaufe alfo they lacke the daily vfe of writing, which is the onely thing that breedeth deepe roote, both in ye witte, for good vnderftanding, and in ye memorie, for fure keep-

ing of all that is learned. Moſt commendable alſo, and that by ye iudgement of all authors, which intreate of theis exerciſes. *Tullie* in the perſon of ɪ. de. Or.
L. *Craſſus*, whom he maketh his example of eloquence and trewe iudgement in learning, doth, not onely praiſe ſpecially, and choſe this way of tranſlation for a yong man, but doth alſo diſcommend and refuſe his owne former wont, in exerciſing *Paraphraſin et Metaphraſin*. *Paraphraſis* is, to take ſome eloquent Oration, or ſome notable common place in Latin, and expreſſe it with other wordes : *Metaphraſis* is, to take ſome notable place out of a good Poete, and turn the ſame ſens into meter, or into other wordes in Proſe. *Craſſus*, or rather *Tullie*, doth miſlike both theſe wayes, bicauſe the Author, either Orator or Poete, had choſen out before, the fitteſt wordes and apteſt compoſition for that matter, and ſo he, in ſeeking other, was driuen to vſe the worſe.

Quintilian alſo preferreth tranſlation before all other exerciſes: yet hauing a luſt, to diſſent, from Quint. x.
Tullie (as he doth in very many places, if a man read his Rhetoricke ouer aduiſedlie, and that rather of an enuious minde, than of any iuſt cauſe) doth greatlie commend *Paraphraſis*, croſſing ſpitefullie *Tullies* iudgement in refuſing the ſame : and ſo do *Ramus* and *Talæus* euen at this day in *France* to. But ſuch ſingularitie, in diſſenting from the beſt mens iudgementes, in liking onelie their owne opinions, is moch miſliked of all them, that ioyne with learning, diſcretion, and wiſedome. For he, that can neither like *Ariſtotle* in Logicke and Philoſophie, nor *Tullie* in Rhetoricke and Eloquence, will, from theſe ſteppes, likelie enough preſume, by like pride, to mount hier, to the miſliking of greater matters : that is either in Religion, to haue a diſſentious head, or in the common wealth, to haue a factious hart: as I knew one a ſtudent in Cambrige, who, for a ſingularitie, began firſt to diſſent, in the ſcholes, from *Ariſtotle*, and ſone after became a peruerſe *Arian*, againſt Chriſt and all true Religion : and

ftudied diligentlie *Origene, Bafileus*, and *S. Hierome*, onelie to gleane out of their workes, the pernicious herefies of *Celfus, Eunomius*, and *Heluidius*, whereby the Church of Chrift, was fo poyfoned withall.

But to leaue thefe hye pointes of diuinitie, furelie, in this quiet and harmeles controuerfie, for the liking, or mifliking of *Paraphrafis* for a yong fcholer, euen as far, as *Tullie* goeth beyond *Quintilian, Ramus* and *Talæus*, in perfite Eloquence, euen fo moch, by myne opinion, cum they behinde *Tullie*, for trew iudgement in teaching the fame.

*Plinius Secundus, a wife Senator, of great experience, excellentlie learned him felfe, a liberall Patrone of learned men, and the purest writer, in myne opinion, of all his age, I except not *Suetonius*, his two fchole-mafters *Quintilian* and *Tacitus*, nor yet his moft ex-cellent learned Vncle, the Elder *Plinius*, doth expreffe in an Epiftle to his frende *Fufcus*, many good wayes for order in ftudie : but he beginneth with tranflation, and preferreth it to all the reft : and becaufe his wordes be notable, I will recite them.

Vtile in primis, vt multi præcipiunt, ex Græco in Lati-num, et ex Latino vertere in Græcum : Quo genere exercitationis, proprietas splendorque verborum, ap-ta structura sententiarum, figurarum copia et ex-plicandi vis colligitur. Præterea, imitatione optimo-rum, facultas similia inueniendi paratur : et quæ legentem, fefelliffent, tranfferentem fugere non pof-funt. Intelligentia ex hoc, et iudicium acquiritur.

Ye perceiue, how *Plinie* teacheth, that by his exer-cife of double tranflating, is learned, eafely, fenfiblie, by litle and litle, not onelie all the hard congruities of Grammer, the choice of apteft wordes, the right fram-ing of wordes and fentences, cumlines of figures and formes, fitte for euerie matter, and proper for euerie tong, but that which is greater alfo, in marking dayly,

* Plinius Se-cundus. Plinius dedit Quintiliano præceptori suo, in matrimonium filiæ, 50000 [60000] numum.

Epist. lib. 7, Epist. 9,

and folowing diligentlie thus, the fteppes of the beft
Aut[h]ors, like inuention of Argumentes, like order in
difpofition, like vtterance in Elocution, is eafelie gathered vp : whereby your fcholer fhall be brought not
onelie to like eloquence, but alfo, to all trewe vnderftanding and right iudgement, both for writing and
fpeaking. And where *Dionyf. Halicarnaffæus* hath
written two excellent bookes, the one, *de delectu opti-
morum verborum*, the which, I feare, is loft, the other,
of the right framing of wordes and fentences, which
doth remaine yet in Greeke, to the great proffet of all
them, that trewlie ftudie for eloquence, yet this waie
of double tranflating, fhall bring the whole proffet of
both thefe bookes to a diligent fcholer, and that eafelie
and pleafantlie, both for fitte choice of wordes, and
apt compofition of fentences. And by theis authorities
and reafons am I moued to thinke, this waie of double
tranflating, either onelie or chieflie, to be fitteft, for the
fpedy and perfit atteyning of any tong. And for fpedy
atteyning, I durft venture a good wager, if a fcholer,
in whom is aptnes, loue, diligence, and conftancie,
would but tranflate, after this forte, one litle booke in
Tullie, as *de fenectute*, with two Epiftles, the firft *ad Q.
fra :* the other *ad Lentulum*, the laft faue one, in the
firft booke, that fcholer, I fay, fhould cum to a better
knowledge in the Latin tong, than the moft part do,
that fpend foui or fiue yeares, in toffing all the rules of
Grammer in common fcholes. In deede this one
booke with thefe two Epiftles, is not fufficient to
affourde all Latin wordes (which is not neceffarie for
a yong fcholer to know) but it is able to furnifhe him
fully, for all pointes of Grammer, with the right placing,
ordering, and vfe of wordes in all kinde of matter.
And why not ? for it is read, that *Dion. Pruffæus*, that
wife Philofopher, and excellent orator of all his tyme,
did cum to the great learning and vtterance that was
in him, by reading and folowing onelie two bookes,
Phædon Platonis, and *Demofthenes* moft notable oration
περὶ παραπρεσβείας. And a better, and nerer example

herein, may be, our moſt noble Queene *Elizabeth*, who
neuer toke yet, Greeke nor Latin Grammer in her
hand, after the firſt declining of a nowne and a verbe,
but onely by this double tranſlating of *Demoſthenes* and
Iſocrates dailie without miſſing euerie forenone, for the
ſpace of a yeare or two, hath atteyned to ſoch a perfite
vnderſtanding in both the tonges, and to ſoch a readie
vtterance of the latin, and that wyth ſoch a iudgement,
as they be fewe in nomber in both the vniuerſities, or
els where in England, that be, in both tonges, comparable with her Maieſtie.   And to conclude in a
ſhort rowme, the commodities of double tranſlation,
ſurelie the mynde by dailie marking, firſt, the cauſe
and matter : than, the wordes and phraſes : next, the
order and compoſition : after, the reaſon and argumentes : than the formes and figures of both the
tonges : laſtelie, the meaſure and compas of euerie
ſentence, muſt nedes, by litle and litle drawe vnto it
the like ſhape of eloquence, as the author doth vſe,
which is re[a]d.

    And thus much for double tranſlation.

Paraphraſis.

Lib. x.   *Paraphraſis*, the ſecond point, is not
onelie to expreſſe at large with moe wordes, but to
ſtriue and contend (as *Quintilian* ſaith) to tranſlate the
beſt latin authors, into other latin wordes, as many or
thereaboutes.

    This waie of exerciſe was vſed firſt by *C. Crabo*, and
taken vp for a while, by *L. Craſſus*, but ſone after,
vpon dewe profe thereof, reiected iuſtlie by *Craſſus*
and *Cicero* : yet allowed and made ſterling agayne by
M. Quintilian : neuertheleſſe, ſhortlie after, by better
aſſaye, diſalowed of his owne ſcholer *Plinius Secundus*,
who termeth it rightlie thus *Audax contentio*.   It is a
bold compariſon in deede, to thinke to ſay better, than
that is beſt.   Soch turning of the beſt into worſe, is
much like the turning of good wine, out of a faire

fweete flagon of filuer, into a foule muftie bottell of ledder: or, to turne pure gold and filuer, into foule braffe and copper.

Soch kinde of *Paraphrafis*, in turning, chopping, and changing, the beft to worfe, either in the mynte or fcholes, (though *M. Brokke* and *Quintilian* both fay the contrary) is moch mifliked of the beft and wifeft men. I can better allow an other kinde of *Paraphrafis*, to turne rude and barbarus, into proper and eloquent: which neuertheleffe is an exercife, not fitte for a fcholer, but for a perfite mafter, who in plentie hath good choife, in copie hath right iudgement, and grounded fkill, as did appeare to be in *Sebaftian Caftalio*, in tranflating *Kemppes* booke *de Imitando Chrifto*.

But to folow *Quintilianus* aduife to *Paraphrafis*, were euen to take paine, to feeke the worfe and fowler way, whan the plaine and fairer is occupied before your eyes.

The olde and beft authors that euer wrote, were content if occafion required to fpeake twife of one matter, not to change the wordes, but ῥητῶς, that is, worde for worde to expreffe it againe. For they thought, that a matter, well expreffed with fitte wordes and apt compofition, was not to be altered, but liking it well their felues, they thought it would alfo be well allowed of others.

A fcholemafter (foch one as I require) knoweth that I fay trewe.

He readeth in *Homer*, almoft in euerie *Homerus.* booke, and fpeciallie in *Secundo et nono Iliados*, not onelie fom verfes, but whole leaues, not to be altered with new, but to be vttered with [Ι]λ $\left\{ \begin{array}{l} \text{2.} \\ \text{9.} \end{array} \right.$ the old felfe fame wordes.

He knoweth, that *Xenophon*, writing *Xenophon.* twife of *Agefilaus*, once in his life, againe in the hiftorie of the Greekes, in one matter, kepeth alwayes the felfe fame wordes. He doth the like, fpeaking of *Socrates*, both in the beginning of his Apologie and in the laft ende of ἀπομνημονευμάτων.

Demosthenes.   *Demosthenes* alfo in 4. *Philippica*, doth borow his owne wordes vttered before in his oration *de Cherfonefo*. He doth the like, and that more at large, in his orations, againft *Andration* and *Timocrates*.

Cicero.   In latin alfo, *Cicero* in fom places, and

Virgilius.   *Virgil* in mo, do repeate one matter, with the felfe fame wordes. Thies excellent authors, did thus, not for lacke of wordes, but by iudgement and fkill : whatfoeuer, other, more curious, and leffe fkilfull, do thinke, write, and do.

Paraphrafis neuertheleffe hath good place in learning, but not, but myne opinion, for any fcholer, but is onelie to be left to a perfite Mafter, eyther to expound openlie a good author withall, or to compare priuatelie, for his owne exercife, how fome notable place of an excellent author, may be vttered with other fitte wordes : But if ye alter alfo, the compofition, forme, and order than that is not *Paraphrafis*, but *Imitatio*, as I will fullie declare in fitter place.

The fcholer fhall winne nothing by *Paraphrafis*, but onelie, if we may beleue *Tullie*, to choofe worfe wordes, to place them out of order, to feare ouermoch the iudgement of the mafter, to miflike ouermoch the hardnes of learning, and by vfe, to gather vp faultes, which hardlie will be left of againe.

The mafter in teaching it, fhall rather encreafe hys owne labo[u]r, than his fcholers proffet : for when the fcholer fhall bring vnto his mafter a peece of *Tullie* or *Cæfar* turned into other latin, then muft the mafter cum to *Quintilians* goodlie leffon *de Emendatione*, which, (as he faith) is the moft profitable part of teaching, but not in myne opinion, and namelie for youthe in Grammer fcholes. For the mafter nowe taketh double paynes : firft, to marke what is amiffe : againe, to inuent what may be fayd better. And here perchance, a verie good mafter may eafelie both deceiue himfelfe, and lead his fchol[l]er[s] into error.

It requireth greater learning, and deeper iudgement, than is to be hoped for at any fcholemafters

hand : that is, to be able alwaies learnedlie and perfitelie.

> *Mutare quod ineptum est :*
> *Tranfmutare quod peruerfum est :*
> *Replere quod deeft ;*
> *Detrahere quod obest :*
> *Expungere quod inane eft.*

And that, which requireth more fkill, and deaper
confideracion.

> *Premere tumentia :*
> *Extollere humilia :*
> *Astringere luxuriantia :*
> *Componere diffoluta.*

The mafter may here onelie ftumble, and perchance
faull in teaching, to the marring and mayning of the
Scholer in learning, whan it is a matter, of moch
readyng, of great learning, and tried iudgement, to
make trewe difference betwixt.

> *Sublime, et Tumidum :*
> *Grande, et immodicum :*
> *Decorum, et ineptum :*
> *Perfectum, et nimium.*

Some men of our time, counted perfite Maifters of
eloquence, in their owne opinion the beft, in other
mens iudgements very good, as *Omphalius* euerie
where, *Sadoletus* in many places, yea alfo my frende
Oforius, namelie in his Epiftle to the Queene and in
his whole booke *de Iufticia,* haue fo ouer reached them
felues, in making trew difference in the poyntes afore
rehearfed, as though they had bene brought vp in
fome fchole in *Afia,* to learne to decline rather then
in *Athens* with *Plato, Ariftotle,* and *Demofthenes,* (from
whence *Tullie* fetched his eloquence) to vnderftand,
what in euerie matter, to be fpoken or written on, is,
in verie deede, *Nimium, Satis, Parum,* that is for to
fay, to all confiderations, *Decorum,* which, as it is the
hardeft point, in all learning, fo is it the faireft and
onelie marke, that fcholers, in all their ftudie, muft
alwayes fhote at, if they purpofe an other day to be,

either founde in Religion, or wife and difcrete in any vocation of the common wealth.

Agayne, in the loweft degree, it is no low point of learning and iudgement for a Scholemafter, to make trewe difference betwixt.

> *Humile et deprefsum:*
> *Lene et remiffum:*
> *Siccum et aridum:*
> *Exile et macrum:*
> *Inaffeĉtatum et negleĉtum.*

In thefe poyntes, fome, louing *Melancthon* well, as he was well worthie, but yet not confidering well nor wifelie, how he of nature, and all his life and ftudie by iudgement was wholly fpent in *genere Difciplinabili*, that is, in teaching, reading, and expounding plainlie and aptlie fchole matters, and therefore imployed thereunto a fitte, fenfible, and caulme kinde of fpeaking and writing, fome I fay, with very well liuyng [likyng?], but not with verie well weying *Melanĉthones* doinges, do frame them felues a ftyle, cold, leane, and weake, though the matter be neuer fo warme and earneft, not moch vnlike vnto one, that had a pleafure, in a roughe, raynie, winter day, to clothe him felfe with nothing els, but a demie bukram caffok, plaine without pl[a]ites, and fingle without lyning : which will neither beare of winde nor wether, nor yet kepe out the funne, in any hote day.

Some fuppofe, and that by good reafon, that *Melanĉthon* him felfe came to this low kinde of writing, by vfing ouer moch *Paraphrafis* in reading : For ftudying therbie to make euerie thing ftreight and eafie, in fmothing and playning all things to much, neuer leaueth, whiles the fence it felfe be left, both lowfe and lafie. And fome of thofe *Paraphrafis* of *Melanĉthon* be fet out in Printe, as, *Pro Archia Poeta, et Marco Marcello* : But a fcholer, by myne opinion, is better occupied in playing or fleping, than in fpendyng time, not onelie vainlie but alfo harmefullie, in foch a kinde of exercife.

Paraphrasis in vse of teaching hath hurt *Melancthons* stile in writing.

If a Mafter woulde haue a perfite example to folow,

how, in *Genere sublimi*, to auoide *Nimium*, or in *Medi-
ocri*, to atteyne *Satis*, or in *Humili*, to exchew *Parum*,
let him read diligently for the firſt, *Secundam* Cicero.
Philippicam, for the meane, *De Natura Deorum*, and
for the loweſt, *Partitiones*. Or, if in an other tong, ye
looke for like example, in like perfection, for all thoſe
three degrees, read *Pro Cteſiphonte, Ad* Demosthenes.
Leptinem, et Contra Olympiodorum, and, what witte,
Arte, and diligence is hable to affourde, ye ſhall
plainely ſee.

For our tyme, the odde man to performe all three
perfitlie, whatſoeuer he doth, and to know the way to
do them ſkilfullie, whan ſo euer he liſt, is, in my poore
opinion, *Iohannes Sturmius*.   Ioan. Stur.

He alſo councelleth all ſcholers to beware of *Paraphraſis*, except it be, from worſe to better, from rude
and barbarous, to proper and pure latin, and yet no
man to exerciſe that neyther, except ſoch one, as is
alreadie furniſhed with plentie of learning, and grounded
with ſtedfaſt iudgement before.

All theis faultes, that thus manie wiſe men do finde
with the exerciſe of *Paraphraſis*, in turning the beſt
latin, into other, as good as they can, that is, ye may
be ſure, into a great deale worſe, than it was, both in right
choice for proprietie, and trewe placing, for good order
is committed alſo commonlie in all common ſcholes,
by the ſcholemaſters, in toſſing and trobling yong wittes
(as I ſayd in the beginning) with that boocherlie feare
in making of Latins.

Therefore, in place of Latines for yong ſcholers,
and *Paraphraſis* for the maſters, I wold haue double
tranſlation ſpecially vſed. For, in double tranſlating
a perfite peece of *Tullie* or *Cæſar*, neyther the ſcholer
in learning, nor ye Maſter in teaching can erre. A
true tochſtone, a ſure metwand lieth before both their
eyes. For, all right congruitie : proprietie of wordes :
order in ſentences : the right imitation, to inuent good
matter, to diſpoſe it in good order, to confirme it with
good reaſon, to expreſſe any purpoſe fitlie and orderlie,

is learned thus, both eafelie and perfitlie: Yea, to miffe fomtyme in this kinde of tranflation, bringeth more proffet, than to hit right, either in *Paraphrafi* or making of Latins. For though ye fay well, in a latin making, or in a *Paraphrafis*, yet you being but in do[u]bte, and vncertayne whether ye faie well or no, ye gather and lay vp in memorie, no fure frute of learning thereby: But if ye fault in tranflation, ye ar[e] eafelie taught, how perfitlie to amende it, and fo well warned, how after to exchew, all foch faultes againe.

Paraphrafis therefore, by myne opinion, is not meete for Grammer fcholes: nor yet verie fitte for yong men in the vniuerfitie, vntill ftudie and tyme, haue bred in them, perfite learning, and ftedfaft iudgement.

There is a kinde of *Paraphrafis*, which may be vfed, without all hurt, to moch proffet: but it ferueth onely the Greke and not the latin, nor no other tong, as to alter *linguam Ionicam aut Doricam* into *meram Atticam*: A notable example there is left vnto vs by a notable learned man *Diony: Halicarn*: who, in his booke, περὶ συντάξεος, doth tranflate the goodlie ftorie of *Candaulus* and *Gyges* in 1 *Herodoti*, out of *Ionica lingua*, into *Atticam*. Read the place, and ye fhall take, both pleafure and proffet, in conference of it. A man, that is exercifed in reading, *Thucydides*, *Xenophon*, *Plato*, and *Demofthenes*, in vfing to turne, like places of *Herodotus*, after like forte, fhold fhortlie cum to fuch a knowledge, in vnderftanding, fpeaking, and writing the Greeke tong, as fewe or none hath yet atteyned in England. The like exercife out of *Dorica lingua* may be alfo vfed, if a man take that litle booke of *Plato*, *Timæus Locrus*, *de Animo et natura*, which is written *Dorice*, and turne it into foch Greeke, as *Plato* vfeth in otherworkes. The booke, is but twoleaues: and the laborwold be, but twoweekes: but furelie the proffet, for eafie vnderftanding, and trewe writing the Greeke tonge, wold conteruaile wyth the toile, that fom men taketh, in otherwife coldlie reading that tonge, two yeares.

And yet, for the latin tonge, and for the exercife of

Paraphrasis, in those places of latin, that can not be bettered, if some yong man, excellent of witte, couragious in will, lustie of nature, and desirous to contend euen with the best latin, to better it, if he can, surelie I commend his forwardnesse, and for his better instruction therein, I will set before him, as notable an example of *Paraphrasis*, as is in Record of learning. *Cicero* him selfe, doth contend, in two sondrie places, to expresse one matter, with diuerse wordes: and that is *Paraphrasis*, saith *Quintillian.* The matter I suppose, is taken out of *Panætius*: and therefore being translated out of Greeke at diuers times, is vttered for his purpose, with diuers wordes and formes: which kind of exercise, for perfite learned men, is verie profitable.

2. De Finib.

a. *Homo enim Rationem habet à natura menti datam quæ, et causas rerum et confecutiones videt, et fimilitudines, transfert, et difiuncta coniungit, et cum præfentibus futura copulat, omnemque complectitur vitæ confequentis ftatum.* **b.** *Eademque ratio facit hominem hominum appetendum, cumque his, natura, et fermone in vfu congruentem: vt profectus à caritate domefticorum ac fuorum, currat longius, et fe implicet, primo Ciuium, deinde omnium mortalium focietati: vtque non fibi foli fe natum meminerit, fed patriæ, fed fuis, vt exigua pars ipfi relinquatur.* **c.** *Et quoniam eadem natura cupiditatem ingenuit homini veri inueniendi, quod facillimè apparet, cum vacui curis, etiam quid in cælo fiat, fcire avemus, etc.*

1. Officiorum.

a *Homo autem, qui rationis est particeps, per quam confequentia cernit, et caufas rerum videt, earumque progreffus, et quafi antecefsiones non ignorat, fimilitudines, comparat, rebufque præfentibus adiungit, atque annectit futuras, facile totius vitæ curfum videt, ad eamque degendam præparat res necefsarias.* **b.** *Eademque natura vi rationis hominem conciliat homini, et ad Orationis et ad vitæ focietatem: ingeneratque imprimis præcipuum* *quendam amorem in eos, qui procreati funt, impellitque vt hominum cœtus et celebrari inter fe, et fibi obediri [a fe obiri] velit, ob eafque caufas studeat par.re ea, quæ fuppeditent ad cultum et ad victum, nec fibi foli, fed coniugi, liberis, cæterifque quos charos habeat, tuerique debeat. c. Quæ cura exfufcitat etiam animos, et maiores ad rem gerendam facit : imprimifque hominis est propria veri inquifitio atque inueftigatio : ita cum fumus neceffarijs negocijs curifque vacui, tum auemus aliquid videre, audire, addif-rere, cognitionemque rerum mirabilium, etc.*

The conference of thefe two places, conteinyng fo excellent a peece of learning, as this is, expreffed by fo worthy a witte, as *Tullies* was, muft needes bring great pleafure and proffit to him, that maketh trew counte, of learning and honeftie. But if we had the *Greke* Author, the firft Patterne of all, and therby to fee, how *Tullies* witte did worke at diuerfe tymes, how, out of one excellent Image, might be framed two other, one in face and fauor, but fomwhat differing in forme, figure, and color, furelie, fuch a peece of worke-manfhip compared with the Paterne it felfe, would better pleafe the eafe of honeft, wife, and learned myndes, than two of the faireft Venuffes, that euer Apelles made.

And thus moch, for all kinde of *Paraphrafis*, fitte or vnfit, for Scholers or other, as I am led to thinke, not onelie, by mine owne experience, but chiefly by the authoritie and iudgement of thofe, whom I my felfe would gladlieft folow, and do counfell all myne to do the fame : not contendyng with any other, that will otherwife either thinke or do.

Metaphrafis.

This kinde of exercife is all one with *Paraphrafis*, faue it is out of verfe, either into profe, or into fome other kinde of meter : or els, out of profe into verfe, *Plato* in *Phædone.* which was *Socrates* exercife and paftime (as *Plato* reporteth) when he was in prifon,

to tranflate *Æfopes Fabules* into verfe. *Quintilian* doth
greatlie praife alfo this exercife : but bicaufe *Tullie*
doth difalow it in young men, by myne opinion, it
were not well to vfe it [in] Grammer Scholes, euen for
the felfe fame caufes, that be recited againft *Paraphrafis*. And therfore, for the vfe or mifufe of it, the
fame is to be thought, that is fpoken of *Paraphrafis*
before. This was *Sulpitius* exercife : and he gathering
vp thereby, a Poeticall kinde of talke, is iuftlie named
of *Cicero, grandis et Tragicus Orator :* which I think
is fpoken, not for his praife, but for other mens warning, to exchew the like faulte. Yet neuertheles, if our
Scholemafter for his owne inftruction, is defirous, to fee
a perfite example hereof, I will recite one, which I
thinke, no man is fo bold, will fay, that he can amend
it : and that is *Chrifes* the Prieftes Oration to the
Grekes, in the beginnyng of *Homers Ilias*, Hom. 1. Il.
turned excellentlie into profe by *Socrates* Pla. 3. Rep.
him felfe, and that aduifedlie and purpofelie for other
to folow : and therfore he calleth this exercife, in the
fame place, μίμησις, that is, *Imitatio*, which is moft
trew : but, in this booke, for teachyng fake, I will
name it *Metaphrafis*, reteinyng the word, that all
teachers, in this cafe, do vfe.

Homerus I. Ιλιαδ.

ὁ γὰρ ἦλθε θοὰς ἐπὶ νῆας Ἀχαιῶν,
λυσόμενός τε θύγατρα, φέρων τ᾽ ἀπερείσι᾽ ἄποινα,
στέμματ᾽ ἔχων ἐν χερσὶν ἑκηβόλου Ἀπόλλωνος,
χρυσέῳ ἀνὰ σκήπτρῳ· καὶ ἐλίσσετο πάντας Ἀχαιοὺς,
Ἀτρείδα δὲ μάλιστα δύω, κοσμήτορε λαῶν.

Ἀτρείδαί τε, καὶ ἄλλοι ἐϋκνήμιδες Ἀχαιοὶ,
ὑμῖν μὲν θεοὶ δοῖεν, Ὀλύμπια δώματ᾽ ἔχοντες,
ἐκπέρσαι Πριάμοιο πόλιν, εὖ δ᾽ οἴκαδ᾽ ἱκέσθαι·
παῖδα δ᾽ ἐμοί λῦσαί τε φίλην, τὰ τ᾽ ἄποινα δέχεσθαι,
ἁζόμενοι Διὸς υἱὸν ἑκηβόλου Ἀπόλλωνα.

ἔνθ᾽ ἄλλοι μὲν πάντες ἐπευφήμησαν Ἀχαιοὶ
αἰδεῖσθαι θ᾽ ἱερῆα, καὶ αγλαὰ δέχθαι ἄποινα·
ἀλλ᾽ οὐκ Ἀτρείδῃ Ἀγαμέμνονι ἥνδανε θυμῷ,

ἀλλὰ κακῶς ἀφίει, κρατερὸν δ' ἐπὶ μῦθον ἔτελλεν.

μή σε, γέρον, κοίλησιν ἐγὼ παρὰ νηυσὶ κιχείω,
ἢ νῦν δηθύνοντ', ἢ ὕστερον αὖτις ἰόντα,
μή νύ τοι οὐ χραίσμῃ σκῆπτρον, καὶ στέμμα θεοῖο.
τὴν δ' ἐγὼ οὐ λύσω, πρίν μιν καὶ γῆρας ἔπεισιν,
ἡμετέρῳ ἐνὶ οἴκῳ, ἐν Ἄργεϊ, τηλόθι πάτρης,
ἱστὸν ἐποιχομένην, καὶ ἐμὸν λέγος ἀντιόωσαν·
ἀλλ' ἴθι, μή μ' ἐρέθιζε· σαώτερος ὥς κε νέηαι.

ὣς ἔφατ'· ἔδδεισεν δ' ὁ γέρων, καὶ ἐπείθετο μύθῳ·
βῆ δ' ἀκέων παρὰ θῖνα πολυφλοίσβοιο θαλάσσης,
πολλὰ δ' ἔπειτ' ἀπάνευθε κιὼν ἠρᾶθ' ὁ γεραιὸς
Ἀπόλλωνι ἄνακτι, τὸν ἠΰκομος, τέκε Λητώ·

κλῦθί' μευ, ἀργυρότοξ', ὃς Χρύσην ἀμφιβέβηκας,
κίλλαν τε ζαθέην, Τενέδοιό τε ἶφι ἀνάσσεις,
σμινθεῦ· ἔι ποτέ τοι χαρίεντ' ἐπὶ νηὸν ἔρεψα,
ἢ εἰ δή ποτέ τοι κατὰ πίονα μηρί' ἔκηα
ταύρων ἠδ' αἰγῶν, τόδε μοι κρήηνον ἐέλδωρ·
τίσειαν Δαναοὶ ἐμὰ δάκρυα σοῖσι βέλεσσιν.

Socrates in 3 *de Rep* ſaith thus.

Φράσω γὰρ ἄνευ μέτρου,
οὐ γὰρ εἰμι ποιητικός.

ἦλθεν ὁ Χρύσης τῆς τε θυγατρὸς λύτρα φέρων καὶ ἱκέτης
τῶν Ἀχαιῶν, μάλιστα δὲ τῶν βασιλέων : καὶ εὔχετο,
ἐκείνοις μὲν τοὺς θεοὺς δοῦναι ἑλόντας τὴν Τροίαν, αὐτοὺς
δὲ σωθῆναι, τὴν δὲ θυγατέρα οἱ αὐτῷ λῦσαι, δεξαμένους
ἄποινα, καὶ τὸν θεὸν αἰδεσθέντας. Τοιαῦτα δὲ εἰπόντος
αὐτοῦ, οἱ μὲν ἄλλοι ἐσέβοντο καὶ συνῄνουν, ὁ δὲ Ἀγα-
μεμνων ἠγρίαινεν, ἐντελλόμενος νῦν τε ἀπιέναι, καὶ αὖθις
μὴ ἐλθεῖν, μὴ αὐτῷ τό τε σκῆπτρον, καὶ τὰ τοῦ θεοῦ
στέμματα οὐκ ἐπαρκέσοι. πρὶν δὲ λυθῆναι αὐτοῦ θυγατέρα,
ἐν Ἄργει ἔφη γηράσειν μετὰ οὐ. ἀπιέναι δὲ ἐκέλευε, καὶ μὴ
ἐρεθίζειν, ἵνα σῶς οἴκαδε ἔλθοι· ὁ δὲ πρεσβύτης ἀκούσας
ἔδεισέ τε καὶ ἀπῄει σιγῇ, ἀποχωρήσας δ' ἐκ τοῦ στρα-
τοπέδου πολλὰ τῷ Ἀπόλλωνι εὔχετο, τάς τε ἐπωνυμίας
τοῦ θεοῦ ἀνακαλῶν καὶ ὑπομιμνῄσκων καὶ ἀπαιτῶν, εἴ τι
πώποτε ἢ ἐν ναῶν οἰκοδομήσειν ἢ ἐν ἱερῶν θυσίας κεχα-
ρισμένον δωρήσαιτο. ὧν δὴ χάριν κατεύχετο τῖσαι τοὺς
Ἀχαιοὺς τὰ ἃ δάκρυα τοῖς ἐκείνου βέλεσιν.

To compare *Homer* and *Plato* together, two wonders of nature and arte for witte and eloquence, is moſt pleaſant and profitable, for a man of ripe iudgement. *Platos* turning of *Homer* in this place, doth not ride a loft in Poeticall termes, but goeth low and ſoft on foote, as proſe and *Pedestris oratio* ſhould do. If *Sulpitius* had had *Platos* conſideration, in right vſing this exerciſe, he had not deſerued the name of *Tragicus Orator,* who ſhould rather haue ſtudied to expreſſe *vim Demosthenes,* than *furorem Poetæ,* how good ſo euer he was, whom he did follow.

And therfore would I haue our Scholemaſter wey well together *Homer* and *Plato,* and marke diligentlie theſe foure pointes, what is kept; what is added ; what is left out : what is changed, either, in choiſe of wordes, or forme of ſentences; which foure pointes, be the right tooles, to handle like a workeman, this kinde of worke : as our Scholer ſhall better vnderſtand, when he hath be[e]ne a good while in the Vniuerſitie : to which tyme and place, I chiefly remitte this kind of exerciſe.

And bicauſe I euer thought examples to be the beſt kinde of teaching, I will recite a golden ſentence out of that Poete, which is next vnto *Homer,* not onelie in tyme, but alſo in worthines : which hath beene a paterne for many worthie wittes to follow, by this kind of *Metaphrasis,* but I will content my ſelfe, with foure workemen, two in *Greke,* and two in *Latin,* ſoch, as in both the tonges, wiſer and worthier, can not be looked for. Surelie, no ſtone ſet in gold by moſt cunning workemen, is in deed, if right counte be made, more worthie the looking on, than this golden ſentence, diuerſlie wrought upon, by ſoch foure excellent Maſters.

Ⱨeſioduſ. 2.

1. οὗτος μὲν πανάριστος, ὃς αὐτῷ πάντα νοήσῃ,
   φρασσάμενος τά κ' ἔπειτα καὶ ἐς τέλος ᾖσιν ἀμείνω
2. ἐσθλὸς δ' αὖ κάκεῖνος, ὃς εὖ εἰπόντι πίθηται.
3. ὃς δέ κε μήτ' αὐτὸς νοέῃ, μήτ' ἄλλου ἀκούων
   ἐν θυμῷ βάλληται, ὁ δ' αὖτ' ἀχρήϊος ἀνήρ.

¶ Thus rudelie turned into bafe Englifh.

1. *That man in wifedome paffeth all,*
   to know the beft who hath a head:
2. *And meetlie wife eeke counted fhall,*
   who yeildes him felfe to wife mens read.
3. *Who hath no witte, nor none will heare,*
   amongeft all fooles the belles may beare.

Sophocles *in Antigone.*

1.   Φήμ' ἔγωγε πρεσβεύειν πολὺ,
   Φῦναι τὸν ἄνδρα πάντ' ἐπιστήμης πλέων:
2. Εἰ δ' οὖν (φιλεῖ γὰρ τοῦτο μὴ ταύτῃ ῥέπειν),
   Καὶ τῶν λεγόντων εὖ καλὸν τὸ μανθάνειν.

Marke the wifedome of *Sophocles*, in leauyng out the laft fentence, becaufe it was not cumlie for the fonne to vfe it to his father.

¶ D. Basileus *in his Exhortation to youth.*

Μέμνησθε τοῦ Ἡσιόδου, ὅς φησι, ἄριστον μὲν εἶναι τὸν παρ' ἑαυτοῦ τὰ δέοντα ξυνορῶντα. 2. Ἐσθλὸν δὲ κἀκεῖνον, τὸν τοῖς, παρ' ἑτέρων ὑποδειχθεῖσιν ἑπόμενον. 3. τὸν δὲ πρὸς οὐδέτερον ἐπιτήδειον ἀχρεῖον εἶναι πρὸς ἅπαντα.

¶ M. Cic. Pro. A. Cluentio.

1. *Sapientifsimum effe dicunt eum, cui, quod opus fit, ipfi veniat in mentem:* 2. *Proxime accedere illum, qui alterius bene inuentis obtemperet.* 3. *In ftulticia contra eft: minus enim ftultus eft is, cui nihil in mentem venit, quam ille, qui, quod ftultè alteri venit in mentem comprobat.*

Cicero doth not plainlie expreffe the laft fentence, but doth inuent it fitlie for his purpofe, to taunt the folie and fimplicitie in his aduerfarie *Actius*, not weying ing wifelie, the fubtle doynges of *Chryfogonus* and *Stalenus.*

¶ Tit. Livius *in Orat. Minutij.* Lib. 22.

1. *Sæpe ego audiui milites; eum primum effe virum, qui ipfe confulat, quid in rem fit:* 2. *Secundum eum, qui*

bene monenti obediat: 3. *Qui, nec ipfe confulere, nec alieri parere fci*[*a*]*t, eum extremi effe ingenij.*

Now, which of all thefe foure, *Sophocles, S. Bafil, Cicero,* or *Liuie,* hath expreffed *Hefiodus* beft, the iudgement is as hard, as the workemanfhip of euerie one is moft excellent in deede. An other example out of the *Latin* tong alfo I will recite, for the worthines of the workeman therof, and that is *Horace,* who hath fo turned the begynning of *Terence Eunuchus,* as doth worke in me, a pleafant admiration, as oft fo euer, as I compare thofe two places togither. And though euerie Mafter, and euerie good Scholer to, do know the places, both in *Terence* and *Horace,* yet I will fet them heare, in one place togither, that with more plea-fure, they may be compared together.

¶ Terentius in Eunucho.

Quid igitur faciam? non eam? ne nunc quidem cum ac-ceffor vltrò? an potius ita me comparem, non perpeti mere-tricum contumelias? exclufit: reuocat, redeam? non, fi me obfecret. PARMENO a little after. *Here, quæ res in se neque confilium neque modum habet vllum, eam confilio regere non potes. In Amore hæc omnia infunt vitia, in-iuriæ, fuffpiciones, inimicitiæ, induciæ, bellum, pax rurfum. Incerta hæc fi tu poftules ratione certa facere, nihilo plus agas, quam fi des operam, vt cum ratione infanias.*

¶ Horatius, lib. Ser. 2. Saty. 3.

Nec nunc cum me vocet vltro,
Accedam? an potius mediter finire dolores?
Exclufit: reuocat, redeam? non fi obfecret. Ecce
Seruus non Paulo fapientior: ò Here, quæ res
Nec modum habet, neque confilium, ratione modóque
Tractari non vult. In amore, hæc funt mala, bellum,
Pax rurfum: hæc fi quis tempeftatis propè ritu
Mobilia, et cæca fluitantia forte, laboret
Reddere certa, fibi nihilò plus explicet, ac fi
Infanire paret certa natione, modóque.

This exercife may bring moch profite to ripe heads,

and ftayd iudgementes: bicaufe in traueling in it, the mynde muft nedes be verie attentiue, and bufilie occupied, in turning and toffing it felfe many wayes: and conferryng with great pleafure, the varietie of worthie wittes and iudgementes togither: But this harme may fone cum therby, and namelie to yong Scholers, leffe, in feeking other wordes, and new forme of fentences, they chance vpon the worfe: for the which onelie caufe, *Cicero* thinketh this exercife not to be fit for yong men.

Epitome.

This is a way of ftudie, belonging, rather to matter, than to wordes: to memorie, than to vtterance: to thofe that be learned alreadie, and hath fmall place at all amonges yong fcholers in Grammer fcholes. It may proffet priuately fome learned men, but it hath hurt generallie learning it felfe, very moch. For by it haue we loft whole *Trogus*, the beft part of *T. Liuius*, the goodlie Dictionarie of *Pompeius feftus*, a great deale of the Ciuill lawe, and other many notable bookes, for the which caufe, I do the more miffike this exercife, both in old and yong.

Epitome, is good priuatelie for himfelfe that doth worke it, but ill commonlie for all other that vfe other mens labor therein: a filie poore kinde of ftudie, not vnlike to the doing of thofe poore folke, which neyther till, nor fowe, nor reape themfelues, but gleane by ftelth, vpon other mens growndes. Soch haue emptie barnes, for deare yeares.

Grammar fcholes haue fewe *Epitomes* to hurt them, except *Epitheta Textoris,* and fuch beggarlie gatheringes, as *Horman, Whittington,* and other like vulgares for making of latines: yea I do wifhe, that all rules for yong fcholers, were fhorter than they be. For without doute, *Grammatica* it felfe, is fooner and furer learned by examples of good authors, than by the naked rewles of *Grammarians.* *Epitome* hurteth more, in the vniuerfities and ftudie of Philofophie: but moft of all, in diuinitie it felfe.

In deede bookes of common places be verie neceſſarie, to induce a man, into an orderlie generall knowledge, how to referre orderlie all that he readeth, *ad
certa rerum Capita*, and not wander in ſtudie.   And
to that end did *P. Lombardus* the maſter of ſentences
and *Ph. Melancthon* in our daies, write two notable
bookes of common places.

But to dwell in *Epitomes* and bookes of common
places, and not to binde himſelfe dailie by orderlie
ſtudie, to reade with all diligence, principallie the
holyeſt ſcripture and withall, the beſt Doctors, and ſo
to learne to make trewe difference betwixt, the authoritie of the one, and the Counſell of the other, maketh
ſo many ſeeming, and ſonburnt miniſters as we haue,
whoſe learning is gotten in a ſommer heat, and waſhed
away, with a Chriſtmas ſnow againe: who neuertheleſſe, are leſſe to be blamed, than thoſe blind buſſardes,
who in late yeares, of wilfull malicioufnes, would neyther
learne themſelues, nor could teach others, any thing
at all.

Paraphraſis hath done leſſe hurt to learning, than
Epitome: for no *Paraphraſis*, though there be many,
ſhall neuer take away *Dauids* Pſalter.   *Eraſmus Paraphraſis* being neuer ſo good, ſhall neuer baniſhe the
New Teſtament.   And in an other ſchole, the *Paraphraſis* of *Brocardus*, or *Sambucus*, ſhal neuer take
Ariſtotles Rhetoricke, nor *Horace de Arte Poetica*, out
of learned mens handes.

But, as concerning a ſchole *Epitome*, he that wo[u]ld
haue an example of it, let him read *Lucian* περὶ κάλλους
which is the verie *Epitome* of *Iſocrates* oration *de
laudibus Helenæ*, whereby he may learne, at the leaſt,
this wiſe leſſon, that a man ought to beware, to be
ouer bold, in altering an excellent mans worke.

Neuertheles, ſome kinde of *Epitome* may be vſed, by
men of ſkilful iudgement, to the great proffet alſo of
others.   As if a wiſe man would take *Halles* C[h]ronicle,
where moch good matter is quite marde with Inden-
ture Engliſhe, and firſt change, ſtrange and inkhorne

tearmes into proper, and commonlie vfed wordes: next, fpecially to wede out that, that is fuperfluous and idle, not onelie where wordes be vainlie heaped one vpon an other, but alfo where many fentences, of one meaning, be fo clowted vp together as though *M. Hall* had bene, not writing the ftorie of England, but varying a fentence in Hitching fchole: furelie a wife learned man, by this way of *Epitome*, in cutting away wordes and fentences, and diminifhing nothing at all of the matter, fhold leaue to mens vfe, a ftorie, halfe as moch as it was in quantitie, but twife as good as it was, both for pleafure and alfo commoditie.

An other kinde of *Epitome* may be vfed likewife very well, to moch proffet. Som man either by luftines of nature, or brought by ill teaching, to a wrong iudgement, is ouer full of words, [and] fentences, and matter, and yet all his words be proper, apt and well chofen: all his fentences be rownd and trimlie framed : his whole matter grownded vpon good reafon, and ftuffed with full arguments, for this intent and purpofe. Yet when his talke fhalbe heard, or his writing be re[a]d, of foch one, as is, either of my two deareft friendes, *M. Haddon* at home, or *Iohn Sturmius* in Germanie, that *Nimium* in him, which fooles and vnlearned will moft commend, fhall eyther of thies two, bite his lippe, or fhake his heade at it.

This fulnes as it is not to be mifliked in a yong man, fo in farder aige, in greater fkill, and weightier affaires, it is to be temperated, or elfe difcretion and iudgement fhall feeme to be wanting in him. But if his ftile be ftill ouer rancke and luftie, as fome men being neuer fo old and fpent by yeares, will ftill be full of youthfull conditions as was Syr *F. Bryan*, and euermore wold haue bene, foch a rancke and full writer, muft vfe, if he will do wifelie the exercife of a verie good kinde of *Epitome*, and do, as certaine wife men do, that be ouer fat and flefhie : who leauing their owne full and plentifull table, go to foiorne abrode from home for a while, at the temperate diet of fome fober man, and fo by litle and

litle, cut away the grofneffe that is in them. As for an
example : If *Oforius* would leaue of his luftines in
ftriuing againſt *S. Auſten*, and his ouer rancke rayling
againſt poore *Luther*, and the troth of Gods doctrine,
and giue his whole ftudie, not to write any thing of his
owne for a while, but to tranflate *Demoſthenes*, with fo
ftraite, faſt, and temperate a ſtyle in latine, as he is in
Greeke, he would becume fo perfit and pure a writer,
I beleue, as hath be[e]ne fewe or none fence *Ciceroes*
dayes : And fo, by doing himfelf and all learned moch
good, do others leffe harme, and Chriftes doctrine
leffe iniury, than he doth : and with all, wyn vnto himfelfe many worthy frends, who agreing with him gladly,
in ye loue and liking of excellent learning, are forie to
fee fo worthie a witte, fo rare eloquence, wholie fpent
and confumed, in ftriuing with God and good men.

Emonges the reſt, no man doth lament him more
than I, not onelie for the excellent learning that I fee
in him, but alfo bicaufe there hath paffed priuatelie
betwixt him and me, fure tokens of moch good will,
and frendlie opinion, the one toward the other.   And
furelie the diftance betwixt London and Lyfbon, fhould
not ftoppe, any kinde of frendlie dewtie, that I could,
eyther fhew to him, or do to his, if the greateſt matter
of all did not in certeyne pointes, feparate our myndes.

And yet for my parte, both toward him, and diuerfe
others here at home, for like caufe of excellent learning,
great wifdome, and gentle humanitie, which I haue feene
in them, and felt at their handes my felfe, where the
matter of difference is mere confcience in a quiet minde
inwardlie, and not contentious malice with fpitefull
rayling openlie, I can be content to followe this rewle,
in miſliking fome one thing, not to hate for anie
thing els.

But as for all the bloodie beaftes, as that   *Pfal.* 80.
fat Boore of the wood : or thofe brauling Bulles of
Bafan: or any lurking *Dorm[o]us*, blinde, not by nature,
but by malice, and as may be gathered of their owne
teftimonie, giuen ouer to blindnes, for giuing ouer God

and his word; or foch as be fo luftie runnegates, as firft, runne from God and his trew doctrine, than, from their Lordes, Mafters, and all dewtie, next, from them felues and out of their wittes, laftly from their Prince, contrey, and all dew allegeance, whether they ought rather to be pitied of good men, for their miferie, or contemned of wife men, for their malicious folie, let good and wife men determine.

And to returne to *Epitome* agayne, fome will iudge moch boldnes in me, thus to iudge of *Oforius* ftyle : but wife men do know, that meane lookers on, may trewelie fay, for a well made Picture : This face had bene more cumlie, if that hie redde in the cheeke, were fomwhat more pure fanguin than it is : and yet the ftander by, can not amend it himfelfe by any way.

And this is not written to the difpraife but to the great commendation of *Oforius*, becaufe Tullie him-felfe had the fame fulnes in him : and therefore went to *Rodes* to cut it away : and faith himfelfe, *recepi me domum prope mutatus, nam quafi referuerat iam oratio.* Which was brought to paffe I beleue, not onelie by the teaching of *Molo Appollomius* but alfo by a good way of *Epitome*, in binding him felfe to tranflate *meros Atticos Oratores*, and fo to bring his ftyle, from all lowfe grofneffe, to foch firme faftnes in latin, as is in *Demof-thenes* in Greeke. And this to be moft trew, may eafelie be gathered, not onelie of *L. Craffus* talke in 1. *de Or.* but fpeciallie of *Ciceroes* owne deede in tranflating *Demofthenes* and *Æfchines* orations περὶ στεφ. to that verie ende and purpofe.

And although a man growndlie learned all readie, may take moch proffet him felfe in vfing, by *Epitome*, to draw other mens workes for his owne memorie fake, into fhorter rowme, as *Conterus* hath done verie well the whole *Metamorphofis* of *Ouid*, and *Dauid Cythræus* a great deale better, the. ix. Mufes of *Herodotus*, and *Melancthon* in myne opinion, far beft of all, the whole ftorie of Time, not onelie to his own vfe, but to other mens proffet and hys great prayfe, yet, *Epitome* is moft

neceffarie of all in a mans owne writing, as we learne
of that noble Poet *Virgill*, who, if *Donatus* fay trewe,
in writing that perfite worke of the *Georgickes*, vfed
dailie, when he had written 40. or 50. verfes, not to
ceafe cutting, paring, and pollifhing of them, till he
had brought them to the nomber of x. or xij.

And this exercife, is not more nedefullie done in a
great worke, than wifelie done, in your common dailie
writing, either of letter, or other thing elfe, that is to fay,
to perufe diligentlie, and fee and fpie wifelie, what is
alwaies more then nedeth: For, twenty to one, offend
more, in writing to moch, than to litle: euen as twentie
to one, fall into ficknefle, rather by ouer mochfulnes,
than by anie lacke or emptinefle.   And therefore is he
alwaies the beft Englifh Phyfition, that beft can geue a
purgation, that is, by way of *Epitome*, to cut all ouer much
away.   And furelie mens bodies, be not more full of ill
humors, than commonlie mens myndes (if they be
yong, luftie, proude, like and loue them felues well, as
moft men do) be full of fan[ta]fies, opinions, errors, and
faultes, not onelie in inward inuention, but alfo in all
their vtterance, either by pen or taulke.

And of all other men, euen thofe that haue ye inuen-
tiueft heades, for all purpofes, and roundeft tonges in
all matters and places (except they learne and vfe this
good leffon of *Epitome*) commit commonlie greater
faultes, than dull, ftaying filent men do.   For, quicke
inuentors, and faire readie fpeakers, being boldned with
their prefent habilitie to fay more, and perchance better
to, at the foden for that prefent, than any other can
do, vfe leffe helpe of diligence and ftudie than they
ought to do: and fo haue in them commonlie, leffe
learning, and weaker iudgement, for all deepe confiderations, than fome duller heades, and flower tonges
haue.

And therefore, readie fpeakers, generallie be not
the beft, playneft, and wifeft writers, nor yet the deepeft
iudgers in weightie affaires, bicaufe they do not tarry to
weye and iudge all thinges, as they fhould: but hauing

their heades ouer full of matter, be like pennes ouer full of incke, which will foner blotte, than make any faire letter at all. Tyme was, whan I had experience of two Ambaffadors in one place, the one of a hote head to inuent, and of a haftie hand to write, the other, colde and ftayd in both: but what difference of their doinges was made by wife men, is not vnknowne to fome perfons. The Bifhop of Winchefter *Steph. Gardiner* had a quicke head, and a readie tong, and yet was not the beft writer in England. *Cicero* in *Brutus* doth wifelie note the fame in *Serg: Galbo*, and *Q. Hortentius*, who were both, hote, luftie, and plaine fpeakers, but colde, lowfe, and rough writers: And *Tullie* telleth the caufe why, faying, whan they fpake, their tong was naturally caried with full tyde and wynde of their witte: whan they wrote their head was folitarie, dull, and caulme, and fo their ftyle was blonte, and their writing colde: *Quod vitium,* fayth *Cicero, peringeniofis hominibus neque fatis doctis plerumque accidit.*

And therfore all quick inuentors, and readie faire fpeakers, muft be carefull, that, to their goodnes of nature, they adde alfo in any wife, ftudie, labor, leafure, learning, and iudgement, and than they fhall in deede, paffe all other, as I know fome do, in whome all thofe qualities are fullie planted, or elfe if they giue ouer moch to their witte, and ouer litle to their labor and learning, they will foneft ouer reach in taulke, and fardeft cum behinde in writing whatfoeuer they take in hand. The methode of *Epitome* is moft neceffarie for foch kinde of men. And thus much concerning the vfe or mifufe of all kinde of *Epitome* in matters of learning.

❊ *Imitatio.*

Imitation, is a facultie to expreffe liuelie and perfitelie that example: which ye go about to fol[l]ow. And of it felfe, it is large and wide: for all the workes of nature, in a maner be examples for arte to folow.

But to our purpofe, all languages, both learned and

mother tonges, be gotten, and gotten onelie by *Imitation.* For as ye vfe to heare, fo ye learne to fpeake :
if ye heare no other, ye fpeake not your felfe : and
whome ye onelie heare, of them ye onelie learne.

And therefore, if ye would fpeake as the beft and
wifeft do, ye muft be conuerfant, where the beft and
wifeft are : but if yow be borne or brought vp in a
rude co[u]ntrie, ye fhall not chofe but fpeake rudelie :
the rudeft man of all knoweth this to be trewe.

Yet neuertheleffe, the rudenes of common and
mother tonges, is no bar for wife fpeaking. For in
the rudeft contrie, and moft barbarous mother language, many be found [yat] can fpeake verie wifelie :
but in the Greeke and latin tong, the two onelie learned
tonges, which be kept, not in common taulke, but in
priuate bookes, we finde alwayes, wifdome and eloquence, good matter and good vtterance, neuer or
feldom a fonder. For all foch Authors, as be fulleft
of good matter and right iudgement in doctrine, be
likewife alwayes, moft proper in wordes, moft apte in
fentence, moft plaine and pure in vttering the fame.

And contrariwife, in thofe two tonges, all writers,
either in Religion, or any fect of Philofophie, who fo
euer be founde fonde in iudgement of matter, be commonlie found as rude in vttering their mynde. For
Stoickes, Anabaptiftes, and Friers : with Epicures,
Libertines and Monkes, being moft like in learning
and life, are no fonder and pernicious in their opinions,
than they be rude and barbarous in their writinges.
They be not wife, therefore that fay, what care I for a
mans wordes and vtterance, if his matter and reafons
be good. Soch men, fay fo, not fo moch of ignorance,
as eyther of fome fingular pride in themfelues, or fome
fpeciall malice or other, or for fome priuate and parciall
matter, either in Religion or other kinde of learning.
For good and choice meates, be no more requifite for
helthie bodies, than proper and apte wordes be for
good matters, and alfo plaine and fenfible vtterance
for the beft and de[e]peft reafons : in which two pointes

ſtandeth perfite eloquence, one of the faireſt and rareſt
giftes that God doth geue to man.

Ye know not, what hurt ye do to learning, that care
not for wordes, but for matter, and ſo make a deuorſe
betwixt the tong and the hart.   For marke all aiges :
looke vpon the whole courſe of both the Greeke and
Latin tonge, and ye ſhall ſurelie finde, that, whan apte
and good wordes began to be neglected, and properties
of thoſe two tonges to be confounded, than alſo began,
ill deedes to ſpring : ſtrange maners to oppreſſe good
orders, newe and fond opinions to ſtriue with olde and
trewe doctrine, firſt in Philoſophie : and after in Religion : right iudgement of all thinges to be peruerted,
and ſo vertue with learning is contemned, and ſtudie
left of : of ill thoughtes cummeth peruerſe iudgement :
of ill deedes ſpringeth lewde taulke.   Which fower mis-
orders, as they mar mans life, ſo deſtroy they good
learning withall.

But behold the goodneſſe of Gods prouidence for
learning : all olde authors and ſectes of Philoſophy,
which were fondeſt in opinion, and rudeſt in vtterance,
as Stoickes and Epicures, firſt contemned of wiſe men,
and after forgotten of all men, be ſo confumed by
tymes, as they be now, not onelie out of vſe, but alſo
out of memorie of man : which thing, I ſurelie thinke,
will ſhortlie chance, to the whole doctrine and all the
bookes of phantaſticall Anabaptiſtes and Friers, and
of the beaſtlie Libertines and Monkes.

Againe behold on the other ſide, how Gods wiſdome
hath wrought, that of *Academici* and *Peripatetici*, thoſe
that were wiſeſt in iudgement of matters, and pureſt in
vttering their myndes, the firſt and chiefeſt, that wrote
moſt and beſt, in either tong, as *Plato* and *Ariſtotle* in
Greeke, *Tullie* in Latin, be ſo either wholie, or ſuffi-
ciently left vnto vs, as I neuer knew yet ſcholer, that
gaue himſelfe to like, and loue, and folowe chieſlie thoſe
three Authors but he proued, both learned, wiſe, and
alſo an honeſt man, if he ioyned with all the trewe
doctrine of Gods holie Bible, without the which, the

other three, be but fine edge tooles in a fole or mad mans hand.

But to returne to *Imitation* agayne : There be three kindes of it in matters of learning.

The whole doctrine of Comedies and Tragedies, is a perfite *imitation*, or faire liuelie painted picture of the life of euerie degree of man. Of this *Imitation* writeth *Plato* at large in *3. de Rep.* but it doth not moch belong at this time to our purpofe.

The fecond kind of *Imitation*, is to folow for learning of tonges and fciences, the beft authors. Here rifeth, emonges proude and enuious wittes, a great controuerfie, whether, one or many are to be folowed : and if one, who is that one : *Seneca*, or *Cicero* : *Saluft* or *Cæfar*, and fo forth in Greeke and Latin.

The third kinde of *Imitation*, belongeth to the fecond : as when you be determined, whether ye will folow one or mo, to know perfitlie, and which way to folow that one : in what place : by what meane and order : by what tooles and inftrumentes ye fhall do it, by what fkill and iudgement, ye fhall trewelie difcerne, whether ye folow rightlie or no.

This *Imitatio*, is *difsimilis materei fimilis tractatio* : and alfo, *fimilis materei difsimilis tractatio*, as *Virgill* folowed *Homer* : but the Argument to the one was *Vlyffes*, to the other *Æneas*. *Tullie* perfecuted *Antonie* with the fame wepons of eloquence, that *Demofthenes* vfed before againft *Philippe*.

Horace foloweth *Pindar*, but either of them his owne Argument and Perfon : as the one, *Hiero* king of *Sicilie*, the other *Auguftus* the Emperor : and yet both for like refpectes, that is, for their coragious ftoutnes in warre, and iuft gouernment in peace.

One of the beft examples, for right *Imitation* we lacke, and that is *Menander*, whom our *Terence*, (as the matter required) in like argument, in the fame Perfons, with equall eloquence, foote by foote did folow.

Som peeces remaine, like broken Iewelles, whereby

men may rightlie efteme, and iuftlie lament, the loffe of the whole.

Erafmus, the ornament of learning, in our tyme, doth wifh that fom man of learning and diligence, would take the like paines in *Demofthenes* and *Tullie*, that *Macrobius* hath done in *Homer* and *Virgill*, that is, to write out and ioyne together, where the one doth imitate the other. *Erafmus* wifhe is good, but furelie, it is not good enough: for *Macrobius* gatherings for the *Æneodos* out of *Homer*, and *Eobanus Heffus* more diligent gatherings for the *Bucolikes* out of *Theocritus*, as they be not fullie taken out of the whole heape, as they fhould be, but euen as though they had not fought for them of purpofe, but fownd them fcatered here and there by chance in their way, euen fo, onelie to point out, and nakedlie to ioyne togither their fentences, with no farder declaring the maner and way, how the one doth folow the other, were but a colde helpe, to the encreafe of learning.

But if a man would take his paine alfo, whan he hath layd two places, of *Homer* and *Virgill*, or of *Demofthenes* and *Tullie* togither, to teach plainlie withall, after this fort.

1. *Tullie* reteyneth thus moch of the matter, thies fentences, thies wordes:

2. This and that he leaueth out, which he doth wittelie to this end and purpofe.

3. This he addeth here.

4. This he diminifheth there.

5. This he ordereth thus, with placing that here, not there.

6. This he altereth, and changeth, either, in propertie of wordes, in forme of fentence, in fubftance of the matter, or in one, or other conuenient circumftance of the authors prefent purpofe. In thies fewe rude Englifh wordes, are wrapt vp all the neceffarie tooles and inftrumentes, where with trewe *Imitation* is rightlie wrought withall in any tonge. Which tooles, I openlie confeffe, be not of myne owne forging, but partlie left

vnto me by the cunni[n]geſt Maſter, and one of the
worthieſt Ientlemen that euer England bred, Syr *Iohn
Cheke*: partelie borowed by me out of the ſhoppe of
the deareſt frende I haue out of England, *Io. St.*
And therefore I am the bolder to borow of him, and
here to leaue them to other, and namelie to my Children: which tooles, if it pleaſe God, that an other day,
they may be able to vſe rightlie, as I do wiſh and daylie
pray, they may do, I ſhal be more glad, than if I were
able to leaue them a great quantitie of land.

This foreſaide order and doctrine of *Imitation*, would
bring forth more learning, and breed vp trewer iudgement, than any other exerciſe that can be vſed, but
not for yong beginners, bicauſe they ſhall not be able
to conſider dulie therof. And trewelie, it may be a
ſhame to good ſtudentes who hauing ſo faire examples
to follow, as *Plato* and *Tullie*, do not vſe ſo wiſe wayes
in folowing them for the obteyning of wiſdome and
learning, as rude ignorant Artificers do, for gayning a
ſmall commoditie. For ſurelie the meaneſt painter
vſeth more witte, better arte, greater diligence, in hys
ſhoppe, in folowing the Picture of any meane mans
face, than commonlie the beſt ſtudentes do, euen in
the vniuerſitie, for the atteining of learning it ſelfe.

Some ignorant, vnlearned, and idle ſtudent: or ſome
buſie looker vpon this litle poore booke, that hath
neither will to do good him ſelfe, nor ſkill to iudge right
of others, but can luſtelie contemne, by pride and ignorance, all painfull diligence and right order in ſtudy, will
perchance ſay, that I am to preciſe, to curious, in marking
and piteling [pidling] thus about the imitation of others :
and that the olde worthie Authors did neuer buſie their
heades and wittes, in folowyng ſo preciſelie, either the
matter what other men wrote, or els the maner how
other men wrote. They will ſay, it were a plaine
ſlauerie, and iniurie to, to ſhakkle and tye a good witte,
and hinder the courſe of a mans good nature with ſuch
bondes of ſeruitude, in folowyng other.

Except ſoch men thinke them ſelues wiſer then

Cicero for teaching of eloquence, they muft be content to turne a new leafe.

The beft booke that euer *Tullie* wrote, by all mens iudgement, and by his owne teftimonie to, in wrytyng wherof, he employed moft care, ftudie, learnyng and iudgement, is his booke *de Orat. ad Q. F.* Now let vs fee, what he did for the matter, and alfo for the maner of writing therof. For the whole booke con-fifteth in thefe two pointes onelie: In good matter, and good handling of the matter. And firft, for the matter, it is whole *Ariftotles*, what fo euer *Antonie* in the fecond, and *Craffus* in the third doth teach. Truft not me, but beleue *Tullie* him felfe, who writeth fo, firft, in that goodlie long Epiftle *ad P. Lentulum*, and after in diuerfe places *ad Atticum.* And in the verie booke it felfe, Tullie will not haue it hidden, but both *Catulus* and *Craffus* do oft and pleafantly lay that ftelth to *Antonius* charge. Now, for the handling of the matter, was *Tullie* fo precife and curious rather to follow an other mans Paterne, than to inuent fome newe fhape him felfe, namelie in that booke, wherein he pur-pofed, to leaue to pofteritie, the glorie of his witte? yea forfoth, that he did. And this is not my geffing and gathering, nor onelie performed by *Tullie* in verie deed, but vttered alfo by *Tullie* in plaine wordes : to teach other men thereby, what they fhould do, in tak-ing like matter in hand.

And that which is efpecially to be marked, *Tullie* doth vtter plainlie his conceit and purpofe therein, by the mouth of the wifeft man in all that companie: for fayth *Scæuola* him felfe, *Cur non imitamur, Craffe, Socratem illum, qui est in Phædro Platonis etc.*

And furder to vnderftand, that *Tullie* did not *obiter* and bichance, but purpofelie and mindfullie bend him felfe to a precife and curious Imitation of *Plato*, con-cernyng the fhape and forme of thofe bookes, marke I pray you, how curious *Tullie* is to vtter his purpofe and doyng therein, writing thus to *Atticus.*

Quod in his Oratorijs libris, quos tantopere laudas,

*perfonam defideras Scæuolæ, non eam temerè dimoui:
Sed feci idem, quod in* πολετεία *Deus ille nofter Plato,
cum in Piræeum Socrates venifset ad Cephalum locuple-
tem et feftiuum Senem, quoad primus ille fermo habere-
tur, adest in difputando fenex: Deinde, cum ipfe quoque
commodifsimè locutus effet, ad rem diuinam dicit fe velle
difcedere, neque poftea reuertitur. Credo Platonem vix
putaffe fatis confonum fore, fi hominem id ætatis in tam
longo fermone diutius retinuiffet: Multo ego fatius hoc
mihi cauendum putaui in Scæuola, qui et ætate et vale-
tudine erat ea qua meminifti, et his honoribus, vt vix
fatis decorum videretur eum plures dies effe in Crafsi
Tufculano. Et erat primi libri fermo non alienus à
Scæuolæ ftudijs: reliqui libri* τεχνολοσίαν *habent, vt
fcis. Huic ioculatoriæ difputationi fenem illum vt noras,
intereffe fanè nolui.*

If *Cicero* had not opened him felfe, and declared
hys owne thought and doynges herein, men that be
idle, and ignorant, and enuious of other mens diligence
and well doinges, would haue fworne that *Tullie* had
neuer mynded any foch thing, but that of a precife
curiofitie, we fayne and forge and father foch thinges
of *Tullie*, as he neuer ment in deed. I write this, not
for nought: for I haue heard fome both well learned,
and otherwayes verie wife, that by their luftie mifliking
of foch diligence, haue drawen back the forwardnes of
verie good wittes. But euen as fuch men them felues,
do fometymes ftumble vpon doyng well by chance and
benefite of good witte, fo would I haue our fcholer
alwayes able to do well by order of learnyng and
right fkill of iudgement.

Concernyng Imitation, many learned men haue
written, with moch diuerfitie for the matter, and therfore with great contrarietie and fome ftomacke amongeft
them felues. I haue read as many as I could get
diligentlie, and what I thinke of euerie one of them, I
will freelie fay my mynde. With which freedome I
truft good men will beare, bicaufe it fhall tend to
neither fpitefull nor harmefull controuerfie.

Cicero. In *Tullie*, it is well touched, ſhortlie taught, not fullie declared by *Ant. in 2. de Orat*: and afterward in *Orat. ad Brutum*, for the liking and miſliking of *Iſocrates*: and the contrarie iudgement of *Tullie* agaynſt *Caluus*, *Brutus*, and *Calidius*, *de genere dicendi Attico et Aſiatico*.

Dio Halicar. Dioniſ. *Halic.* περὶ μιμήσεως. I feare is loſt: which Author next *Ariſtotle*, *Plato*, and *Tullie*, of all other, that write of eloquence, by the iudgement of them that be beſt learned, deſerueth the next prayſe and place.

Quintil. *Quintilian* writeth of it, ſhortly and coldlie for the matter, yet hotelie and ſpitefullie enough, agaynſt the Imitation of *Tullie*.

Eraſmus. *Eraſmus*, beyng more occupied in ſpying other mens faultes, than declaryng his owne aduiſe, is miſtaken of many, to the great hurt of ſtudie, for his authoritie ſake. For he writeth rightlie, rightlie vnderſtanded: he and *Longolius* onelie differing in this, that the one ſeemeth to giue ouermoch, the other ouer litle, to him, whom they both, beſt loued, and chiefly allowed of all other.

Budæus. *Budæus* in his Commentaries roughlie and obſcurelie, after his kinde of writyng: and for the matter, caryed ſomewhat out of the way in ouermuch miſliking the Imitation of *Tullie*.

Ph. Melanch. *Phil. Melanĉthon*, learnedlie and trewlie.

Ioa. Camer. *Camerarius* largely with a learned iudgement, but ſumewhat confuſedly, and with ouer rough a ſtile.

Sambucus. *Sambucus*, largely, with a right iudgement but ſomewhat a crooked ſtile.

Cortesius. Other haue written alſo, as *Corteſius* to
P. Bembus. *Politian*, and that verie well: *Bembus ad*
IoanSturmius. *Picum* a great deale better, but *Ioan. Sturmius de Nobilitate literata, et de Amiſſa dicendi ratione*, farre beſt of all, in myne opinion, that euer tooke this matter in hand. For all the reſt, declare chiefly this point, whether one, or many, or all, are to

be followed: but *Sturmius* onelie hath moſt learnedlie
declared, who is to be followed, what is to be followed, and the beſt point of all, by what way and
order, trew Imitation is rightlie to be exerciſed.   And
although *Sturmius* herein doth farre paſſe all other, yet
hath he not ſo fullie and perfitelie done it, as I do
wiſhe he had, and as I know he could.   For though
he hath done it perfitelie for precept, yet hath he not
done it perfitelie enough for example: which he did,
neither for lacke of ſkill, nor by negligence, but of
purpoſe, contented with one or two examples, bicauſe
he was mynded in thoſe two bookes, to write of it
both ſhortlie, and alſo had to touch other matters.

   Barthol. Riccius Ferrarienſis alſo hath written learnedlie, diligentlie and verie largelie of this matter euen as
hee did before verie well *de Apparatu linguæ Lat.*   He
writeth the better in myne opinion, bicauſe his whole
doctrine, iudgement, and order, ſemeth to be borowed out of *Io. Stur.* bookes.   He addeth alſo examples, the beſt kinde of teaching: wherein he doth
well, but not well enough: in deede, he committeth
no faulte, but yet, deſerueth ſmall praiſe.   He is
content with the meane, and followeth not the beſt:
as a man, that would feede vpon Acornes, whan he
may eate, as good cheape, the fineſt wheat bread.   He
teacheth for example, where and how, two or three
late *Italian* Poetes do follow *Virgil*: and how *Virgil*
him ſelfe in the ſtorie of *Dido*, doth wholie Imitate
Catullus in the like matter of *Ariadna*: Wherein I
like better his diligence and order of teaching, than
his iudgement in choiſe of examples for *Imitation*.
But, if he had done thus: if he had declared where
and how, how oft and how many wayes *Virgil* doth
folow *Homer*, as for example the comming of *Vlyſſes*
to *Alcynous* and *Calypſo*, with the comming of *Æneas*
to *Cart[h]age* and *Dido*: Likewiſe the games running,
wreſtling, and ſhoting, that *Achilles* maketh in *Homer*,
with the ſelfe ſame games, that *Æneas* maketh in
Virgil: The harneſſe of *Achilles*, with the harneſſe of

Æneas, and the maner of making of them both by *Vulcane*: The notable combate betwixt *Achilles* and *Hector*, with as notable a combate betwixt *Æneas* and *Turnus*. The going downe to hell of *Vlyffes* in *Homer*, with the going downe to hell of *Æneas* in *Virgil*: and other places infinite mo, as fimilitudes, narrations, meffages, difcriptions of perfons, places, battels, tempeftes, fhipwrackes, and common places for diuerfe purpofes, which be as precifely taken out of *Homer*, as euer did Painter in London follow the picture of any faire perfonage. And when thies places had bene gathered together by this way of diligence than to haue conferred them together by this order of teaching, as, diligently to marke what is kept and vfed in either author, in wordes, in fentences, in matter: what is added: what is left out: what ordered otherwife, either *præponendo, interponendo*, or *postponendo*: And what is altered for any refpect, in word, phrafe, fentence, figure, reafon, argument, or by any way of circumftance: If *Riccius* had done this, he had not onely bene well liked, for his diligence in teaching, but alfo iuftlie commended for his right iudgement in right choice of examples for the beft *Imitation*.

Riccius alfo for *Imitation* of profe declareth where and how *Longolius* doth folow *Tullie*, but as for *Longolius*, I would not haue him the patern of our *Imitation*. In deede: in *Longolius* fhoppe, be proper and faire fhewing colers, but as for fhape, figure, and naturall cumlines, by the iudgement of beft iudging artificers, he is rather allowed as one to be borne withall, than efpecially commended, as one chieflie to be folowed.

If *Riccius* had taken for his examples, where *Tullie* him felfe foloweth either *Plato* or *Demofthenes*, he had fhot than at the right marke. But to excufe *Riccius*, fomwhat, though I can not fullie defend him, it may be fayd, his purpofe was, to teach onelie the Latin tong, when thys way that I do wifh, to ioyne *Virgil* with *Homer*, to read *Tullie* with *Demofthenes* and *Plato*, requireth a cunning and perfite Mafter in both the tonges. It is my wifh in deede, and that by good reafon: For who fo euer will write well of any matter, muft labor to expreffe that, that is perfite, and not to ftay and content himfelfe with the meane: yea, I fay farder, though it not be vnpofible, yet it is verie rare. and maruelous hard, to proue excellent in the Latin tong, for him that is not alfo well feene in the Greeke tong. *Tullie* him felfe, moft excellent of nature, moft diligent in labor, brought vp from his cradle, in that place, and in that tyme, where and whan the Latin tong moft florifhed naturallie in euery mans mouth, yet was not his owne tong able it felfe to make him fo cunning in his owne tong, as he was in deede: but the knowledge and *Imitation* of the Greeke tong withall.

This he confeffeth himfelfe: this he vttereth in many places, as thofe can tell beft, that vfe to read him moft.

Therefore thou, that fhoteft at perfection in the Latin tong, think not thy felfe wifer than *Tullie* was, in choice of the way, that leadeth rightlie tc the fame: thinke not thy witte better than *Tullies* was, as though that may ferue thee that was not fufficient for him. For euen as a hauke flieth not hie with one wing: euen fo a man reacheth not to excellency with one tong.

I haue bene a looker on in the Cokpit of learning thies many yeares: And one Cock onelie haue I knowne, which with one wing, euen at this day, doth paffe all other, in myne opinion, that euer I faw in any pitte in England, though they had two winges. Yet neuer-theleffe, to flie well with one wing, to runne faft with one leg, be rather, rare Maiftreis moch to be merueled at, than fure examples fafelie to be folowed. A Bufhop that now liueth, a good man, whofe iudgement in Religion I better like, than his opinion in perfitnes in other learning, faid once vnto me: we haue no nede now of the Greeke tong, when all thinges be tranflated into Latin. But the good man vnderftood not, that euen the beft tranflation, is, for mere neceffitie, but an euill imped wing to flie withall, or a heuie ftompe leg

of wood to go withall: ſoch, the hier they flie, the
ſooner they falter and faill: the faſter they runne, the
ofter they ſtumble, and ſorer they fall. Soch as will
nedes ſo flie, may flie at a Pye, and catch a Dawe:
And ſoch runners, as commonlie, they ſhoue and ſhol-
der to ſtand formoſt, yet in the end they cum behind
others and deſerue but the hopſhakles, if the Maſters
of the game be right iudgers.

Therefore in peruſing thus, ſo many diuerſe bookes
for *Imitation,* it came into my head that a
verie profitable booke might be made *de
Imitatione,* after an other ſort, than euer yet was at-
tempted of that matter, conteyning a certaine fewe
fitte preceptes, vnto the which ſhoulde be gathered
and applied plentie of exa*m*ples, out of the choiſeſt
authors of both the tonges. This worke would ſtand
rather in good diligence, for the gathering, and right
iudgement for the apte applying of thoſe examples:
than any great learning or vtterance at all.

Optima ratio Imitationis. (margin note)

The doing thereof, would be more pleaſant, than
painfull, and would bring alſo moch proffet to all that
ſhould read it, and great praiſe to him would take it in
hand, with iuſt deſert of thankes.

Eraſmus, giuyng him ſelfe to read ouer
all Authors *Greke* and *Latin,* ſeemeth to
haue preſcribed to him ſelfe this order of readyng:
that is, to note out by the way, three ſpeciall pointes:
All Adagies, all ſimilitudes, and all wittie ſayinges
of moſt notable perſonages: And ſo, by one labour,
he left to poſteritie, three notable bookes, and namelie
two his *Chiliades, Apophthegmata,* and *Similia.* Likewiſe, if a good ſtudent would bend him ſelfe to read diligently ouer Tullie, and with him alſo at the ſame tyme,

Eraſmus order in his ſtudie. (margin note)

as diligently *Plato,* and *Xenophon,* with
his bookes of Philoſophie, *Iſocrates,*
and *Demoſthenes* with his orations, and
Ariſtotle with his Rhetorickes: which
fiue of all other, be thoſe, whom *Tullie* beſt loued, and
ſpecially followed: and would marke diligently in *Tullie,*
where he doth *exprimere* or *effingere* (which be the verie

Plato.
Xenophon.
Cicero *Iſocrates.*
Demoſth.
Ariſtotles. (margin note)

proper wordes of Imitation) either, *Copiam Platonis* or *venuſtatem Xenophontis, ſuauitatem Iſocratis,* or *vim Demoſthenes, propriam et puram ſubtilitatem Ariſtotelis,* and not onelie write out the places diligentlie, and lay them together orderlie, but alſo to conferre them with ſkilfull iudgement by thoſe few rules, which I haue expreſſed now twiſe before : if that diligence were taken, if that order were vſed, what perfite knowledge of both the tonges, what readie and pithie vtterance in all matters, what right and deepe iudgement in all kinde of learnyng would follow, is ſcarſe credible to be beleued.

Theſe bookes, be not many, nor long, nor rude in ſpeach, nor meane in matter, but next the Maieſtie of Gods holie word, moſt worthie for a man, the louer of learning and honeſtie, to ſpend his life in. Yea, I haue heard worthie *M. Cheke* many tymes ſay : I would haue a good ſtudent paſſe and iorney through all Authors both *Greke* and *Latin* : but he that will dwell in theſe few bookes onelie : firſt, in Gods holie Bible, and than ioyne with it, *Tullie* in *Latin*, *Plato*, *Ariſtotle* : *Xenophon*: *Iſocrates*: and *Demoſthenes* in *Greke*: muſt nedes proue an excellent man.

Some men alreadie in our dayes, haue put to their helping handes, to this worke of Imitation. *Perionus.* As *Perionius, Henr. Stephanus in dictionario* *H. Steph.* *Ciceroniano*, and *P. Victorius* moſt praiſe- *P. Victorius.* worthelie of all, in that his learned worke conteyning xxv. bookes *de varia lectione*: in which bookes be ioyned diligentlie together the beſt Authors of both the tonges where one doth ſeeme to imitate an other.

But all theſe, with *Macrobius, Heſſus,* and other, be no more but common porters, caryers, and bringers of matter and ſtuffe togither. They order nothing : They laye before you, what is done : they do not teach you, how it is done : They buſie not them ſelues with forme of buildyng : They do not declare, this ſtuffe is thus framed by *Demoſthenes*, and thus and thus by *Tullie*, and ſo likewiſe in *Xenophon, Plato* and *Iſocrates* and

I

Ariſtotle. For ioyning *Virgil* with *Homer* I haue ſufficientlie declared before.

Pindarus. .... The like diligence I would wiſh to be
Horatius. .... taken in *Pindar* and *Horace* an equall
match for all reſpectes.

In Tragedies, (the goodlieſt Argument of all, and for
the vſe, either of a learned preacher, or a Ciuill Ientleman, more profitable than *Homer, Pindar, Virgill,* and
Horace : yea comparable in myne opinion, with the doc-
Sophocles. ... trine of *Ariſtotle, Plato,* and *Xenophon,*) the
Euripides. ... *Grecians, Sophocles* and *Euripides* far ouer
Seneca. ..... match our *Seneca* in Latin, namely in
οἰκονομίᾳ *et Decoro,* although *Senacaes* elocution and
verſe be verie commendable for his tyme. And for the
matters of *Hercules, Thebes, Hippolytus,* and *Troie,* his
Imitation is to be gathered into the ſame booke, and to
be tryed by the ſame touchſtone, as is ſpoken before.

In hiſtories, and namelie in *Liuie,* the like diligence
of Imitation, could bring excellent learning, and breede
ſtayde iudgement, in taking any like matter in hand.
Tit. Liuius. .... Onely *Liuie* were a ſufficient taſke for
one mans ſtudie, to compare him, firſt with his fellow
Dion. Hali- .. for all reſpectes, *Dion. Halicarnaſſæus* : who
carn. .... both, liued in one tyme : toke both one
hiſtorie in hande to write : deſerued both like prayſe
Polibius. ..... of learnynge and eloquence. Than with
Polybius that wiſe writer, whom *Liuie* profeſſeth to
follow : and if he would denie it, yet it is plaine, that
the beſt part of the thyrd *Decade* in *Liuie,* is in a
maner tranſlated out of the thyrd and reſt of *Polibius* :
Thucidides. .... Laſtlie with *Thucydides,* to whoſe Imita-
tation *Liuie* is curiouſlie bent, as may well appeare by
1. *Decad.* ...... that one Oration of thoſe of *Campania,*
Lib. 7. .... aſking aide of the *Romanes* agaynſt the
Samnites, which is wholie taken, Sentence, Reaſon,
Argument, and order, out of the Oration of *Corcyra,*
Thucid. 10. .. aſking like aide of the *Athenienſes* againſt
them of *Corinth.* If ſome diligent ſtudent would take
paynes to compare them togither, he ſhould eaſelie

perceiue, that I do fay trew. A booke, thus wholie
filled with examples of Imitation, firft out of *Tullie*,
compared with *Plato, Xenophon, Ifocrates, Demofthenes*
and *Ariftotle* : than out of *Virgil* and *Horace*, with
Homer and *Pindar* : next out of *Seneca* with *Sophocles*
and *Euripides* : Laftlie out of *Liuie*, with *Thucydides*,
Polibius and *Halicarnaffæus*, gathered with good dili
gence, and compared with right order, as I haue
expreffed before, were an other maner of worke for all
kinde of learning, and namely for eloquence, than be
thofe cold gatheringes of *Macrobius, Heffus, Perionius,
Stephanus*, and *Victorius*, which may be vfed, as I fayd
before, in this cafe, as porters and caryers, deferuing
like prayfe, as foch men do wages ; but onely *Sturmius*
is he, out of whom, the trew furuey and whole worke-
manfhip is fpeciallie to be learned.

I truft, this my writyng fhall giue fome good ftudent
occafion, to take fome peece in hand of this worke of
Imitation. And as I had rather haue any Opus de
do it, than my felfe, yet furelie my felfe recta imitandi
rather than none at all. And by Gods ratione.
grace, if God do lend me life, with health, free layfure
and libertie, with good likyng and a merie heart, I will
turne the beft part of my ftudie and tyme, to toyle in
one or other peece of this worke of Imitation.

This diligence to gather examples, to giue light and
vnderftandyng to good preceptes, is no new inuention,
but fpeciallie vfed of the beft Authors and oldeft
writers. For *Ariftotle* him felfe, (as *Diog.* Aristoteles.
Laertius declareth) when he had written that goodlie
booke of the *Topickes*, did gather out of ftories and
Orators, fo many examples as filled xv. bookes, onelie
to expreffe the rules of his *Topickes*. Thefe were the
Commentaries, that *Ariftotle* thought fit for Commentarij
hys *Topickes* : And therfore to fpeake as Græci et Latini
in Dialect.
I thinke, I neuer faw yet any Commen- Aristotelis.
tarie vpon *Ariftotles* Logicke, either in *Greke* or
Latin, that euer I lyked, bicaufe they be rather
fpent in declaryng fcholepoynt rules, than in gather

ing fit examples for vſe and vtterance, either by
pen or talke. For precepts in all Authors, and
namelie in *Ariſtotle*, without applying vnto them,
the Imitation of examples, be hard, drie, and cold,
and therfore barrayn, vnfruitfull and vnpleaſant. But
Ariſtotle, namelie in his *Topickes* and *Elenches*, ſhould
be, not onelie fruitfull, but alſo pleaſant to, if examples
out of *Plato*, and other good Authors, were diligentlie
gathered, and aptlie applied vnto his moſt perfit pre-

Precepta in
Aristot.   ceptes there. And it is notable, that my
frende *Sturmius* writeth herein, that there

Exempla in
Platone.   is no precept in *Ariſtotles Topickes*, wherof
plentie of examples be not manifeſt in *Platos* workes.
And I heare ſay, that an excellent learned man, *Tomi-
tanus* in *Italie*, hath expreſſed euerie fallacion in
Ariſtotle, with diuerſe examples out of *Plato*. Would
to God, I might once ſee, ſome worthie ſtudent of
Ariſtotle and *Plato* in Cambridge, that would ioyne in
one booke the preceptes of the one, with the examples
of the other. For ſuch a labor, were one ſpeciall peece
of that worke of Imitation, which I do wiſhe were
gathered together in one Volume.

Cambrige, at my firſt comming thither, but not at
my going away, committed this fault in reading the
preceptes of *Ariſtotle* without the examples of other
Authors: But herein, in my time thies men of worthie
memorie, *M. Redman, M. Cheke, M. Smith, M. Haddon, M. Watſon*, put ſo to their helping handes, as
that vniuerſitie, and all ſtudents there, as long as
learning ſhall laſt, ſhall be bounde vnto them, if that
trade in ſtudie be trewlie folowed, which thoſe men
left behinde them there.

By this ſmall mention of Cambridge, I am caryed
into three imaginations: firſt, into a ſweete remembrance of my tyme ſpent there: than, into ſom carefull
thoughts, for the greuous alteration that folowed ſone
after: laſtlie, into much ioy to heare tell, of the good
recouerie and earneſt forwardnes in all good learning
there agayne.

To vtter theis my thoughts fomwhat more largelie, were fomwhat befide my matter, yet not very farre out of the way, bycaufe it fhall wholy tend to the good encoragement and right confideration of learning, which is my full purpofe in writing this litle booke: whereby alfo fhall well appeare this fentence to be moft trewe, that onelie good men, by their gouernment and example, make happie times, in euery degree and ftate.

Doctor *Nico. Medcalfe*, that honorable *D. Nic. Medcalf.* father, was Mafter of *S. Iohnes* Colledge, when I came thether: A man meanelie learned him-felfe, but not meanely affectioned to fet forward learn-ing in others. He found that Colledge fpending fcarfe two hundred markes by [the] yeare: he left it fpend-ing a thoufand markes and more. Which he procured, not with his mony, but by his wifdome; not charge-ablie bought by him, but liberallie geuen by others by his meane, for the zeale and honor they bare to learning. And that which is worthy of memorie, all thies giuers were almoft Northenmen: who being liberallie rewarded in the feruice of their Prince, beftowed it as liberallie for the good of their Contrie. Som men thought therefore, that *D. Medcalfe* was parciall to Northrenmen, but fure I am of this, that Northrenmen were parciall, in doing more good, and geuing more landes to ye forderance of *The parcialitie* learning, than any other contrie men, *of Northren men in S.Iohnes* in thofe dayes, did: which deede fhould *colledge.* haue beene, rather an example of goodnes, for other to folowe, than matter of malice, for any to enuie, as fome there were that did. Trewly, *D. Med-calfe* was parciall to none: but indifferent to all: a mafter for the whole, a father to euery one, in that Colledge. There was none fo poore, if he had, either wil in goodnes, or wit to learning, that could lacke being there, or fhould depart from thence, for any need. I am witnes my felfe, that mony many times was brought into yong mens ftudies by ftrangers whom they knew not.   In which doing, this worthy *Nicolaus* folowed the fteppes of good olde *S. Nicolaus*, that learned Bifhop.   He was a Papiſt in deede, but would to God, amonges all vs Proteſtants I might once fee but one, that would winne like praiſe, in doing like good, for the aduauncement of learning and vertue.   And yet, though he were a Papiſt, if any yong man, geuen to new learning (as they termed it) went beyond his fellowes, in witte, labor, and towardnes, euen the fame, neyther lacked, open praiſe to encorage him, nor priuate exhibition to mainteyne hym, as worthy Syr *I. Cheke*, if he were aliue would beare good witnes and fo can many mo.   I my felfe one of the meaneſt of a great number, in that Colledge, becauſe there appeared in me fom fmall ſhew of towardnes and diligence, lacked not his fauor to forder me in learning.

And being a boy, newe Bacheler of arte, I chanced amonges my companions to fpeake againſt the Pope : which matter was than in euery mans mouth, bycauſe *D. Haines* and *D. Skippe* were cum from the Court, to debate the fame matter, by preaching and difputation in the vniuerfitie.   This hapned the fame tyme, when I ſtoode to be felow there: my taulke came to *D. Medcalfes* eare: I was called before him and the Seniores: and after greuous rebuke, and fome puniſhment, open warning was geuen to all the felowes, none to be fo hardie to geue me his voice at that election. And yet for all thofe open threates, the good father himfelfe priuilie procured, that I ſhould euen than be chofen felow.   But, the election being done, he made countinance of great difcontentation thereat.   This good mans goodnes, and fatherlie difcretion, vfed towardes me that one day, ſhall neuer out of my remembrance all the dayes of my life.   And for the fame caufe, haue I put it here, in this fmall record of learning.   For next Gods prouidence, furely that day, was by that good fathers meanes, *Dies natalis*, to me, for the whole foundation of the poore learning I haue, and of all the furderance, that hetherto elfe where I haue obteyned.

This his goodnes ftood not ftill in one or two, but flowed aboundantlie ouer all that Colledge, and brake out alfo to norifhe good wittes in euery part of that vniuerfitie: whereby, at this departing thence, he left foch a companie of fellowes and fcholers in *S. Iohnes* Colledge, as can fcarfe be found now in fome whole vniuerfitie: which, either for diuinitie, on the one fide or other, or for Ciuill feruice to their Prince and con-trie, haue bene, and are yet to this day, notable orna-ments to this whole Realme: Yea *S. Iohnes* did then fo florifh, as Trinitie college, that Princelie houfe now, at the firft erection, was but *Colonia deducta* out of *S. Iohnes,* not onelie for their Mafter, fellowes, and fcholers, but alfo, which is more, for their whole, both order of learning, and difcipline of maners: and yet to this day, it neuer tooke Mafter but fuch as was bred vp before in *S. Iohnes:* doing the dewtie of a good *Colonia* to her *Metropolis,* as the auncient Cities of Grece and fome yet in Italie, at this day, are accuftomed to do.

S. Iohnes ftoode in this ftate, vntill thofe heuie tymes, and that greuous change that chanced. An. 1553. whan mo perfite fcholers were difperfed from thence in one moneth, than many yeares can reare vp againe. For, whan *Aper de Sylua* had Psal. 80. paffed the feas, and faftned his foote againe in England, not onely the two faire groues of learning in England were eyther cut vp, by the roote, or troden downe to the ground and wholie went to wracke, but the yong fpring there, and euerie where elfe, was pitifullie nipt and ouertroden by very beaftes, and alfo the faireft ftanders of all, were rooted vp, and caft into the fire, to the great weakening euen at this day of Chriftes Chirch in England, both for Religion and learning.

And what good could chance than to the vni-uerfities, whan fom of the greateft, though not of the wifeft nor beft learned, nor beft men neither of that fide, did labor to perfwade, that ignorance was better than knowledge, which they ment, nor for the laitie onelie, but alfo for the greateft rable of their fpiritualitie, what other pretenfe openlie fo euer they made: and therefore did fom of them at Cambrige (whom I will not name openlie,) caufe hedge prieftes fette oute of the contrie, to be made fellowes in the vniuerfitie: faying, in their talke priuilie, and declaring by their deedes openlie, that he was, felow good enough for their tyme, if he could were a gowne and a tipet cumlie, and haue hys crowne fhorne faire and roundlie, and could turne his Portreffe and pie readilie: whiche I fpeake not to reproue any order either of apparell, or other dewtie, that may be well and indifferentlie vfed, but to note the miferie of that time, whan the benefites prouided for learning were fo fowlie mifufed. And what was the frute of this feade? Verely, iudgement in doctrine was wholy altered: order in difcipline very fore changed: the loue of good learning, began fodenly to wax cold: the knowledge of the tonges (in fpite of fome that therein had florifhed) was manifeftly contemned: and fo, ye way of right ftudie purpofely peruerted: the choice of good authors of mallice confownded. Olde fophiftrie (I fay not well) not olde, but that new rotten fophiftrie began to beard and fholder logicke in her owne tong: yea, I know, that heades were caft together, and counfell deuifed, that *Duns*, with all the rable of barbarous queftioniftes, fhould haue difpoffeffed of their place and rowmes, *Ariftotle*, *Plato*, *Tullie*, and *Demofthenes*, when good *M. Redman*, and thofe two worthy ftarres of that vniuerfitie, *M. Cheke*, and *M. Smith*, with their fcholers, had brought to florifhe as notable in Cam-

Aristoteles. brige, as euer they did in Grece and in
Plato. Italie: and for the doctrine of thofe fowre,
Cicero.
Demost. the fowre pillers of learning, Cambrige
than geuing place to no vniuerfitie, neither in France, Spaine, Germanie, nor Italie. Alfo in outward behauiour, than began fimplicitie in apparell, to be layd afide. Courtlie galantnes to be taken vp: frugalitie in diet was priuately mifliked: Towne going
Shoting.   to good cheare openly vfed: honeft paf

times, ioyned with labor, left of in the fieldes: vnthrifty
and idle games haunted corners, and occupied the
nightes: contention in youth, no where for learning:
factions in the elders euery where for trifles: All which
miferies at length, by Gods prouidence, had their end
16. *Nouemb.* 1558. Since which tyme, the yong fpring
hath fhot vp fo faire, as now there be in Cambrige
againe, many goodly plantes (as did well appeare at
the Queenes Maiefties late being there) which are
like to grow to mightie great timber, to the honor of
learning, and great good of their contrie, if they may
ftand their tyme, as the beft plantes there were wont
to do: and if fom old dotterell trees, with ftanding ouer
nie them, and dropping vpon them, do not eithei
hinder, or crooke their growing, wherein my feare is
ye leffe, feing fo worthie a Iuftice of an Oyre hath the
prefent ouerfight of that whole chace, who was himfelfe fomtym, in the faireft fpring that euer was there
of learning, one of the forwardeft yong plantes, in all
that worthy College of *S. Iohnes*: who now by grace
is growne to foch greatneffe, as, in the temperate and
quiet fhade of his wifdome, next the prouidence of
God, and goodnes of one, in theis our daies, *Religio*
for finceritie, *literæ* for order and aduauncement,
Respub. for happie and quiet gouernment, haue to
great rejoyfing of all good men, fpeciallie repofed
them felues.

Now to returne to that Queftion, whether one, a
few, many or all, are to be followed, my aunfwere
fhalbe fhort: All, for him that is defirous to know all:
yea, the worft of all, as Queftioniftes, and all the barbarous nation of fcholemen, helpe for one or other
confideration : But in euerie feparate kinde of learning and ftudie, by it felfe, ye muft follow, chofelie a
few, and chieflie fome one, and that namelie in our
fchole of eloquence, either for penne or talke. And
as in portracture and paintyng wife men chofe not that
workman, that can onelie make a faire hand, or a well
facioned legge, but foch [a] one, as can furnifh vp fullie

all the fetures of the whole body, of a man, woman and child: and with all is able to, by good fkill, to giue to euerie one of thefe three, in their proper kinde, the right forme, the trew figure, the naturall color, that is fit and dew, to the dignitie of a man, to the bewtie of a woman, to the fweetnes of a yong babe: euen likewife, do we feeke foch one in our fchole to folow, who is able alwayes, in all matters, to teach plainlie, to delite pleafantlie, and to cary away by force of wife talke, all that fhall heare or reade him: and is fo excellent in deed, as witte is able, or wifhe can hope, to attaine vnto: And this not onelie to ferue in the *Latin* or *Greke* tong, but alfo in our own Englifh language. But yet, bicaufe the prouidence of God hath left vnto vs in no other tong, faue onelie in the *Greke* and *Latin* tong, the trew preceptes, and perfite examples of eloquence, therefore muft we feeke in the Authors onelie of thofe two tonges, the trewe Paterne of Eloquence, if in any other mother tongue we looke to attaine, either to perfit vtterance of it our felues, or fkilfull iudgement of it in others.

And now to know, what Author doth medle onelie with fome one peece and member of eloquence, and who doth perfitelie make vp the whole bodie, I will declare, as I can call to remembrance the goodlie talke, that I haue had oftentymes, of the trew difference of Authors, with that Ientleman of worthie memorie, my deareft frend, and teacher of all the litle poore learning I haue, Syr *Iohn Cheke.*

The trew difference of Authors is beft knowne, *per diuerfa genera dicendi,* that euerie one vfed. And therefore here I will deuide *genus dicendi,* not into thefe three, *Tenuè, mediocrè, et grande,* but as the matter of euerie Author requireth, as

in Genus { *Poeticum.* *Hiftoricum.* *Philofophicum.* *Oratorium.*

Thefe differre one from an other, in choice of wordes, in framyng of Sentences, in handling of Argumentes, and vfe of right forme, figure, and number, proper and fitte for euerie matter, and euerie one of thefe is diuerfe alfo in it felfe, as the firft.

$$Poeticum, in \begin{cases} Comicum. \\ Tragicum. \\ Epicum. \\ Melicum. \end{cases}$$

And here, who foeuer hath bene diligent to read aduifedlie ouer, *Terence, Seneca, Virgil, Horace,* or els *Ariftophanus, Sophocles, Homer,* and *Pindar,* and fhall diligently marke the difference they vfe, in proprietie of wordes, in forme of fentence, in handlyng of their matter, he fhall eafelie perceiue, what is fitte and *decorum* in euerie one, to the trew vfe of perfite Imitation. Whan *M. Watfon* in S. Iohns College at Cambrige wrote his excellent Tragedie of *Abfalon, M. Cheke,* he and I, for that part of trew Imitation, had many pleafant talkes togither, in comparing the preceptes of *Ariftotle* and *Horace de Arte Poetica,* with the examples of *Euripides, Sophocles,* and *Seneca.* Few men, in writyng of Tragedies in our dayes, haue fhot at this marke. Some in *England,* moe in *France, Germanie,* and *Italie,* alfo haue written Tragedies in our tyme: of the which, not one I am fure is able to abyde the trew touch of *Ariftotles* preceptes, and *Euripides* examples, faue onely two, that euer I faw, *M. Watfons Abfalon,* and *Georgius Buckananus Iephthe.* One man in Cambrige, well liked of many, but beft liked of him felfe, was many tymes bold and bufie, to bryng matters vpon ftages, which he called Tragedies. In one, wherby he looked to wynne his fpurres, and whereat many ignorant felowes faft clapped their handes, he began the *Protafis* with *Trochæijs Octonarijs*: which kinde of verfe, as it is but feldome and rare in Tragedies, fo is it neuer vfed, faue onelie in *Epitafi*: whan the Tragedie is hieft and hoteft, and full of greateft troubles. I remember ful well what *M. Watſon* merelie ſayd vnto me of his blindneſſe and boldnes in that behalfe although otherwiſe, there paſſed much frendſhip betwene them. *M. Watſon* had an other maner [of] care of perfection, with a feare and reuerence of the iudgement of the beſt learned : Who to this day would neuer ſuffer, yet his *Abſalon* to go abroad, and that onelie, bicauſe, in *locis paribus*, *Anapeſtus* is twiſe or thriſe vſed in ſtede of *Iambus*. A ſmal faulte, and ſuch [a] one, as perchance would neuer be marked, no neither in *Italie* nor *France*. This I write, not ſo much, to note the firſt, or praiſe the laſt, as to leaue in memorie of writing, for good example to poſteritie, what perfection, in any tyme, was, moſt diligentlie ſought for in like maner, in all kinde of learnyng, in that moſt worthie College of S. Iohns in Cambrige.

$$\text{Historicum in} \begin{cases} \textit{Diaria.} \\ \textit{Annales.} \\ \textit{Commentarios.} \\ \textit{Iuſtam Hiſtoriam.} \end{cases}$$

For what proprietie in wordes, ſimplicitie in ſentences, plainneſſe and light, is cumelie for theſe kindes, *Cæſar* and *Liuie*, for the two laſt, are perfite examples of Imitation : And for the two firſt, the old paternes be loſt, and as for ſome that be preſent and of late tyme, they be fitter to be read once for ſome pleaſure, than oft to be perſued, for any good Imitation of them.

$$\text{Philoſophicum in} \begin{cases} \textit{in Sermonem, as officia} \\ \qquad \textit{Cic. et Eth. Ariſt.} \\ \textit{Contentionem.} \end{cases}$$

As, the Dialoges of *Plato*, *Xenophon*, and *Cicero*: of which kinde of learnyng, and right Imitation therof, *Carolus Sigonius* hath written of late, both learnedlie and eloquentlie: but beſt of all my frende *Ioan. Stur mius* in hys Commentaries vpon *Gorgias Platonis*, which booke I haue in writyng, and is not yet ſet out in Print.

$$\text{Oratorium in}\ \begin{cases} \textit{Humile.} \\ \textit{Mediocre.} \\ \textit{Sublime.} \end{cases}$$

Examples of thefe three, in the *Greke* tong, be plenti-full and perfite, as *Lycias*, *Ifocrates*, and *Demofthenes*: and all three, in onelie *Demofthenes*, in diuerfe orations as *contra Olimpiodorum, in Leptinem, et pro Ctefiphonte*. And trew it is, that *Hermogenes* writeth of *Demofthenes*, that all formes of Eloquence be perfite in him. In *Ciceroes* Orations, *Medium et fublime* be moft excellentlie hand-led, but *Humile* in his Orations is feldome fene. Yet neuertheleffe in other bookes, as in fome part of his offices, and fpecially *in Partitionibus*, he is comparable *in hoc humili et difciplinabili genere*, euen with the beft that euer wrote in *Greke*. But of *Cicero* more fullie in fitter place. And thus, the trew difference of ftiles, in euerie Author, and euerie kinde of learnyng may eafelie be knowne by this diuifion.

$$\text{in Genus}\ \begin{cases} \textit{Poeticum.} \\ \textit{Hiftoricum.} \\ \textit{Philofophicum.} \\ \textit{Oratorium.} \end{cases}$$

Which I thought in this place to touch onelie, not to profecute at large, bicaufe, God willyng, in the *Latin* tong, I will fullie handle it, in my booke *de Imitatione*.

Now, to touch more particularlie, which of thofe Authors, that be now moft commonlie in mens handes, will fone affourd you fome peece of Eloquence, and what maner a peece of eloquence, and what is to be liked and folowed, and what to be mifliked and efchewed in them : and how fome agayne will furnifh you fully withall, rightly, and wifely confidered, fom-what I will write as I haue heard Syr *Iohn Cheke* many tymes fay.

The Latin tong, concerning any part of pureneffe of it, from the fpring, to the decay of the fame, did not endure moch longer, than is the life of a well aged man, fcarfe one hundred yeares from the tyme of the laſt *Scipio Africanus* and *Lælius*, to the Empire of *Auguſtus*. And it is notable, that *Vellius Paterculus* writeth of *Tullie*, how that the perfection of eloquence did fo remayne onelie in him and in his time, as before him, were few, which might moch delight a man, or after him any, worthy admiration, but foch as *Tullie* might haue feene, and fuch as might haue feene *Tullie*. And good caufe why: for no perfection is durable. En-creafe hath a time, and decay likewife, but all perfit ripeneffe remaineth but a moment: as is plainly feen in fruits, plummcs and cherries: but more fenfibly in flowers, as Rofes and fuch like, and yet as trewlie in all greater matters. For what naturallie, can go no hier, muſt naturallie yeld and ſtoupe againe.

Of this ſhort tyme of any pureneffe of the Latin tong, for the firſt fortie yeare of it, and all the tyme before, we haue no peece of learning left, faue *Plautus* and *Terence*, with a litle rude vnperfit pamflet of the elder *Cato*. And as for *Plautus*, except the fcholemaſter be able to make wife and ware choice, firſt in proprietie of wordes, than in framing of Phrafes and fentences, and chieflie in choice of honeſtie of matter, your fcholer were better to play, then learne all that is in him. But furelie, if iudgement for the tong, and direction for the maners, be wifely ioyned with the diligent reading of *Plautus*, than trewlie *Plautus*, for that pureneffe of the Latin tong in Rome, whan Rome did moſt floriſh in wel doing, and fo thereby, in well fpeaking alfo, is foch a plentifull ſtoreho[u]ſe, for common eloquence, in meane matters, and all priuate mens affaires, as the Latin tong, for that refpect, hath not the like agayne. Whan I remember the worthy tyme of Rome, wherein *Plautus* did liue, I muſt nedes honor the talke of that tyme, which we fee *Plautus* doth vfe.

Terence is alfo a ſtorehoufe of the fame tong, for an other tyme, following foone after, and although he be not fo full and plentiful as *Plautus* is, for multitude of matters, and diuerſitie of wordes, yet his wordes, be

chofen fo purelie, placed fo orderly, and all his ftuffe
fo neetlie packed vp, and wittely compaffed in euerie
place, as, by all wife mens iudgement, he is counted
the cunninger workeman, and to haue his fhop, for the
rowme that is in it, more finely appointed, and trimlier
ordered, than *Plautus* is.

Three thinges chiefly, both in *Plautus* and *Terence*,
are to be fpecially confidered The matter, the vtterance, the words, the meter.   The matter in both, is
altogether within the compaffe of the meaneft mens
maners, and doth not ftretch to any thing of any great
weight at all, but ftandeth chiefly in vtteryng the
thoughtes and conditions of hard fathers, foolifh
mothers, vnthrifty yong men, craftie feruantes, fotle
bawdes, and wilie harlots, and fo, is moch fpent, in
finding out fine fetches, and packing vp pelting matters,
foch as in London commonlie cum to the hearing of
the Mafters of Bridewell.   Here is bafe ftuffe for that
fcholer, that fhould be cum hereafter, either a good
minifter in Religion, or a Ciuill Ientleman in feruice
of his Prince and contrie : except the preacher do
know foch matters to confute them, whan ignorance
furelie in all foch thinges were better for a Ciuill
Ientleman, than knowledge.   And thus, for matter,
both *Plautus* and *Terence*, be like meane painters, that
worke by halfes, and be cunning onelie, in making the
worft part of the picture, as if one were fkilfull in
painting the bodie of a naked perfon, from the nauell
downward, but nothing elfe.

For word and fpeach, *Plautus* is more plentifull, and
Terence more pure and proper : And for one refpect,
Terence is to be embraced aboue all that euer wrote in
hys kinde of argument : Bicaufe it is well known, by
good recorde of learning, and that by *Ciceroes* owne
witnes that fome Comedies bearyng *Terence* name,
were written by worthy *Scipio*, and wife *Lælius*, and
namely *Heauton* : and *Adelphi*.   And therefore as oft
as I reade thofe Comedies, fo oft doth found in myne
eare, the pure fine talke of Rome, which was vfed by

the floure of the worthieſt nobilitie that euer Rome bred. Let the wifeſt man, and beſt learned that liueth, read aduiſedlie ouer, the firſt ſcene of *Heauton*, and the firſt ſcene of *Adelphi*, and let him conſideratlie iudge, whether it is the talke of a ſeruile ſtranger borne, or rather euen that milde eloquent wiſe ſpeach, which *Cicero* in *Brutus* doth ſo liuely expreſſe in *Lælius*. And yet neuertheleſſe, in all this good proprietie of wordes, and pureneſſe of phraſes which be in *Terence*, ye muſt not follow him alwayes in placing of them, bicauſe for the meter ſake, ſome wordes in him, ſomtyme, be driuen awrie, which require a ſtraighter placing in plaine proſe, if ye will forme, as I would ye ſhould do, your ſpeach and writing, to that excellent perſitneſſe, which was onely in *Tullie*, or onelie in *Tullies* tyme.

The meter and verſe of *Plautus* and *Terence* be verie meane, and not to be followed : which is not their reproch, but the fault of the tyme, wherein they wrote, whan no kinde of Poetrie, in the Latin tong, was brought to perfection, as doth well appeare in the fragmentes of *Ennius*, *Cerilius*, and others, and euiden[t]lie in *Plautus* and *Terence*, if thies in Latin be compared with right ſkil, with *Homer*, *Euripides*, *Ariſtophanes*, and other in Greeke of like ſort. *Cicero* him ſelfe doth complaine of this vnperfitnes, but more plainly *Quintilian*, ſaying, *in Comœdia maximè claudicamus, et vix leuem conſequimur vmbram* : and moſt earneſtly of all *Horace in Arte Poetica*, which he doth namely *propter carmen Iambicum*, and referreth all good ſtudentes herein to the Imitation of the Greeke tong, ſaying.

> *Exemplaria Græca*
> *noƈturna verſate manu, verſate diurna.*

This matter maketh me gladly remember, my ſweete tyme ſpent at Cambrige, and the pleaſant talke which I had oft with *M. Cheke*, and *M. Watſon*, of this fault, not onely in the olde Latin Poets, but alſo in our new Engliſh Rymers at this day. They wiſhed as *Virgil* and *Horace* were not wedded to follow the faultes of

former fathers (a fhrewd mariage in greater matters)
but by right *Imitation* of the perfit Grecians, had
brought Poetrie to perfitneffe alfo in the Latin tong,
that we Englifhmen likewife would acknowledge and
vnderfland rightfully our rude beggerly ryming, brought
firft into Italie by *Gothes* and *Hunnes*, whan all good
verfes and all good learning to, were deftroyd by
them : and after caryed into France and Germanie :
and at laft receyued into England by men of excellent
wit in deede, but of fmall learning, and leffe iudgement in that behalfe.

But now, when men know the difference, and haue
the examples, both of the beft, and of the worft, furelie,
to follow rather the *Gothes* in Ryming, than the Greekes
in trew verfifiyng, were euen to eate ackornes with
fwyne, when we may freely eate wheate bread emonges
men. In deede, *Chaufer*, *Th. Norton*, of Briftow, my
L. of Surrey, *M. Wiat*, *Th. Phaer*, and other Ientleman, in tranflating *Ouide*, *Palingenius* and *Seneca*, haue
gonne as farre to their great praife, as the copie they
followed could cary them, but, if foch good wittes, and
forward diligence, had bene directed to follow the beft
examples, and not haue bene caryed by tyme and
cuftome, to content themfelues with that barbarous
and rude Ryming, emonges their other worthy praifes,
which they haue iuftly deferued, this had not bene the
leaft, to be counted emonges men of learning and fkill,
more like vnto the Grecians, than vnto the Gothians,
in handling of their verfe.

In deed, our Englifh tong, hauing in vfe chiefly,
wordes of one fyllable which commonly be long, doth
not well receiue the nature of *Carmen Heroicum*,
bicaufe *dactylus*, the apteft foote for that verfe, conteining one long and two fhort, is feldom therefore
found in Englifh : and doth alfo rather ftumble than
ftand vpon *Monafyllabis*. *Quintilian* in hys learned
Chapiter *de Compofitione*, geueth this leffon
de Monafyllabis, before me : and in the fame place
doth iuftlie inuey againft all Ryming, if there be any,

who be angrie with me, for miſliking of Ryming, may be angry for company to, with *Quintilian* alſo, for the ſame thing: And yet *Quintilian* had not ſo iuſt cauſe to miſlike of it than, as men haue at this day.

And although *Carmen Exametrum* doth rather trotte and hoble, than runne ſmothly in our Engliſh tong, yet I am ſure, our Engliſh tong will receiue *carmen Iambicum* as naturallie, as either *Greke* or *Latin*. But for ignorance, men can not like, and for idlenes, men will not labor, to cum to any perfitnes at all. For, as the worthie Poetes in *Athens* and *Rome*, were more carefull to ſatiſfie the iudgement of one learned, than raſhe in pleaſing the humor of a rude multitude, euen ſo if men in England now, had the like reuerend regard to learning ſkill and iudgement, and durſt not preſume to write, except they came with the like learnyng, and alſo did vſe like diligence, in ſearchyng out, not onelie iuſt meaſure in euerie meter, as euerie ignorant perſon may eaſely do, but alſo trew quantitie in euery foote and ſillable, as onelie the learned ſhalbe able to do, and as the *Grekes* and *Romanes* were wont to do, ſurelie than raſh ignorant heads, which now can eaſely recken vp fourten ſillabes, and eaſelie ſtumble on euery Ryme, either durſt not, for lacke of ſuch learnyng: or els would not, in auoyding ſuch labor, be ſo buſie, as euerie where they be: and ſhoppes in London ſhould not be ſo full of lewd and rude rymes, as commonlie they are. But now, the ripeſt of tonge, be readieſt to write: And many dayly in ſetting out bookes and bal[l]ettes make great ſhew of bloſſomes and buddes, in whom is neither, roote of learning, nor frute of wiſedome at all. Some that make *Chaucer* in Engliſh and *Petrarch* in *Italian*, their Gods in verſes, and yet be not able to make trew difference, what is a fault, and what is a iuſt prayſe, in thoſe two worthie wittes, will moch miſlike this my writyng. But ſuch men be euen like followers of *Chaucer* and *Petrarke*, as one here in England did folow Syr *Tho. More*: who, being moſt vnlike vnto him, in wit and learnyng, neuertheles in wearing his gowne awrye vpon the one fhoulder, as Syr *Tho. More* was wont to do, would nedes be counted lyke vnto him.

This miflikyng of Ryming, beginneth not now of any newfangle fingularitie, but hath bene long mifliked of many, and that of men, of greateft learnyng, and deepeft iudgement. And foch, that defend it, do fo, either for lacke of knowledge what is beft, or els of verie enuie, that any fhould performe that in learnyng, whereunto they, as I fayd before, either for ignorance, can not, or for idlenes will not, labor to attaine vnto.

And you that prayfe this Ryming, bicaufe ye neither haue reafon, why to like it, nor can fhew learning to defend it, yet I will helpe you, with the authoritie of the oldeft and learnedft tyme. In *Grece*, whan Poetrie was euen as the hieft pitch of perfitnes, one *Simmias Rhodius* of a certaine fingularitie wrote a booke in ryming *Greke* verfes, naming it ᾠὸν, conteyning the fable how *Iupiter* in likenes of a fwan, gat that egge vpon *Leda*, whereof came *Caftor*, *Pollux* and faire [*H*]*elena*. This booke was fo liked, that it had few to read it, but none to folow it: But was prefentlie contemned: and fone after, both Author and booke, fo forgotten by men, and confumed by tyme, as fcarce the name of either is kept in memorie of learnyng: And the like folie was neuer folowed of any, many hondred yeares after vntill ye *Hunnes* and *Gothians*, and other barbarous nations, of ignorance and rude fingularitie, did reuiue the fame folie agayne.

The noble Lord *Th.* Earle of Surrey, The Earle of Surrey. firft of all Englifh men, in tranflating the *Gonfaluo Periz.* fourth booke of *Virgill*: and *Gonfaluo Periz* that excellent learned man, and Secretarie to kyng *Philip* of *Spaine*, in tranflating the *Vliffes* of *Homer* out of *Greke* into *Spanifh*, haue both, by good iudgement, auoyded the fault of Ryming, yet neither of them hath fullie hit[t]e perfite and trew verfifying. In deed, they obferue iuft number, and euen feete: but here is the fault, that their feete: be feete without ioyntes, that is to fay, not diftinct by trew quantitie of fillabes: And fo, foch feete, be but numme [benummed] feete: and be, euen as vnfitte for a verfe to turne and runne roundly withall, as feete of braffe or wood be vn-weeldie to go well withall. And as a foote of wood, is a plaine fhew of a manifeft maime, euen fo feete, in our Englifh verfifing, without quantitie and ioyntes, be fure fignes, that the verfe is either, borne deformed, vnnaturall and lame, and fo verie vnfeemlie to looke vpon, except to men that be gogle eyed them felues.

The fpying of this fault now is not the curiofitie of Englifh eyes, but euen the good iudgement alfo of the beft that write in thefe dayes in *Italie*: and namelie *Senese Felice Figlincci*, who, writyng vpon *Ariftotles Ethickes* fo excel-lentlie in *Italian*, as neuer did yet any one in myne opinion either in *Greke* or *Latin*, amongeft other thynges doth moft earneftlie inuey agaynft the rude ryming of verfes in that tong: And whan foeuer he expreffed *Ariftotles* preceptes, with any example, out of *Homer* or *Euripides*, he tranflateth them, not after the Rymes of *Petrarke*, but into foch kinde of perfite verfe, with like feete and quantitie of fillabes, as he found them before in the *Greke* tonge: exhortyng earneftlie all the *Italian* nation, to leaue of their rude barbariouf-neffe in ryming, and folow diligently the excellent *Greke* and *Latin* examples, in trew verfifiyng.

And you, that be able to vnderftand no more, then ye finde in the *Italian* tong: and neuer went farder than the fchole of *Petrarke* and *Arioftus* abroad, or els of *Chaucer* at home, though you haue pleafure to wander blindlie ftill in your foule wrong way, enuie not others, that feeke, as wife men haue done before them, the faireft and righteft way: or els, befide the iuft reproch of malice, wifemen fhall trewlie iudge, that you do fo, as I haue fayd and fay yet agayne vnto you, bicaufe, either, for idlenes ye will not, or for ignorance ye can not, cum by no better your felfe.

And therfore euen as *Virgill* and *Horace* deferue moft worthie prayfe, that they fpying the vnperfitnes in

Ennius and *Plautus*, by trew Imitation of *Homer* and *Euripides*, brought Poetrie to the fame perfitnes in *Latin*, as it was in *Greke*, euen fo thofe, that by the fame way would benefite their tong and contrey, deferue rather thankes than difprayfe in that behalfe.

And I reioyce, that euen poore England preuented *Italie*, firft in fpying out, than in feekyng to amend this fault in learnyng.

And here, for my pleafure I purpofe a litle, by the way, to play and fporte with my Mafter *Tully*: from whom commonlie I am neuer wont to diffent. He him felfe, for this point of learnyng, in his verfes doth halt a litle by his leaue. He could not denie it, if he were aliue, nor thofe defend hym now that loue him beft. This fault I lay to his charge: bicaufe once it pleafed him, though fomwhat merelie, yet oueruncurteflie, to rayle vpon poore Eng- Tullies faying against Eng- land. land, obiecting both, extreme beggerie, and mere barbarioufnes vnto it, writyng thus vnto his frend *Atticus*: There is not one fcruple of filuer Ad Att. Lib. iv. Ep. 16. in that whole Ifle, or any one that knoweth either learnyng or letter.

But now mafter *Cicero*, bleffed be God, and his fonne Iefus Chrift, whom you neuer knew, except it were as it pleafed him to lighten you by fome fhadow, as couertlie in one place ye confeffe faying: *Veritatis tantum vmbram confectamur*, as your Mafter Offic. *Plato* did before you: bleffed be God, I fay, that fixten hundred yeare after you were dead and gone, it may trewly be fayd, that for filuer, there is more cumlie plate, in one Citie of England, than is in foure of the proudeft Cities in all *Italie*, and take *Rome* for one of them. And for learnyng, befide the knowledge of all learned tongs and liberall fciences, euen your owne bookes *Cicero*, be as well read, and your excellent eloquence is as well liked and loued, and as trewlie folowed in England at this day, as it is now, or euer was, fence your owne tyme, in any place of *Italie* either at *Arpinum*, where ye were borne, or els at *Rome* where ye were brought vp. And a litle to brag with you *Cicero*, where you your felfe, by your leaue, halted in fome point of learnyng in your owne tong, many in England at this day go ftreight vp, both in trewe fkill, and right doing therein.

This I write, not to reprehend *Tullie*, whom, aboue all other, I like and loue beft, but to excufe *Terence*, becaufe in his tyme, and a good while after, Poetrie was neuer perfited in *Latin*, vntill by trew *Imitation* of the Grecians, it was at length brought to perfection: And alfo thereby to exhorte the goodlie wittes of England, which apte by nature, and willing by defire, geue them felues to Poetrie, that they, rightly vnderftanding the barbarous bringing in of Rymes, would labor, as *Virgil* and *Horace* did in Latin, to make perfit alfo this point of learning, in our Englifh tong.

And thus much for *Plautus* and *Terence*, for matter, tong, and meter, what is to be followed, and what to be exchewed in them.

After *Plautus* and *Terence*, no writing remayneth vntill *Tullies* tyme, except a fewe fhort fragmentes of *L. Craffus* excellent wit, here and there recited of *Cicero* for example fake, whereby the louers of learnyng may the more lament the loffe of foch a worthie witte.

And although the Latin tong did faire blome and bloffome in *L. Craffus*, and *M. Antonius*, yet in *Tullies* tyme onely, and in Tullie himfelfe chieflie, was the Latin tong fullie ripe, and growne to the hieft pitch of all perfection.

And yet in the fame tyme, it began to fade and ftoupe, *Tullie* him felfe, in *Brutus de Claris Oratoribus*, with weeping wordes doth witneffe.

And bicaufe, emong[e]ft them of that tyme, there was fome difference, good reafon is, that of them of that tyme, fhould be made right choice alfo. And yet let the beft *Ciceronian* in Italie read *Tullies* familiar epiftles aduifedly ouer, and I beleue he fhall finde fmall difference, for the Latin tong, either in propriety of wordes or framing of the ftile, betwixt *Tullie*, and thofe that write vnto him. As *Ser. Sulpitius, A. Cecinna,*

M. Cælis, M. et D. Bruti, A. Pollia, L. Plancus, and
diuerſe other: read the epiſtles of *L. Plancus*   Epi. Planci x.
in *x. Lib.* and for an aſſay, that Epiſtle lib. Epist. 8.
namely to the *Co[n]ſſ.* and whole *Senate,* the eight Epiſtle
in number, and what could be, eyther more eloquentlie,
or more wiſelie written, yea by *Tullie* himſelfe, a man
may iuſtly doubt.   Thies men and *Tullie,* liued all in
one tyme, were like in authoritie, not vnlike in learning
and ſtudie, which might be iuſt cauſes of this their
equalitie in writing: And yet ſurely, they neyther were
in deed, nor yet were counted in mens opinions, equall
with *Tullie* in that facultie.   And how is the difference
hid in his Epiſtles? verelie, as the cunning of an expert
Seaman, in a faire calme freſh Ryuer, doth litle differ
from the doing of a meaner workman therein, euen ſo,
in the ſhort cut of a priuate letter, where, matter is
common, wordes eaſie, and order not moch diuerſe,
ſmall ſhew of difference can appeare. But where *Tullie*
doth ſet vp his ſaile of eloquence, in ſome broad deep
Argument, caried with full tyde and winde, of his witte
and learnyng, all other may rather ſtand and looke after
him, than hope to ouertake him, what courſe ſo euer
he hold, either in faire or foule.   Foure men onely
whan the Latin tong was full ripe, be left vnto vs, who
in that tyme did floriſh, and did leaue to poſteritie, the
fruite of their witte and learning: *Varro, Saluſt, Cæſar,*
and *Cicero.*   Whan I ſay, theſe foure onely, I am not
ignorant, that euen in the ſame tyme, moſt excellent
Poetes, deſeruing well of the Latin tong, as *Lucretius,
Catulius, Virgill,* and *Horace,* did write: But, bicauſe,
in this litle booke, I purpoſe to teach a yong ſcholer,
to go, not to daunce: to ſpeake, not to ſing, (whan
Poetes in deed, namelie *Epici* and *Lyrici,* as theſe be,
are fine dauncers, and trime ſingers,) but *Oratores* and
Historici, be thoſe cumlie goers, and faire and wiſe
ſpeakers, of whom I wiſhe my ſcholer to wayte vpon
firſt, and after in good order, and dew tyme, to be
brought forth, to the ſinging and dauncing ſchole:
And for this conſideration, do I name theſe foure, to
be the onelie writers of that tyme.

¶ *Varro.*

Varro.   *Varro*, in his bookes *de lingua Latina, et Analogia* as thefe be left mangled and patched vnto vs, doth not enter there in to any great depth of eloquence, but as one caried in a fmall low veffell him felfe verie nie the common fhore, not much vnlike the fifher men of Rye, and Hering men of Yarmouth.   Who deferue by common mens opinion, fmall commendacion, for any cunning fa[y]ling at all, yet neuertheles in thofe bookes of *Varro* good and neceffarie ftuffe, for that meane kinde of Argument, be verie well and learnedlie gathered togither.

De Rep.   His bookes of Hufbandrie, are moch to
Ruftica.   be regarded, and diligentlie to be read, not onelie for the proprietie, but alfo for the plentie of good wordes, in all contrey and hufbandmens affaires: which can not be had, by fo good authoritie, out of any other Author, either of fo good a tyme, or of fo great learnyng, as out of *Varro*.   And yet bicaufe, he was fourfcore yeare old, whan he wrote thofe bookes, the forme of his ftyle there compared with *Tullies* writyng, is but euen the talke of a fpent old man: whofe wordes commonlie fall out of his mouth, though verie wifelie, yet hardly and coldie, and more heauelie alfo, than fome eares can well beare, except onelie for age, and authorities fake.   And perchance, in a rude contrey argument, of purpofe and iudgement, he rather vfed, the fpeach of the contrey, than talke of the Citie.

And fo, for matter fake, his wordes fometyme, be fomewhat rude: and by the imitation of the elder *Cato*, old and out of vfe: And beyng depe ftept in age, by negligence fome wordes do fo [e]fcape and fall from him in thofe bookes, as be not worth the taking vp, by him, that is carefull to fpeak or write trew Latin, as that
Lib. 3. *Cap.* 1.   fentence in him, *Romani, in pace à rufticis alebantur, et in bello ab his tuebantur*.   A good ftudent muft be therfore carefull and diligent, to read with

iudgement ouer euen thofe Authors, which did write in
the moft perfite tyme: and let him not be affrayd to
trie them, both in proprietie of wordes, and forme of
ftyle, by the touch ftone of *Cæfar* and *Cicero*, whofe
puritie was neuer foiled, no not by the fentence of thofe,
that loued them worft.

All louers of learnyng may fore lament The loue of
the loffe of thofe bookes of *Varro*, which he Warroes
wrote in his yong and luftie yeares, with good bookes.
leyfure, and great learnyng of all partes of Philofophie:
of the goodlieft argumentes, perteyning both to the
common wealth, and priuate life of man, as, *de Ratione
studij, et educandis liberis*, which booke, is oft recited,
and moch prayfed, in the fragmentes of *Nonius*, euen for
authoritie fake. He wrote moft diligentlie and largelie,
alfo the whole hiftorie of the ftate of *Rome*: the myf-
teries of their whole Religion: their lawes, cuftomes,
and gouernement in peace: their maners, and whole
difcipline in warre: And this is not my geffing, as one
in deed that neuer faw thofe bookes, but euen, the
verie iudgement, and playne teftimonie of *Tullie* him
felfe, who knew and read thofe bookes, in thefe wordes:
*Tu ætatem Patriæ: Tu defcriptiones temporum: Tu
facrorum, tu facerdotum Iura: Tu domesticam, tu belli-
cam difciplinam: Tu fedem Regionum, locorum, tu
omnium diuinarum humanarumque rerum* In Acad.
nomina, genera, officia, caufas aperuifti. etc. Queft.

But this great loffe of *Varro*, is a litle recompenfed
by the happy comming of *Dionyfius Halicarnaffæus* to
Rome in *Auguftus* dayes: who getting the poffeffion of
Varros librarie, out of that treafure houfe of learning,
did leaue vnto vs fome frute of *Varros* witte and diligence, I meane, his goodlie bookes *de Antiquitatibus
Romanorum.* *Varro* was fo eftemed for his excellent
learnyng, as *Tullie* him felfe had a reuerence to his
iudgement in all dou[b]tes of learnyng. And *Antonius
Triumuir*, his enemie, and of a contrarie Cic. ad Att.
faction, who had power to kill and bannifh whom he
lifted, whan *Varros* name amongeft others was brought

in a fchedule vnto him, to be noted to death, he tooke his penne and wrote his warrant of fauegard with thefe moft goodlie wordes, *Viuat Varro vir doctiffimus.*   In later tyme, no man knew better: nor liked and loued more *Varros* learnyng, than did *S. Auguftine*, as they do well vnderftand, that haue diligentlie read ouer his learned bookes *de Ciuitate Dei*: Where he hath this moft notable fentence: Whan I fee, how much *Varro* wrote, I meruell much, that euer he had any leafure to read: and whan I perceiue how many thinges he read, I meruell more, that euer he had any leafure to write. etc.

And furelie, if *Varros* bookes had remained to pofteritie, as by Gods prouidence, the moft part of *Tullies* did, than trewlie the *Latin* tong might haue made good comparifon with the *Greke*.

Saluste.

Salust *Saluft*, is a wife and worthy writer: but he requireth a learned Reader, and a right confiderer of him.   My deareft frend, and beft mafter that euer I

Syr Iohn Chekes iudgement and counsell for readyng of *Saluste*. had or heard in learning, Syr *I. Cheke*, foch a man, as if I fhould liue to fee England breed the like againe, I feare, I fhould liue ouer long, did once giue me a leffon for *Saluft*, which, as I fhall neuer forget my felfe, fo is it worthy to be remembred of all thofe, that would cum to perfite iudgement of the Latin tong. He faid, that *Saluft* was not verie fitte for yong men, to learne out of him, the puritie of the Latin tong: becaufe, he was not the pureft in proprietie of wordes, nor choifeft in aptnes of phrafes, nor the beft in framing of fentences: and therefore is his writing, fayd he neyther plaine for the matter, nor fenfible for mens vnderftanding.   And what is the caufe thereof, Syr, quoth I.   Verilie faid he, bicaufe in *Saluft* writing, is more Arte than nature, and more labor than Arte: and in his labor alfo, to moch toyle, as it were, with

an vncontented care to write better than he could, a
fault common to very many men.   And therefore he
doth not expreffe the matter liuely and naturally with
common fpeach as ye fee *Xenophon* doth in Greeke,
but it is caried and driuen forth artificiallie, after to
learned a forte, as *Thucydides*, doth in his orations.
And how cummeth it to paffe, fayd I, that *Cæfar* and
Ciceroes talke, is fo naturall and plaine, and *Saluft*
writing fo artificiall and darke, whan all they three
liued in one tyme ?   I will freelie tell you my fanfie
herein, faid he : furely, *Cæfar* and *Cicero*, befide a
fingular prerogatiue of naturall eloquence geuen vnto
them by God, both two, by vfe of life, were daylie
orators emonges the common people, and greateft
councellers in the Senate houfe : and therefore gaue
themfelues to vfe foch fpeach as the meaneft fhould
well vnderftand, and the wifeft beft allow : folowing
carefullie that good councell of *Ariftotle, loquendum vt
multi, fapiendum vt pauci.   Saluft* was no foch man,
neyther for will to goodnes, nor fkill by learning : but
ill geuen by nature, and made worfe by bringing vp,
fpent the moft part of his youth very miforderly in
ryot and lechery.   In the company of foch, who, neuer
geuing theyr mynde to honeft doyng, could neuer
inure their tong to wife fpeaking.   But at [ye] laft cummyng to better yeares, and b[u]ying witte at the deareft
hand, that is, by long experience of the hurt and fhame
that commeth of mifcheif, moued, by the councell of
them that were wife, and caried by the example of foch
as were good, firft fell to honeftie of life, and after to
the loue to ftudie and learning : and fo became fo new
a man, that *Cæfar* being dictator, made him Pretor in
Numidia where he abfent from his contrie, aand not
inured with the common talke of Rome, but fhut vp
in his ftudie, and bent wholy to reading, did write the
ftorie of the Romanes.   And for the better accom-
plifhing of the fame, he re[a]d *Cato* and *Pifo* in Latin
for gathering of matter and troth : and *Thucydides* in
Greeke for the order of his ftorie, and furnifhing of his

ftyle. *Cato* (as his tyme required) had more troth for
the matter, than eloquence for the ftyle. And fo
Saluft, by gathering troth out of *Cato*, fmelleth moch
of the roughnes of his ftyle : euen as a man that eateth
garlike for helth, fhall cary away with him the fauor of
it alfo, whether he will or not. And yet the vfe of old
wordes is not the greateft caufe of *Saluftes* [his] roughnes
and darkneffe : There be in *Saluft* fome old wordes in
Lib. 8. Cap. 3.
De Ornata. deed as *patrare bellum, ductare exercitum*,
well noted by *Quintilian*, and verie much
mifliked of him : and *fupplicium* for *fupplicatio*, a word
fmellyng of an older ftore, than the other two fo mifliked by *Quint* : And yet is that word alfo in *Varro*,
fpeaking of Oxen thus, *boues ad victimas faciunt, atque
ad Deorum fupplicia* : and a few old wordes mo. Read
Salufte and *Tullie* aduifedly together : and in wordes
ye fhall finde fmall difference : yea *Saluft* is more geuen
to new wordes, than to olde, though fom olde writers
fay the contrarie : as *Claritudo* for *Gloria* : *exactè* for
perfectè : *Facundia* for *eloquentia*. Thies two laft wordes
exactè and *facundia* now in euery mans mouth, be
neuer (as I do remember) vfed of *Tullie*, and therefore
I thinke they be not good : For furely *Tullie* fpeaking
euery where fo moch of the matter of eloquence,
would not fo precifely haue abfteyned from the word
Facundia, if it had bene good : that is proper for the
tong, and common for mens vfe. I could be long, in
reciting many foch like, both olde and new wordes in
Saluft : but in very dede neyther oldnes nor newneffe
The cause why
Salust is not
like Tully. of wordes maketh the greateft difference
betwixt *Saluft* and *Tullie*, but firft ftrange
phrafes made of good Latin wordes, but
framed after the Greeke tonge, which be neyther
choifly borowed of them, nor properly vfed by him :
than, a hard compofition and crooked framing of his
wordes and fentences, as a man would fay, Englifh
talke placed and framed outlandifh like. As for
example firft in phrafes, *nimius et animus* be two vfed
wordes, yet *homo nimius animi*, is an vnufed phrafe.

Vulgus, et amat, et fieri, be as common and well known
wordes as may be in the Latin tong, yet *id quod vulgò
amat fieri,* for *solet fieri,* is but a ſtrange and grekyſh
kind of writing. *Ingens et vires* be proper wordes, yet
vir ingens virium is an vnproper kinde of ſpeaking and
ſo be likewiſe,

> { *æger conſilij.*
> { *promptiſsimus belli.*
> { *territus animi.*

and many ſoch like phraſes in *Saluſt,* borowed as I
ſayd not choiſly out of Greeke, and vſed therefore vn-
properlie in Latin. Againe, in whole ſentences, where
the matter is good, the wordes proper and plaine, yet
the ſenſe is hard and darke, and namely in his prefaces
and oration[s], wherein he vſed moſt labor, which fault
is likewiſe in *Thucydides* in Greeke, of whom *Saluſt*
hath taken the greateſt part of his darkeneſſe. For
Thucydides likewiſe wrote his ſtorie, not at home in
Gre[e]ce, but abrode in Italie, and therefore ſmelleth of
a certaine outlandiſh kinde of talke, ſtrange to them
of *Athens,* and diuerſe from their writing, that liued in
Athens and Gre[e]ce, and wrote the ſame tyme that
Thucydides did, as *Lyſias, Xenophon, Plato,* and
Iſocrates, the pureſt and playneſt writers, that euer
wrote in any tong, and beſt examples for any man to
follow whether he write, Latin, Italian, French, or
Engliſh. *Thucydides* alſo ſemeth in his writing, not ſo
much benefited by nature, as holpen by Arte, and
caried forth by deſire, ſtudie, labor, toyle and ouer
great curioſitie: who ſpent xxvii. yeares in writing his
eight bookes of his hiſtory. *Saluſt* likewiſe wrote out
of his contrie, and followed the faultes of *Thuc.* to moch: and boroweth of him ſom
kinde of writing, which the Latin tong can not well beare, as *Caſus nominatiuus* in diuerſe places
abſolutè poſitus, as in that place of *Iugurth,* ſpeaking *de
Leptitanis, itaque ab imperatore facilè quæ petebant adepti,
miſſæ ſunt eò cohortes Ligurum quatuor.* This thing in

Dionyſ. Haly-
car. ad Q. Tub.
de Hiſt. Thuc.

participles, vſed ſo oft in *Thucyd*[*ides*] and other Greeke
authors to, may better be borne with all, but *Saluſt*
vſeth the ſame more ſtrangelie and boldlie, as in thies
wordes, *Multis ſibi quiſque imperium petentibus.* I
beleue, the beſt Grammarien in England can ſcarſe
giue a good reule, why *quiſque* the nominatiue caſe,
without any verbe, is ſo thruſt vp amongeſt ſo many
oblique caſes. Some man perchance will ſmile, and
laugh to ſcorne this my writyng, and call it idle curioſitie, thus to buſie my ſelfe in pickling about theſe
ſmall pointes of Grammer, not fitte for my age, place
and calling, to trifle in: I truſt that man, be he neuer ſo
great in authoritie, neuer ſo wiſe and learned, either,
by other mens iudgement, or his owne opinion, will
yet thinke, that he is not greater in England, than
Tullie was at *Rome*, not yet wiſer, nor better learned
than *Tullie* was him ſelfe, who, at the pitch of three
ſcore yeares, in the middes[t] of the broyle betwixt
Cæſar and *Pompeie*, whan he knew not, whether to
ſend wife and children, which way to go, where to hide
him ſelfe, yet, in an earneſt letter, amongeſt his
Ad. Att. Lib. 7.
Epistola. 3. earneſt councelles for thoſe heuie tymes
concerning both the common ſtate of his
contrey, and his owne priuate great affaires he was
neither vnmyndfull nor aſhamed to reaſon at large,
and learne gladlie of *Atticus*, a leſſe point of Grammer
than theſe be, noted of me in *Saluſt*, as, whether he
would write, *ad Piræea, in Piræea*, or *in Piræeum*, or
Piræeum ſine præpoſitione: And in thoſe heuie tymes,
he was ſo carefull to know this ſmall point of Grammer,
that he addeth theſe wordes *Si hoc mihi ζήτημα per-
ſolueris, magna me moleſtia liberaris.* If *Tullie*, at that
age, in that authoritie, in that care for his contrey, in
that ieopardie for him ſelfe, and extreme neceſſitie of
hys deareſt frendes, beyng alſo the Prince of Eloquence
hym ſelfe, was not aſhamed to deſcend to theſe low
pointes of Grammer, in his owne naturall tong, what
ſhould ſcholers do, yea what ſhould any man do, if he
do thinke well doyng, better than ill doyng: And

had rather be, perfite than meane, fure than doubte-
full, to be what he fhould be, in deed, not feeme what
he is not, in opinion. He that maketh perfitnes in
the *Latin* tong his marke, muft cume to it by choice
and certaine knowledge, not ftumble vpon it by
chance and doubtfull ignorance. And the right fteppes
to reach vnto it, be thefe, linked thus orderlie together,
aptnes of nature, loue of learnyng, diligence in right
order, conftancie with pleafant moderation, and alwayes to learne of them that be beft, and fo fhall you
iudge as they that be wifeft. And thefe be thofe
reules, which worthie Mafter *Cheke* dyd impart vnto
me concernyng *Saluft*, and the right iudgement of the
Latin tong.

¶ *Cæfar.*

Cæfar for that litle of him, that is left vnto vs, is
like the halfe face of a *Venus*, the other part of the
head beyng hidden, the bodie and the reft of the
members vnbegon, yet fo excellentlie done by *Apelles*,
as all men may ftand ftill to mafe and mufe vpon it,
and no man ftep forth with any hope to performe
the like.

His feuen bookes *de bello Gallico*, and three *de bello
Ciuili* be written, fo wifelie for the matter, fo eloquentlie for the tong, that neither his greateft enemies could
euer finde the leaft note of parcialitie in him (a meruelous wifdome of a man, namely writyng of his owne
doynges) nor yet the beft iudgers of the *Latin* tong,
nor the moft enuious lookers vpon other mens writ-
ynges, can fay any other, but all things be moft
perfitelie done by him.

Brutus, Caluus, and *Calidius,* who found fault with
Tullies fulnes in woordes and matter, and that rightlie,
for *Tullie* did both, confeffe it, and mend it, yet in
Cæfar, they neither did, nor could finde the like, or
any other fault.

And therfore thus iuftlie I may conclude of *Cæfar,*

that where, in all other, the beſt that euer wrote, in any tyme, or in any tong, in *Greke* and *Latin*, I except neither *Plato, Demoſthenes*, nor *Tullie*, ſome fault is iuſtlie noted, in *Cæſar* onelie, could neuer yet fault be found.

Yet neuertheles, for all this perfite excellencie in him, yet it is but in one member of eloquence, and that but of one ſide neither, whan we muſt looke for that example to fol[l]ow, which hath a perfite head, a whole bodie, forward and backward, armes and legges and all.

FINIS.

Printed in Great Britain by T. and A. CONSTABLE LTD. at the University Press, Edinburgh